PRAISE FOR

IN THE BLOOD: BOOK ONE OF THE BLOOD ROYAL SAGA

2018 SILVER STAKE AWARD WINNER
INTERNATIONAL VAMPIRE FILM AND ARTS FESTIVAL

2018 MIDWEST BOOK AWARDS

"…reminded me of the movie, **The Hunger** and there's a real sense of authenticity to the vampires. That's hard to pull off when you're writing about (presumably) imaginary creatures. Definitely one to check out if you like your vampires sans-sparkles, particularly if you're a fan of Anne Rice's **Vampire Chronicles**."

– **Philip Harris**, Author of **The Leah King Trilogy** and **Serial Killer Z**

"While set in the present day, the book contains some of the rich, enticing details of historical fiction - with vampires! One part road trip novel, one part vampire adventure, **In the Blood** sets the stage for more with great characters and twists that will leave you wanting to pick up the next book. Fans of the Sookie Stackhouse mysteries and **Interview with the Vampire** will enjoy this glimpse into a reimagined Marie Antoinette."

– **E.F. Schraeder**, Author of **The Hunger Tree** and **Chapter Eleven**

Trial By Blood

Book Three of The Blood Royal Saga

Delia Remington

EAGLE HEIGHTS PRESS

Fayette, MO

For my tribe.

For the cheerleaders.

For those who taught me.

For the Room 217 Writer gang.

For the women who blazed a trail.

For those who will follow after.

For you, beloved reader.

Thank you.

PART I

The Tomb by the Pounding Sea

Byron

"You have got to be kidding me." Sybill was carrying my sword cane and goggling at the view of the gravestones beyond the open gates as they slowly creaked open.

"Well, I didn't have much choice given the circumstances, did I?" I shook my head, but my tone softened when I saw Marie struggling out of the boat onto the shore of the cemetery island of San Michele. The entire front of her white dress was soaked in blood, and her hands were shaking. "Help her, would you? I think she's in shock."

Sybill looked back and then hurried to her side, speaking softly to Marie and wrapping an arm around her waist to help steady her. "Hey, it's okay. We're safe."

"We will never be safe. And they have him. They'll kill him, you know. They'll kill him. It's all my fault. I ruined his life." Stumbling, Marie clung to Sybill with white knuckles as though if she let go she might collapse completely. "I'm a disaster to you and everyone else."

"Hush. Don't talk like that. This isn't your fault."

I cleared my throat, and Sybill looked up at me with a sour expression. "Get inside. I'll get rid of the boat."

As soon as they were safely behind the high walls, I started the boat engine, lashed the wheel so the prow was aimed toward the lagoon, and loosed the lines. The boat headed off unmanned out across the water, and I prayed it wouldn't be found too near us.

"Wasn't that our ride?" Sybill said.

I entered the gates and swung them shut behind us with a loud clank. "That was going to lead them straight to us. Now come let me get you both settled someplace safe."

"Does it get any more cliché than this? A graveyard? Seriously, you're not really expecting us to stay here, are you?" Her eyes were distressed and panicky, but there was nothing for it.

"I expect you to have survival instincts. You want to go on living? Well, this is the best I've got. I'm sorry I didn't have time to find us first class accommodations. I was a little busy saving our lives."

Marie began crying softly, and she went limp in Sybill's arms.

"Oh Jeez." Sybill lost her grip, and Marie slipped down onto the stones in a heap. "Help me with her, would you?"

I hurried over and picked Marie up. She rested her head on my shoulder, arms around my neck like a child. Though she was not heavy, the extra weight made my foot ache, but I kept silent about it, trying not to let the pain show on my face. There was nothing else for it. Marie was in no shape to walk. "Hurry. We need to get out of sight."

We made our way out of the entrance and into the first high walled enclosure. There was a semicircular row of open doors that led into family crypts, and paths fanned out toward them like spokes in a wheel. Sybill wrinkled her nose. "You're not going to put us in one of those, are you? They stink."

I shook my head, walking straight up the paved center path toward an archway. "This is too close. We need to go further in."

The narrow avenue of stone pavement continued on to the center of the second enclosure, but smaller gravel paths made a grid of walkways between row upon row of gravestones. The paths were flanked by pointed and fragrant cypress trees, drenching the whole place in long patches of deep shadow. I could see the dome of the church to my left, its spires gleaming in the moonlight. Stopping beneath the arch, Sybill gaped open-mouthed, then whispered as she hurried to catch up to me. "This is creepy. I don't want to stay here."

I snorted and kept walking. "Creepy is the least of our worries. You're a vampire. What do you think is going to hurt you here?"

"Ghosts?" She looked around with wide eyes.

"Tsk. No such thing."

"How do you know?"

"Two hundred years of experience. Now stop talking, and let me think." I paused by a dry stone fountain, the water having been shut off until spring. Nothing moved besides us, and the only sound was of the wind in the trees and our feet on the gravel. I turned slowly, looking at our options. Many of the crypts were designed to hold cremated remains in tiny vaults on the wall. No good. There were no fresh graves, and I knew that even if that were an option, Sybill would never agree to lie buried in a box until I returned. That left only one choice. I walked over to a nearby bench and set Marie down carefully. "Just wait here a moment."

Sybill came to sit beside her, eyeing me with uncertainty.

Ignoring her, I turned away and walked over to the door of one of the four large family tombs that stood facing one another across the intersection of paths. The door was padlocked to keep out vandals and tourists. I swore under my breath, then turned back to look at Sybill. "Do you have any hairpins?"

"What?"

"Hairpins. This door is locked."

She smiled in surprise. "You're a regular James Bond, aren't you?"

"I don't know what that means." I shook my head, holding out my hand toward her. "Just tell me if you have any or not. I would rather not break this lock if I don't have to."

"I don't," she said, taking off her wig to reveal her startling blonde spiky hair, so in contrast with her gown, "but I'm sure Marie does."

Without saying anything to Marie who was sitting still, staring out vacantly across the graveyard, Sybill reached up and pulled two hairpins out of Marie's wig. Marie blinked, but didn't say anything. "Here," said Sybill, bringing them over and placing them into my palm. "You sure you know what you're doing?"

"Watch and learn," I said.

It didn't take long before the lock clicked and the hasp slid open. I pocketed the lock, then pushed the door back, revealing the interior of the crypt. The air was close and musty inside. Clearly, no one had entered in quite some time. The flowers on the tomb had mummified, and there was a fine layer of dust over everything. Still, as I looked around, I could see it was light tight. "This will do."

Sybill peeked in. "No way. It's not big enough for all three of us."

"I won't be inside."

"What? Where are you going?" Her eyes were wildly searching mine and full of fear.

"Someone has to get word to Polidori and Mozart. They need to get out of there before the coven arrives. Marie needs you. That means me."

"But...how? You got rid of the boat."

I laughed. "You really don't know anything about me, do you? I'm a strong swimmer. I can make it there before long."

"Swimming?" She gripped my arm tightly. "But it's so far."

I patted her hand reassuringly. "First of all, I swam across the Hellespont almost two hundred years ago. I've had centuries of practice since then. And secondly, do you really think I could drown? We don't have to breathe, remember? I'll be fine. Trust me."

"But what if they're already at San Lazarro?"

"Then Mozart and Polidori will need rescuing, won't they?" I smiled and leaned in to kiss her forehead. "I'm sorry things went so wrong tonight. This was not how I pictured our date ending."

She stared up at me. "This wasn't how I pictured it either."

"Oh? What did you think would happen?" I stepped in closer, brushing back a lock of hair from her forehead.

Biting her lip, she shook her head. "I don't know. I guess I hadn't thought it through that far. I just wanted to have a good time, really."

I nodded. "So did I."

"Rotten timing."

"That it is."

Just then, a clock rang out four times. "Speaking of time, I'm running out of it. I have to hurry if I'm going to be there before dawn."

She reached a hand up and touched my cheek. "Thank you for saving us. You were amazing. Like Zorro or something."

"I'll teach you sometime, just like I said. In the meantime, let's get you both inside."

And like that, we parted, focusing on the task at hand. Standing on either side of Marie, we hoisted her to her feet and then walked her into the tomb together. Sybill helped me lower her down onto the floor, brushing away the patina of grime and spiderwebs covering the stone slabs.

"I'll be back as soon as I can," I said, kissing Marie on the forehead. Then I turned and stroked Sybill's hair one time before handing her my sword cane with solemnity. "Take care of yourselves."

She nodded, and I backed away before wasting any more precious time. I pulled the door shut, and then pulled the padlock out of my pocket. I knew the caretakers would notice if the crypt appeared to have been tampered with. I couldn't risk exposing Sybill and Marie to the sun because of a careless mistake. I had to trust I would be back the following night to free them. Silently, so Sybill wouldn't become alarmed, I slid the lock into the hasp on the door and clicked it shut.

Talking of swimming to San Lazzaro was a far different prospect than actually doing it. I'd learned to navigate these waters by boat, certainly. Swimming was something else entirely. I'd behaved as though it were of no consequence, but as I stood there staring down at the dark water, I realized I had no real idea of the exact distance. I suppose that's what I got for trying to prove I had everything under control.

"Go on, you bastard," I said to myself. "They're counting on you. The sooner you dive in, the sooner it's over. Not like it'll kill you, and you've lived through worse."

For the most part, it was true, but the last bit was debatable. After all, Venice had used the lagoon as an open sewer for centuries, counting on the tides to wash the muck out to sea. Muttering curses, I sat on the edge of the quay, removed my boots, and then slipped into the water. Though the cold didn't bother me, I certainly didn't like it either, but the smell made me want to retch. Dead fish and slime and petrol and a cloying scent I didn't wish to ponder too closely. As I left the cemetery behind on my way toward the deeper channel, I decided this whole venture was the most idiotic thing I'd ever attempted, and the list of possible candidates for that designation was long.

Physical discomfort aside, the logistics of swimming the distance to San Lazzaro were a significant hurdle to overcome. In the dark, being eye level with the waves rather than at the helm of a boat, one island looks much like another. I had to rely on instinct and intuition to guide me, hoping I wouldn't be too late to accomplish my mission.

Fait Accompli

Ernestine

Despite the closeness growing between Raul and the Marquis, I believed Raul and I could work side-by-side without rancor. That is, until I witnessed the Marquis calling him "son" and giving him a place of importance and responsibility. Raul had not earned such recognition. He had not spent long years proving his worth.

It seemed to me, the Marquis' sudden interest in his new plaything had only a few possible causes. Perhaps this was one of his games, an amusement at my expense. He enjoyed pitting people against one another and watching them squirm. Then again, perhaps he was testing my loyalty.

I refused to believe he actually preferred Raul's company over mine. The boy was too ignorant and weak to be the source of interesting conversation, at least as far as I could see, and he had very little else to recommend him other than an eagerness I found difficult to believe. Raul had developed an annoying enthusiasm for following orders, and I didn't trust his sincerity. It seemed impossible to think the Marquis was taken in by such an abrupt about face.

Whatever the Marquis was up to, however, it wouldn't do for me to speak these things aloud. If I seemed jealous, I would only look weak and uncertain of my position. Moreover, it would indicate I had let my emotions cloud my thinking, which was a cardinal sin in the Master's eyes. The only prudent response, therefore, was to take no notice whatsoever and instead demonstrate my usefulness and dedication.

With a renewed determination, I headed to my office for the first time since my arrival. Sitting behind my desk, I reached into my briefcase and pulled out my cell phone. I pushed the button to call Mozart first. No answer. He was supposed to be sticking with the queen. Clearly something had gone awry with that plan, and he had not informed us. That meant either he had changed sides or been killed. Killed would be very inconvenient. I left a message, telling him to call immediately.

Next, I called Robespierre, my father's friend in Venice. I had known the man for years. Indeed, he was one of those responsible for freeing him from prison during The Terror, and the two had been working together for years to track down the queen, intent on making her pay for her crimes. When we'd discovered she and her protege had traveled to Venice, the man had volunteered to be installed among the coven in order to gather more information. So long as Casanova was head of the coven, we couldn't move to bring her into custody, but we had made inroads with some members who were sympathetic to our cause, and Robespierre had gone with the intent of apprehending her.

However, the voice who answered the other end of the line was not Robespierre at all. Instead, it was a woman who spoke.

"Who is this?" I said. "I need Robespierre right away."

"Monsieur Robespierre is dead."

I sat up in my seat. "What? How?"

"Killed in the line of duty."

"By whom?"

"A man aiding the escape of the former queen, Marie Antoinette," the woman said. "They fled and have not yet been apprehended."

Had Mozart betrayed us? "What man? Was he Austrian? German maybe? Short and ugly?"

"We believe it was an Englishman. Dark haired and handsome. He had a woman with him."

Not Mozart then. This was an as yet unknown, accomplice. "What else can you tell me?"

"Signore Casanova has been taken into custody by the coven. He is believed to have been working with the queen, though as yet, this is speculation. The coven is keeping him in the prison of the Doge's Palace."

"Do we have access to him?"

"Access is restricted to only a select few. They refuse any outside interference into the matter."

"Get to him. I don't care how you do it. I need the name of the man who killed Robespierre. Contact me at this number when it is done."

A shambles. That's what it was. Incompetence on every side, and I was left to repair the damage from a distance.

Once again, I dialed Mozart. This time, he answered. He was insolent and argumentative, but I ignored his audacious behavior, giving him strict instructions to go to Venice and take control of the situation. Sending Mozart to regain order in a chaotic situation was ludicrous at best. I knew it. He was wrong in every way for the job. No one would respect him or believe he held any sort of authority in Venice on my behalf.

Mozart, however, didn't realize any of that. His ego made him believe he was actually important enough to be given that level of responsibility. No one else would have credited it, but his self-centeredness and inflated sense of importance lent my instructions real weight in his mind.

Truthfully, I never said it with the intent of his succeeding. My real purpose was not to render him into a lieutenant under my command. No word of mine could ever make that happen. I simply wanted to know where his loyalties lay. Would he do as he was told, or would he show his hand as a traitor?

All the time he'd been embedded with Marie, I had harbored my suspicions. He'd given me too many delays, deflections, and excuses to convince me he could be trusted to bring Marie to us. Yet he hadn't actually been pushed to the sticking point until this crisis. It was time to force his hand. While I would have preferred another way of obtaining the truth from him, this opportunity presented itself, and I wasn't about to let him weasel his way out this time.

He fancied himself charming, believing he had me fooled, but I had seen through him from the first. He was only being used to spy on Marie out of convenience, not because he was the ideal man for the job.

Punishment, though, he did fear, and he was coward enough to be useful to me, despite my distaste for the little man. Mozart was ugly, boorish, and puffed up with a false sense of aggrandizement based on his musical genius. Despite that genius, I found him tedious. He skated the edge of what I would tolerate from a subordinate. If I hadn't been so impatient to work someone into Marie's good graces, I'd have chosen someone else. But they had a history, the fugitive queen and that ugly little man, and so I'd been forced to make do in spite of my misgivings.

Given what I knew of the man, I thought it far more likely for him to throw in his lot with the fugitive queen than to do my bidding. In a way, I was hoping for it. I didn't trust him and hadn't from the first. An open betrayal on his part would give me all the reason I needed to punish him right along with her once we had them surrounded and in custody.

Just as I hung up the phone, Raul's voice came from the doorway at my back. "Rough day at the office?"

I turned to find him standing, leaning against the frame of the door with arms crossed, a crooked smirk tugging at the corner of his mouth.

"You here to gloat or are you willing to be useful?"

"The Master sent me to offer my help," he said.

Raising a brow, I scoffed openly. "Aren't you solicitous? What's brought on this sudden change of heart?"

He shrugged, licking his lips as he considered his answer, then his eyes met mine directly. "Maybe I'm ready to make my own choices for once."

I laughed, chuckling at the irony in his statement. "Well, what do you know? You might just get to be a real boy after all. And what makes you think I'm going to trust you?"

"What choice do you have, Ernestine?" He said these words coolly, slipping his hands into his pockets as he stepped forward into the room, looking back at me with challenge in his eyes. "I'm the best chance you have to catch her. You need me. So...here I am."

"Mmm. Here you are." Lips pursed, I kept my gaze firmly fixed on his, studying his expression for any sign of weakness. "Very well. I want you to make a list for me. Write down the name of every person you've heard her mention in the time since she kidnapped you."

As I spoke, I stepped to the desk and brought out a notepad and pen, handing it over to him.

He stared down at the paper, then furrowed his brow. "You're kidding, right?"

"Not kidding." I shook my head, then gestured toward the chair in front of my desk. "Have a seat. And be thorough."

"This is ridiculous," he said, his lips curling as though he'd tasted something bad, but he sat all the same, placing the notepad on the edge of the desk. "There's got to be a hundred names at least."

"Write," I said firmly. "You and I both know she was far too secretive for the list to be that long. Probably most of the names will be useless. But somewhere along the way, she may have slipped up and told you something she shouldn't. I'm counting on that. You said you wanted to be useful. So write."

Raul sighed. I saw the last bit of resistance he had left fall away. He set his jaw and began making a list.

"Thank you," I whispered, reaching down to pat his shoulder with approval. "You're doing the right thing. You'll see."

His eyes darted in my direction and then back down at the paper, his hand still moving without stopping. "Don't thank me. I'm not doing it for you."

"Oh?" I said. "Then why are you doing it?"

The pen kept scratching over the page, never faltering even as he answered me. "Because fuck her, that's why. And fuck you too for all I care. I don't give a shit about you any more than you care about me. I'm doing this because I want to and because he asked me. That's it. It's not complicated."

"You're angry." It was a statement, not a question.

"Maybe, but that doesn't matter either. And its got nothing to do with why I changed my mind about helping you find her." His mouth twitched, and for a moment I wondered if he was lying.

I moved to sit behind my desk, watching him write. "So you want vengeance. Is that it? You think I'm going to bring you some sort of justice or closure? I hate to break it to you, but there's no way I can punish her for all her crimes."

He looked up then, pausing with pen in hand. "No, but you can punish her for the one that matters most to me."

"And what might that be? She hurt a lot of people in so many ways. I can't keep track of them all." I crossed my legs, leaning back in my seat. "What crime against you is the one you think is so important?"

"It's got nothing to do with what she did to me," he said. "I made my choice, even though I didn't know what she meant. I was tricked, yeah, but still...I gave my consent."

Tilting my head to one side, I peered at him curiously. "Then what's this about?"

"Sybill."

I blinked. "The human girl?"

He nodded. "The dead human girl. And yes."

Snorting with laughter, I shook my head. "Now who's ridiculous."

He rolled his eyes, and then looked back down at the paper and began writing once more. "I don't expect you to understand. I'm doing this for her. Marie's the reason she's dead, and that pisses me off."

"Petty vengeance."

"Sure," he said, his voice flat, as if all the emotion had been stomped out of it. "Call it that. I don't care. Whatever. You asked my reason. I'm giving it. I don't expect you to understand."

I smirked, crossing my arms over my chest with smug satisfaction. "Oh, I understand. She took away your toy and broke it, and now you want her to suffer."

"You're such a romantic, Ernestine."

I grinned and laughed, shaking my head. "Just make your list."

"Yes," he said. "It's better if we stop talking now."

"Are you trying to tell me what to do now, pretty boy?" I teased, knowing it would get under his skin for me to talk down to him. After all, wasn't that how Marie had treated him? Like a child? As though he were incapable of adult rational thought?

He didn't take the bait, and I found that annoying. I'd wanted to see him get defensive with me. Instead, he smiled and kept on writing in silence. I watched him for several long moments, but there was nothing further to say without admitting to myself and to him that I cared about his reaction. When he gave none, I sighed at last, and then rose to leave him alone to finish his list, turning my attention back to planning my strategy for what to do next.

JUSTIFIED

Mozart

Standing with the phone in the palm of my hand, I stared down at it, frozen for a moment as I pondered the instructions from the Marquis' spokeswoman. Go into Venice, she'd said. Take control of the situation until her people arrived. Robespierre was dead. She wasn't asking. She was telling.

Incredulous. That was how I felt. Incredulous and horrified.

I never knew Robespierre. His death was of no consequence to me. But ordering me to step forward and take an active role in the Marquis' name meant she expected me to reveal my true purpose at Marie's side. To declare myself openly as one of the Marquis' minions. It meant betraying not just Marie and her family but Casanova as well. My maker.

Guilt weighed heavily on me as I contemplated those instructions.

I had been willing to share information that was of little consequence. It seemed harmless. In all the former calls between me and the Marquis' enforcer, I had managed to skirt around active engagement in their plans. I'd made excuses, pretending to have made several failed attempts to capture

Marie, when in fact I'd had no real intention of doing anything beyond saving my own neck. My companions, including Marie, hadn't suspected the truth yet.

The Marquis, however, was growing impatient with my failure to deliver on my promises. Living under the Marquis' thumb, knowing at any moment he might choose to squash me if I didn't cooperate, meant I was in a constant state of distrust, suspecting everyone to be a spy who might report back to him. That anxiety wore me down, though I'd learned to put on a façade of easygoing humor to keep the sharks from smelling fresh blood. Though I'd told myself I was clever enough to play both sides, I wasn't skilled at manipulating people, and it was only a matter of time before I would be discovered. Eventually, I would have to choose sides. However, I hoped to delay that decision as long as possible.

I liked imagining I had freedom of choice. Clearly, though, my supposed freedom was an illusion, and the call forced me to face that reality. There wasn't time for me to waste debating. I had to make a decision. Follow orders and take an active part in helping Marie's enemies, or defy those orders and help her escape.

Following each choice to its logical conclusion, there was no good outcome for me either way. If I did as the Marquis instructed, I would hurt everyone I cared about and lose the few friends I had left. If I stayed with Marie, however, I only doubled their incentive to chase us both and made it more likely we'd be caught.

Only one alternative remained. To do neither and flee instead.

Thus, I found myself in a stolen boat, going not toward the city but in the opposite direction entirely, heading for the nearest shore to get as far from Venice and Marie and all of this mess as possible.

I admit it was cowardly. I never claimed to be a fighter. Self-preservation kicked in, and my feet were moving on instinct before I consciously made a decision. I make no excuses. I know the sort of man I am, and a hero is not in my makeup. Heroes get themselves killed. I was a survivor. Simple as that.

Of course I felt guilty leaving Marie the way I did. My loyalty was strong enough, I couldn't bring myself to follow through on the Marquis' instructions, but I had to be realistic. As separate targets, there was at least a hope their resources would be too stretched to bring us both in. That was the lie I told myself as I sped away into the night toward the mainland.

Marie would hate me, I knew. I would regret it always. At least I had defied the Marquis and I wouldn't be directly involved in her capture, even if I was abandoning her. She might not believe there was anything good in me, and to be honest I often doubted it myself. Still, I might at least hinder the speed at which the Marquis mustered his forces to close his trap, and that might be enough to enable her escape.

Was I trying to justify myself? Absolutely. Did I believe my own rhetoric? Not as much as I wished I could. But I knew all my own tricks and weaknesses, and it's difficult not to think the worst of myself when I have seen the depths of my own craven lack of courage.

The lights of Venice at my back, I sped over the dark waters of the lagoon toward the mainland of Italy. As I pulled into a small harbor and tied off the lines of the little motorboat, I told myself what I was doing was for the best for everyone. I needed to believe that, even if it wasn't entirely true. Lifting my bag onto the wooden dock, I spared a look over my shoulder at the city beyond the waves. I would never see Marie again. I was sure of it.

"Goodbye, old girl," I whispered. "Good luck."

My feet on dry land at last, I walked away, jaw set with determination, and as I climbed on board the city bus to the train station, I reached a hand down in my jacket pocket, closing my fingers around the small glass vials that were my insurance in case I was captured. I prayed I would never need it.

THE BRIDGE OF SIGHS

Casanova

Water dripped somewhere in the darkness.

"Hello?" I called, and as I stepped closer to the locked door of my prison cell, the chains binding my wrists and ankles rattled against the stone floor in the damp chill.

No answer came, so I moved closer, peering out of the tiny, barred, square opening in the heavy door. My limited view of the hall beyond showed only a wan light from a distant chamber. It was the only source of illumination, though I could see an unused ceiling fixture overhead, a bare bulb hanging from a wire. From the dust and grime covering its surface, I doubted it had seen much use, and it was most certainly a fire hazard to any who might attempt to turn it on.

This was not the first time I had seen the inside of a cell, but I had been foolish enough to believe such days were behind me.

"Perfect," I muttered, heaving a sigh before backing away from the door again.

With a shuffling step, I wandered back into the deep shadows of the small room, looking around at my surroundings. There was a wooden bench, a cot with a ragged wool blanket, and a bucket. Apparently, we were still living in the Dark Ages down here.

"Whoever designed these cells had a serious lack of imagination," I said as I sat heavily on the cot, my voice echoing on the stones despite my whispering tones.

"I wouldn't say that too loud," came a disembodied voice from the corner. "I think you'll find they have plenty of imagination when it comes to dealing with prisoners."

I squinted, tilting my head to one side and peering into the shadows. "I beg your pardon?" I said, hoping to draw my hidden companion closer.

"Torture, obviously," came the voice again, this time with a hint of dark amusement at my expense. "I thought the great Giacomo Casanova would be quicker than that."

The voice was familiar somehow, but I couldn't put a name or face to it. Whoever this person was, they knew mine right enough, though. Frowning, I glared into the dark corner.

"You have me at a disadvantage, friend," I said.

"Seems to me we are both at a disadvantage," the voice said. "And we are not friends."

I rose and took a step toward my comrade, and as I did so, I saw a hunched figure take shape out of the gloom, sitting on the cold stone floor with knees drawn up and long hair hiding the face.

I shook my head. "No, I mean..."

"I know what you meant," said the voice. "Do you really not recognize me? Ouch. That hurts, Gio. Truly it does. Your word sent me here, after all."

"My word?" I said, brow furrowing as I puzzled over this pronouncement.

"Mmm. I believe your exact statement was 'Take him away.' A bit non-specific, now that I think about it. Is this not 'away' enough for you? Perhaps you thought I'd be taken to a tropical island and marooned there. Wouldn't that be an adventure, eh?"

The figure rose to his feet, tucking his hair behind his ears, and then stepped close enough I could finally make out his features. It wasn't a face I thought I would see again, and I gasped audibly, unable to hide my shock and surprise.

"Kit?" I said. "It can't be."

"Can't it?" he said, raising a brow. He smiled then, and in that moment I saw the mischievous man I'd known so many years ago. Christopher Marlowe, erstwhile playwright and fellow hedonist. "Well, perhaps I should tell them they've got the wrong man, then. I'm sure if you back me up, they'll let me go home again."

I took a stumbling step backward, chains jangling as I raised my hands defensively. "I thought you were…"

"Dead? No, sadly, you didn't allow me that luxury." He laughed, a bitter sound like the dry crackle of old paper. His cheeks were hollowed, and his eyes were sunken deep in their sockets, making his face a mask of death. He must have seen the horror in my expression because in a moment he had me pressed to the wall, lips curled back in a snarl, grasping me with a strength I wouldn't have believed anyone so skeletal could have mustered. "Your words had consequences, Gio. Did you even think of me once in all that time? We were friends once, you and I."

"Once," I said, forcing myself to look back at him and not flinch. "That was before I realized what you really were."

"Oh? And what is that, exactly? And have a care, old friend." There was an edge of warning in his tone, and he leaned in closer until his nose nearly touched mine. His breath smelled of death. "Call me monster, and I shall have to remind you of your oaths to me. Oaths you broke without a second thought. I, who should have been like a brother to you but for your betrayal."

"Betrayal," I repeated, scoffing softly. "Is that what you call it?"

"Indeed. There is no other word so fitting." His eyes glinted in the darkness with an inhuman sheen.

I stared back into the void of his gaze. "And the fact you lied to me from the moment we met? What of that?"

"Necessity." He hissed the word, the susurrus syllables echoing in the small chamber. "You would have done the same in my shoes, Gio. Vain to deny it."

"Is this how you justify what you did? Even now? Have you truly no sense of guilt after all these years?" Raising my hands to his shoulders, I pushed him back, eyes narrowing. "You called me friend, and still you ensnared me in your web of lies. There is no friendship in what you did to me, nor to the countless others you misled over the centuries. How can you stand there, blaming me for your troubles? You have no one to blame but yourself for the way you have ended up."

He laughed again, but it was dark and mirthless, and as he did so I could see his fangs prominent and menacing. "Ah, Gio. So quick to point the hypocritical finger. And yet here we are, side by side again. Tell me, blood brother, do you truly believe we are so different? Our fates appear to tell a different tale."

"I did not betray my own race...my own kin. That is your crime, Kit." For emphasis, I pointed a finger emphatically at him, slashing the air before me as if with a sword.

With a snort, he looked away for the briefest of moments, then returned his baleful gaze in my direction once more. "Let me guess. You're here because of a woman. Am I right?"

I said nothing, only looked back at him coldly, but my silence was answer enough. He laughed again, shaking his head. "Of course I'm right. You bloody fool. They have always been your weakness. Tell me at least that you loved her. Give this old sentimental heart one last laugh at your expense."

"You have no heart," I said, but the bitterness in my voice betrayed my resentment at having been found out.

"You and I both know that is untrue," he said, his voice softening just slightly, and for the briefest of moments I almost felt sorry for him.

To cover my reaction, I looked away, glancing around the cell, my eyes finally adjusting to my surroundings. What I saw made me shiver with recognition. I whispered incredulously, "No. Not possible."

"Do I have to recount the time..."

Raising a hand, I cut him off, shaking my head. "Hush. I'm not talking about you. This cell. I have been in this cell before. This is the one I escaped from years ago. Long before I met you."

"Well, that's a bit ironic," he said sardonically, but I could hear the tiniest bit of hope in his voice.

Biting my lip, I glanced toward the ceiling. "Shut up. I need to think."

"Think about escape, you mean? Take all the time you need. I'll be over here when you're ready to try it." Returning to his corner, he sank back down on his haunches, sitting folded like a heap of dirty rags and bone.

I began pacing, muttering under my breath as I tried to recall exactly how I'd gotten away the last time.

A few minutes passed that way, and then I heard his voice again from the shadows. "Is this going to take long? Not to rush the thinking. It's just it's been a week since my last feeding, and you're starting to look like a walking lunch. No offense."

"Shut up," I repeated, not looking over at him as I turned away and closed my eyes, trying to remember all the details. "You're distracting me."

"Far be it for me to distract an artist," he said. "Out of curiosity's sake, how long did it take you to escape last time?"

Glancing over, I snapped. "A year."

"Ah. Excellent. I'll just wait here then, shall I?"

That mocking tone irritated me, and I turned away again, hissing, "Silent."

He clicked his tongue, then heaved a heavy sigh. "Oh aye. As the grave."

Necessity Makes Strange Bedfellows

Byron

I arrived at San Lazzaro when the moon was sinking on the horizon, entering through the secret side archway where Polidori kept his little boat moored for his clandestine comings and goings. My bare feet left wet tracks on the cold marble. Had I been human, the cold water would have been the death of me, but as it was, I found my late night swim merely a nuisance to be borne.

I padded dripping to Polly's chambers, not pausing even to gather my things or to change clothes. Naturally, my appearance was a shock to him.

"What on earth...have you taken leave of your senses? Surely the ball wasn't as terrible as all that," he said, eyes popping wide as he closed his journal to stare at me.

"Worse," I said quietly. "Gather your things. We're leaving."

"I beg your pardon?"

The horror and outrage in his tone was so immediate and extreme, it was all I could do not to laugh at him. Instead, I turned away and began walking back toward the stairs. "Honestly, you should listen when I say something the first time. It's a bloody nuisance repeating myself. You heard me. Pack. Now. I'll be back in twenty minutes. Whatever isn't in your bags will be left behind."

"But..." he spluttered. "Now see here..."

"No. No time. Got to go do some packing of my own before they arrive. Don't dawdle. I'll explain later."

He rushed forward and grasped my wrist to force me to stop. "Before who arrives? What is happening? Where are the others? You can't just come swanning in here making pronouncements without a word of explanation. And for the record, I know about you and Sybill."

I froze and blinked at him. "You what?"

"I saw you together. In the library. I know." Pronouncing this last word slowly, he gave it weight, and I had the feeling he guessed about my having kissed her too.

"I haven't...," I protested. "We aren't..."

Tilting his head, he raised an eyebrow. "I know what I saw. I'm not stupid."

I scrubbed a hand down my face with a sigh. "I just wanted to make her smile. It's Carnival, so we went to the masquerade ball together. That's all. She was so sad. I couldn't bear the ache I saw in her eyes."

He frowned. "Mmm-hmm. And Marie? Where was she all this time?"

"Signore Casanova invited her to be his guest for the evening."

It was his turn to be stunned. "A date? She and Casanova?"

I laughed. "Yes, dear boy. If you like."

"I don't," he said, shaking his head. "I don't like it at all."

"I'm afraid you have no choice in the matter. Doesn't matter anyway. He was imprisoned last night."

He gaped at me. "Imprisoned? What? How? Why?"

I stifled the urge to tell him he looked like a fish. "He was with Marie."

"So?"

"So apparently some people don't like it. Casanova was taken prisoner, and they would have taken Marie as well if I hadn't stepped in and put a stop to it."

"How did you stop them?"

I shrugged. "I killed the men who were trying to hold her."

Polidori pursed his lips, crossing his arms over his chest. "You cut off their heads, you mean. Right in the middle of the ballroom, I suppose. What a bloody mess."

"They were going to try to capture Marie no matter what I did," I said. "I had a duty to defend her. Surely you can understand that. I couldn't let them imprison her. She has suffered enough. So I got her out of there, and Sybill went with us. We escaped and stole a boat, and I hid them in the cemetery before coming to get you."

Pacing, he clicked his tongue. "Genius plan. Now we have no place to go."

My nostrils flared. "What would you have done in my place?"

"I don't know." He threw up his hands in frustration. "Maybe not killed people? Kept away from public places? Stayed out of sight? Any of those choices would do."

I gave an exasperated sigh. "We're wasting time. We have to leave here tonight. Casanova was taken away, god knows where, and I had to fight my way out of there. I managed to find a safe place for Marie and Sybill to hide temporarily, but we need a more permanent location to use as a sanctuary. They'll be coming for us. Marie's enemies, I mean. No doubt, some of them are on their way here as I stand here chatting. So if you don't mind, I'd prefer to continue this conversation elsewhere."

"But who are they," he insisted.

"I don't know Polly," I said, rolling my eyes. "I didn't linger to ask all their names. I was too busy trying not to be killed or incarcerated to have time for social niceties. The only man I knew was the Revolutionary, Robespierre, but I'm afraid I cut his head rather off before he got around to introductions. Now please, pack. I'm sure my grand heroics won't go unpunished, and I would rather not be here when they come to put my head on a spike, if it's all the same to you."

If I had struck him across the face, he could hardly have looked more shocked. I pulled my arm from his grasp, nodded, and then turned away once more to climb the stairs. I heard him muttering and cursing, but he had lost all will to argue with me further.

My next stop was Wolf's room, but I found it empty and all his things – suitcase, notes, everything – had simply vanished as if his presence had been a mirage. All that remained to assure me I hadn't stumbled into the wrong quarters by mistake was a sealed envelope with Marie's name scrawled in hasty letters across the front.

"Oh hell," I said, reaching to pick up the envelope as if it were a bomb set to explode at the slightest touch. I had no business opening the letter to read its contents, but I didn't have to be a soothsayer to know the gist of what it might say, nor did it take much imagination to envision what Marie's expression would be upon receiving the note. Damn him. Now I was doomed to be the bearer of bad tidings along with the disdain and rancor that went along with the task. Bloody coward. Leaving me to clean up his mess.

With a scowl, I turned and left for my own quarters, cursing the man under my breath. No time to warn him now. He would have to fend for himself and hope for the best.

In my way, I had liked him well enough. He was no Casanova, of course, but then neither was I, whatever my reputation might have been to the contrary. There wasn't time to gather all our belongings. I had to think not only for myself, but also for Marie and Sybill. Whatever could not be carried would have to remain behind. My one consolation was that I would not need to get wet a second time.

I toweled off quickly in my room, changed into attire more suited to our new circumstances, and then began tossing a few books and sentimental items into a bag. I also carefully packed the computer Sybill and I had bought along with the small printer. They took up the bulk of the bag, but clothing could be easily replaced. No sense making a fuss over such things.

From there, I hurried to Marie's room and then to Sybill's. Neither of them were dressed inconspicuously, so I gathered a change of clothing for each of them. Inside Sybill's underwear drawer, I found a neatly hidden .38 revolver. My brows rose.

"Well, it seems you are able to take care of yourself after all," I said, smiling to myself.

I placed the gun inside my jacket pocket, making a mental note to remind her about it later. Sybill's drawing materials I bundled neatly, knowing she would want them above all else, but as I was preparing to make a hasty retreat, the guitar she and I had bought for Raul caught my eye, and I paused for a moment, debating.

I wasn't sure such an item could be carried, but I remembered her expression when I placed it into her hands. She had looked on me and thought me selfless, and for a moment I had felt worthy of such a description. Still, there was very little likelihood as far as I could see that my brother of sorts might join us at last. Though I had not voiced my fears aloud, the odds of his still being alive after being captured by the Marquis seemed slim at best.

I'll admit to a pang of jealousy at the thought of her giving him the guitar, of it being a retained connection between them.

Not so selfless after all.

Despite my feelings, however, I couldn't bear to be the reason for her disappointment either, and so I opted for the middle road. I carried the guitar along with the rest of my burdens down the hall until I found Brother Jerome's room. Though the monks might wish us gone, he would be sad to see me leave after all these years. Despite his vow of silence, or perhaps because of it, he had been a true confidant to me.

He answered the door on my second knock, looking up at me with wide eyes.

Sheepishly, I held out the guitar towards him. "I know I have no right to ask this of you, but I find myself in need of aid, and I wondered if you might be prevailed upon to do the job as a matter of Christian charity. This instrument cannot travel with me at present, but I would take it as a token of our friendship if you would hold it for me until I can return to claim it. All else we have left behind may be sold to support your good works, but this I should very much like to have back when circumstances permit."

Nodding, he smiled broadly, and then he bowed his head, reaching to take the guitar from me.

The humble way he behaved made me ashamed I had no gift to give him as a token of my esteem, but he would not have accepted one anyway, for such was his devotion to the order, he cared little for himself.

I held out a hand to him in thanks, and he took it to shake, not recoiling from the coldness of my fingers. "I will miss our sparring," I said simply. "Take care of yourself, Brother Jerome."

He nodded once more, and then he made the sign of the cross as if in benediction over me.

Under any other circumstances, I might have scoffed or made a sarcastic remark, but his sincerity was touching, and I could not bring myself to mock his gesture. Instead, I smiled and then stepped away, gathering the bags once more. "Thank you, my friend."

Out of time, I hurried back to Polidori's dungeons where I found him still in the midst of packing his belongings. He already had three large trunks full of medical instruments and was in the process of opening a fourth.

"I don't know who you think will help carry those or what boat you have on hand to bear such a burden. I have enough to carry of my own, and I won't be helping you."

He looked up with a pained expression like a wounded animal, and I took pity on him, though what I'd said could not be changed.

"Maybe I can stay," he said in a tone that was near to whining. "No one even knows about me except the monks, and I'm no trouble to them. I'll just stay behind and —"

I cut him off right there. I had to. There was no more time.

"Polly, you can't be here when they arrive. They will take you in. They will try to get information from you. They will use the usual methods, and you know what will happen. Stop fighting it. Please. Marie and Sybill are waiting for rescue inside a crypt on the island of San Michele. Our enemies are coming. We must be gone before they get here. Take only what is essential. Leave the rest. I will buy replacement equipment, but you are the only thing in this room that is irreplaceable." Worry etched across my face, I set down my burdens and held out a hand toward him. "Please."

He hesitated, pain and misery in his eyes, looking down at my outstretched hand before turning to cast his gaze over the room. This place held his life's work, and I knew how deeply walking away from it would hurt him. One moment more of hesitation passed. Then he sighed and nodded. Though he only took my hand and squeezed it for a few brief seconds, it was enough and told me his time for arguing was past.

"Choose only what cannot be replaced," I said, seeing his forlorn expression. "Leave the rest. There's no help for it. I will purchase whatever equipment you require. You have my word."

I heard him whine softly, so I leaned close to whisper. "I understand. I am leaving behind my books and my translation work."

That ended the last of his complaints. With a sigh, he gathered up his notes and papers, then walked over to the cabinet where his glass vials were kept, bringing them down carefully to place into a portable cooler. I looked over at the clock that hung on his wall. I'd been at the monastery nearly an hour, and our enemies would be closing in.

"Is that everything?" I said, struggling to keep my impatience from showing in my tone.

"It's missing," he said, vials rattling as he shuffled them about, reading the labels.

"What is missing?"

He gave me a harried look. "The vaccine! It's not here."

"What? All of it?"

"Yes, all of it. Someone came in and took it."

I rolled my eyes. I'd heard him before make similar paranoid assertions when something of his went missing, only to find it later exactly where he had left it. "Polly, who would possibly have taken your vaccine? No one knows about it except us. Even the monks have no knowledge of your research."

"Someone talked. Maybe Casanova...."

"He doesn't know it exists, and regardless he's been imprisoned for the last few hours. So unless he has magic powers, there is no way he could have gotten in here to take your things. And before you suggest it, no, none of his associates would have had time to get here. There is no one else. You have simply misplaced it. That's all. Don't you have any extra stashed away somewhere?"

"That is beside the point. And no, I have not misplaced it. I have been meticulous with these vials. I am telling you, it's been stolen."

I sighed heavily and shook my head. "Whatever. I don't want to argue. If you have more elsewhere, then let it go."

"But if it gets into the wrong hands..."

I finally lost the last shred of my patience. "Then it does! It is not worth dying over. Grab your things, and let's go."

"You don't understand."

"No, you're right," I said, picking up the bags and walking toward the door. "I don't. And I don't care to."

"It's nearly dawn," he said, glancing up at the clock. "We can't go now."

I gritted my teeth, counted to three, and then growled. "We have to. They will send humans here after us. Stop stalling. We are losing what little time we have quibbling over this. Grab your bag. Shut your mouth. Go get in the damn boat.

"You're an ass," he said, but he gathered his belongings all the same.

"Astute observation, but irrelevant."

With that, I turned away and started up the stairs. I could hear him behind me, muttering, but he followed and climbed into the little motorboat sullenly, glaring daggers in my direction as I loaded my burdens aboard and then loosed the lines. I pointedly ignored him, stepping aboard and starting the motor, and we sped off out into the dark night in silence.

He was right, though, much as I hated to admit it. Dawn was nipping at our heels, and collecting Marie and Sybill would be impossible until the following evening. Unfortunately, I also had no way of contacting them. For several minutes, I pondered over what to do in silence. Then, biting my lip, I turned the boat sharply away, heading instead for the lights of the nearby long fingerlike island of Lido.

"Where are you going?" said Polidori, looking over at me sharply, pointing behind us. "The cemetery of San Michele is back that way."

"Change of plans," I said with a note of finality. "There's no time to fetch the ladies before dawn. It's too risky. You and I will find a room in a hotel for the day. Marie and Sybill will have to remain where they are for now, and we can collect them in the evening."

His jaw dropped, and he stared at me open mouthed. "You're abandoning them among the dead? How can you even think of it? The groundskeepers may stumble upon them. Or someone wishing to visit the departed may discover the two of them hiding inside the tomb. What do you think will happen if they are found? You can't leave them in that place."

"I must," I said, keeping my eyes fixed on the shoreline ahead. "I don't like it, but if we go now, we all risk being caught or severely burned. They are both resourceful women, and I have to trust they can take care of themselves for the time being. You must do the same."

He made a noise of disgust, looking back over his shoulder, but he knew I was right. The sky was already beginning to lighten, and we had no more time to discuss it. Lido was dotted with hotels along the shore, but I opted for a more inconspicuous one. Ducking into one of the small canals leading toward the center of the island, I pulled in front of a hotel that looked as though its heyday was over a century ago, hastily tying up to the mooring.

"You must be joking," Polidori said dubiously as he began unloading his things onto the shore.

"It's only for a few nights," I said. "And you must admit, our enemies would never look here for the former queen and her family."

He snorted, but had to acquiesce the point. "No, they certainly would not."

The night clerk at the desk was dozing, clearly still waiting for his morning replacement to arrive. His tired state was to our advantage, however, as he was too exhausted to pay close attention to our appearance. He had two rooms left, he said, on opposite ends of the second floor. Sight unseen, I took them, paying in cash for a week, and with keys in hand, Polidori and I stepped into the rickety elevator with our baggage.

"These will do for now," said Polidori once the doors closed, "but what will we do tomorrow when we have doubled in number?"

I looked over at him with a brow raised. "You and I are sharing, Polly. The ladies will have the one facing the water while we take the room without a view."

He took a moment to digest this information, blinking slowly. "You. And I. Together. In one room."

I was still laughing when the elevator door opened. "We will survive it, I'm sure."

Following me to the door, he waited for me to unlock it, and when we stepped inside to see how close the walls were on either side of the one double bed, he shot me a look of wide eyed horror.

"I'm not so sure," he said.

"Come now, doctor," I said, setting down my burdens and moving to pull the curtains closed. "Buck up. After all, it's nothing you haven't seen before."

He blinked. "This is a very bad idea."

"We shall just have to make the best of it," I said with a shrug. Before he could say anything more, I removed my shoes and laid down on top of the covers fully clothed, closing my eyes. "Get the lights, won't you, old boy? There's a good man."

GALVANIZED

Raul

Hunting Marie was the framework I was building a new life around. For the first time in nearly thirty years, my existence had meaning. The Marquis had given me that. His words transformed my thinking. No longer would I see myself as a victim, cursing what Marie had done to me. I was galvanized with purpose. One thing I realized with startling clarity – I had all the time in the world to dedicate myself to ensuring she finally met with the justice she deserved.

Marie had destroyed my future the night she made me what I was, but the Marquis had given me a new one, and I was energized by this new vision of who I could become and what I was capable of doing with his guidance. I had never felt such freedom. Freedom from guilt, fear, restraint. He made me realize I was holding onto an outmoded view of myself. By letting go of what I'd lost, I was free to embrace who and what I had become and to plan a new path toward the future. It was a revelation, and I threw myself into this new life with gusto. He had given me the role of a lifetime, and it fulfilled me in a way nothing else ever had.

I had even almost forgiven Ernestine too. With this newfound perspective, I understood her fervor and drive, and while we might never be close friends, I found to my surprise we were slowly building mutual trust. Looking back at all she'd put me through, her actions began to make sense given the urgency of her mission. She'd done what she believed was necessary. I'd hated her for throwing me in that cell, for what I'd perceived as her attempts to manipulate me. In perspective, however, I saw she'd simply been frustrated and desperate to capture Marie. Being so close and losing her made Ernestine do things she might not have under other circumstances.

Even the death of Crystal, I began to comprehend in a new light. After all, she saw Crystal as another of Marie's pawns. Morever, to vampires, the morals of the human world were no longer applicable. I'd been holding onto a world view that didn't fit my immortal life, and it was time I let go and saw things without guilt and shame for my true nature. I had been inappropriately emotionally attached to Crystal. The Marquis made me realize killing was part of what we were. We weren't beholden to the same laws as human beings. At last I understood that truth, and so I could forgive Ernestine.

I could even begin to forgive myself for the things I'd carried in my heart as a burden of guilt and shame. What I'd done to that boy in Forest Park wasn't murder. I was a predator. It was natural for me to need to feed. Judging myself was a form of self-hatred. A kind of eating disorder. I couldn't help or change what I was, and I didn't need to blame myself for acting in accordance with the natural order, any more than a grizzly bear should feel guilty for eating a salmon or than a hawk should feel shame for eating a mouse. I wasn't a human anymore, and it was time I started thinking of myself in a new way.

As for the Marquis, I wanted nothing more than to deserve the attention he gave me. I didn't feel I needed to prove myself to him so much as I wanted to prove to myself that my life had worth and purpose. He called me "son," and while the word had made me inwardly cringe due to the years of abuse I'd suffered under those who had used it, when I heard it from his lips the connotations were new and deeply meaningful. Each time he praised me, it warmed me from within. A quiet joy took root in my soul, knowing I had a place at his side. I belonged. I was part of something important. I was learning to find my own strengths and to appreciate the abilities I'd gained. I discovered peace in surrendering to a higher purpose. The Marquis never demanded my obedience. I gave it willingly, and I was proud to serve him. I never felt so powerful as when I let him take control and guide me. I lived for his praise. I never felt so understood and appreciated as I did when he smiled at me for a job well done. From the moment I woke each night until I lay down to rest at dawn, I strove to please him. I called him "Master" because that was what he was to me. He was teaching me. He had wisdom acquired over centuries, and I was grateful he'd chosen to share it with me.

I had turned in my list of names to Ernestine and was back in my room thinking over my change in fortune when a knock came at my door. Before I could rise from the bed to answer it, however, the door opened and in walked the Marquis, smiling benevolently with the pride of a father who had just seen his young child demonstrate a skill he has worked hard to cultivate.

"I heard what you did. I am quite proud of you, my boy. Quite proud indeed." As he spoke, he stepped closer, crossing the room to stand by my bed.

Sitting up, I turned to face him, swinging my legs over the side of the bed to place my feet on the floor. "Thank you, Master. I only hope it will help."

"Come, son," he said, reaching to clap a hand on my shoulder. "Walk with me. I have work for you."

"Of course," I said, beaming as I rose and followed him out of the room. My heart felt light, and where before I might have been filled with dread or anxiety, those feelings were replaced with anticipation.

Together, we strode out onto the tower. When we reached the parapet overlooking the city below, we stopped, and he turned to face me directly. "You have come so far in such a short time, my son. Tell me, how do you find it here? Are you happy?"

"Hell yeah!" I said, not pausing to think before the words came tumbling out. Afraid I'd spoken too quickly or that I sounded immature and foolish,

I shifted on my feet, looking down, and as my hair fell over my face, I reached up to push it back behind my ear self-consciously. "I mean, yes. Really, I am. This place is great, and I feel like I get it now, you know? Like really get what we are. What I am. I'm not afraid of it anymore."

He laughed and nodded with a knowing glance. "It is liberating to finally accept yourself as you are. No artificial constraints. No need to fill other people's expectations. Just be who you are, completely."

"Yeah. Yeah, it is," I said, looking up at his encouragement. "I feel like this giant weight is just...gone. Thanks for that."

Shaking his head, he patted my shoulder reassuringly. "No need to thank me, dear boy. Watching you remove your own shackles so you can be who you were meant to be...strong, confident, determined...is all the thanks I need."

Those words were more praise than my own father had ever given me, and all the attributes he ascribed to me were things Marie had tried to stifle and control. For a moment, I was so filled with humility and gratitude, I couldn't speak. I looked down again and cleared my throat, tucking my hair behind my ear a second time.

"You don't need that, you know, son," he said quietly.

I knit my brows, looking up into his eyes once more. "Need what?"

"Something to hide behind. That's what your hair is, isn't it? A shield?" With a steady gaze, he watched as I blinked at him. "You don't need to hide in order to defend yourself from me or anyone else. You have an inner strength. It shines through. You're no Sampson, to put it biblically."

That image made me laugh. "You know how many times Marie tried to get me to cut my hair? She chased me around the house once with scissors, threatening to cut it off in my sleep."

"Ah. Well, if it means so much to you..." He shrugged, his words trailing off, and he smiled at me with a gentleness like nothing I'd ever known.

"No, no," I said quickly. "I...I get what you're saying. You're right. I don't need it anymore."

His grin widened as if I'd given him a gift. "If it's what you want."

"Yeah," I said. "Yeah, it is. It's just a nuisance anyway. I'm not a kid anymore. It's time I stopped looking like one."

As I spoke these words, I thought about the clothes I'd been wearing since I had come to this place. While I lived with Marie, jeans and old t-shirts had been my style, if you could call it that. The way I dressed was exactly what I'd worn when I'd been turned, as though time had frozen with me still not completely an adult. Here, though, without those old things to fall back on, I had grown accustomed to the tailored wardrobe I'd been given. The black and dark grey fabrics made me feel more sophisticated and serious, and in turn I'd been treated that way, not just by the Marquis but Ernestine too.

"Is that what you brought me up here for?" I said. "To talk to me about my appearance?"

"Ha!" With a sudden burst of laughter, he shook his head. "No. I told you, I have a job for you. You seemed eager, and I thought of a way you might be useful."

"Anything," I said.

His brows rose slightly at that statement, but only for a second, and then he nodded. "Very well. I have spoken with Ernestine. I think you are ready to be given some responsibilities. I can trust you, can't I, son?"

"Of course." I said, standing a little straighter. "I want to help."

He smiled with approval, reaching out to touch my cheek for a moment. "That's my boy. She said she didn't think you were ready, but I knew better. You're a smart young man, and I know you want to do the right thing. Isn't that right?"

I tugged at my sleeves to straighten them. "Yes, Master. That's all I ever wanted."

"Such a smart lad. It's so lucky I found you when I did."

For a second, I almost corrected him. Technically, he hadn't found me. I'd been imprisoned by his daughter and brought to his dungeon.

But I didn't want to argue with him, and the truth of how I'd come to be standing next to him seemed unimportant. All that mattered was the fact I was there. No sense quibbling.

"Yes, Master," I said quietly.

He smiled again as if I'd given the right answer to a quiz I hadn't known I was taking. "Good. I want you to be my lieutenant."

My eyes practically popped out of my head. "But...what about your daughter, Ernestine?"

"What about her?" he said, as lightly as if we were discussing the weather.

"Won't she feel like I'm taking her job? I don't want on her bad side."

He snickered. "Are you afraid of her still? I thought you had put your fears behind you."

"I'm not afraid," I said. "It's just....I don't think she'll take too kindly to me stepping in on her turf, you know?"

"Oh, I see. So you think there will be a proverbial pissing contest, hmm?"

It was my turn to laugh this time. "The thought had crossed my mind, yes."

"Ernestine has enough to do right now. She could use some help. And if she doesn't agree, we shall just have to show her, won't we?"

"Show her?" I said, the words coming out with hesitation.

"Indeed. Prove your mettle."

I had the sudden mental image of a cage-match fight between the two of us, and I didn't like my odds in that scenario at all, though I didn't want to confess it aloud. "I don't know what you mean," I said, but I feared I knew all too well.

"Don't you? Well, then perhaps I've been too hasty. Maybe you aren't ready after all." He shrugged, turning as if to walk away. "Ah well."

"No," I said, stepping forward. "I want to do it. If it's what you need, I can do it."

Rounding back to face me once more, he grinned again, showing a little fang. "There's that positive attitude. Excellent. See, now that wasn't so hard, was it?"

"No, Master," I said. "Just tell me what you want from me. I'll do it."

"Good man. Really excellent." He clapped his hands together decisively. "It's settled then. Tomorrow, you'll report to me when you wake. I've got other work for Ernestine. You and I will do great things together, son. Amazing things. You'll see."

I didn't know what things he was talking about, nor was I sure what I'd agreed to do, exactly. His request was a little vague. Still, I wasn't about to let on I had concerns. I would just have to work hard to show that I was capable of anything he needed from me. Whatever it took, I would do it. I was determined not to complain or question. I needed to trust. If I could do that, I told myself, everything would go perfectly.

Rather than ask for details, I simply said yes, and he put his arm around me with affection.

"Come, my boy. Let's go down into the city and satisfy your hunger, shall we? Don't want you distracted when it counts, do we? Got to keep up your strength."

It was on the tip of my tongue to ask if that was wise, given the recent hunt we'd done there only a few days earlier, but my hesitation was the voice of the old me. Full of silly sentiment, I knew he'd say. I was determined not to fall back into those old behaviors. Instead, therefore, I went with him. We slaked our thirst, carousing the rest of the night, and didn't return to the castle until nearly dawn.

Marie wouldn't have recognized me if she'd seen me, and I was glad. I didn't want or need her approval anymore.

A Question of Trust

Sybill

I had just drifted off to sleep sitting up, Byron's sword cane on my lap, when I was jerked awake by the sound of Marie frustratedly rattling the door, muttering. I sat up, ready to pull the blade to fight off any intruders. "What's wrong? Are they here?"

Scowling, she kicked the door with an exclamation that would have made a sailor blush. "He has locked us in here! That is what is wrong." She kicked again.

Rising quickly to my feet, I set the cane aside and moved to stand next to her. "No way." I pushed against the doors and met with immediate and firm resistance.

"Way." Flinging up her hands angrily, Marie kicked once more.

"Well, maybe they have one of those bells in case you get buried alive. You know, like in those Edgar Allan Poe stories."

She rounded on me, hands on her hips. "And who exactly do you think would answer such a bell?"

Panic flared in me, but I tried to rationalize our situation. "Byron said he would be back soon."

"The last time he said he would see me soon was in Greece. I did not see him for almost two hundred years."

I shook my head. "No. He wouldn't leave us. He'll be back."

"Hmpf." She clicked her tongue, crossing her arms. "If he is not captured or killed."

The enormity of that possibility yawned before me like a hole I might tumble down and never reach the bottom. "Don't say that! Don't even think it. He'll be here."

"I have been the damsel in distress before. It always ends badly. In the end, you cannot trust anyone to swoop in and save you. Sometimes you have to rescue yourself."

"Oh, that's rich coming from you." I rolled my eyes.

Her eyes bored into me, even in the gloom of the darkened tomb, but she thought better of whatever she wanted to say to me. Instead of snapping back, she let out a deep breath and replied in a much more even tone. "Sybill, he has been gone all day. We are trapped. He may be coming. He may not. There is a limit to how long we can wait to find out. We need to stop arguing and find a way to escape on our own."

"What time is it?" I had no clear idea how long we had been there waiting, and it suddenly occurred to me that it might already be daylight outside.

She checked her watch. "It's six o'clock. Nearly dawn."

I bit my lip, trying to think. "What's your plan?"

My question seemed to stun her. She regarded me silently for several seconds. "What do you mean? I want to get us out of here."

"Yes, but then what?"

"Then we can find a safe place to hide."

"But we're already in one. I mean, I don't like being locked in either, but if we don't have another place to go that's safer, and we are too close to dawn to be on the move, then we might as well stick to Byron's plan and at least give him until tomorrow night before we try busting out of here."

"Do you want to sleep in here?" She looked around, dubiously.

"No, but it's better than frying outside, right? Plus, if we start wandering off, he won't know where to find us. It complicates the whole thing."

She frowned, and for a second I thought she was going to argue with me. Instead, she shook her head and sat back down on the dusty floor, long skirts billowing out around her. "All right. We will do it your way. But if he is not here by midnight tomorrow, we need to find our way out."

I nodded, squeezing in beside her. "Deal. You know, this whole no phone thing is annoying as hell. When we get out of here, first thing we're doing is getting some burner phones for everyone."

"Burner phones? I fail to see how setting them on fire is helpful." I opened my mouth to speak, but she held up her hand and shook her head. "No, please. Don't explain. Not now. My mind is too busy thinking about other things to concentrate." She looked down at the front of her dress and scowled at the blood stains on the white satin.

"These dresses are ridiculous." I squirmed, the tight corset making it difficult to move my torso into a comfortable seated position.

"They were not designed with narrow escapes in mind."

"Or, like, moving at all, really. How did you stand it?"

"My job was to look pretty, not to be active." She shook her head. "You are right, though. I had nearly forgotten how difficult they were to get in and out of. We will need a change of clothes."

"Can you help me loosen this a little?" I said, frowning and straining with effort. "Ugh. I can't reach to get out of this thing. It's making me claustrophobic."

She turned to face me. "Fine. Sit up and turn around so I can get to the laces."

"Thanks." I scooted so my back was to her, and I could feel her fingers give the laces a tug. As the strings slowly loosened, I sighed and smiled, finally able to slouch into a more natural posture. "Oh god, that's better. You're a lifesaver."

She snorted. "That's debatable. But I'm glad you are more comfortable, at any rate."

I turned back around and smiled. "Want me to do yours?"

"No, thank you." Shaking her head, she settled back against the wall. "I can wait until we have something else to put on."

I shrugged. "Suit yourself."

"Indeed."

A few moments passed in silence. I finally got up my courage to ask the question which had been on my mind ever since our frantic, bloody skirmish in the ballroom. "So, who was that guy, anyway?"

She looked up at me. "Who?"

"The creep Byron killed," I said. "The one who knew you."

Her brow went up. "You mean Robespierre?"

"Should I know that name?" I said, trying not to feel insulted by her implication of my ignorance.

With a look of horror, she looked away for a moment and muttered, "What do they teach in those American schools these days?"

"Hey! No picking on the public school girl. We can't all be queens, you know. And anyway, that's all French history. Not something we spent a lot of time on, me being American and all. Besides, history class was boring. I doodled in my notebook through it, mostly."

She covered her mouth and laughed. "I can imagine."

"Mmm. Mrs. Macgill hated my guts for that. Every report card said the same thing. 'Sybill is bright, but daydreams too much.' I couldn't help it. She read right out of the book in this horrible monotone, acting as though we didn't have eyes of our own, then gave us workbook pages to fill out." I rolled my eyes. "I drew pictures to stay awake. Had to do something. Kids who fell asleep got sent to the principal's office."

Marie gazed back at me with interest, as though she found something in my story she could relate to, despite the centuries between our ages. "And what happened then? Did they cane you?"

"What?" I grimaced and shook my head. "No. They called my daddy. I knew better than to ever let that happen."

She nodded. "I see."

"So tell me about this dude," I said, returning to my original question, determined not to let her sidetrack me from answering.

Raising an eyebrow at my word choice, she repeated, "Dude?"

I sighed and glared pointedly. "Robespierre."

She settled back against the wall with a little smile on her face as though she'd won some small victory in making me say his name. "All right. What do you know about the French Revolution?"

I counted facts on my fingers. "Um, guillotines. The Bastille. You said 'Let them eat cake' and they put you in jail for it."

"I never said that," she said.

"What?" I stared at her with wide eyes.

She smiled at my reaction. "Total fabrication. I never said it."

Dumbfounded, I sat up cross-legged and leaned my elbows on my knees. "That's crazy. Why would they make that up?"

She shrugged. "The winning side can put whatever words in your mouth they please. They made up all sorts of things about me. I am not sure why that one stuck. You would think there were more juicy lies to latch onto, but there is no anticipating what will appeal to the masses sometimes."

"Hmm," I said, pondering that for a moment before returning to the topic once again. "So, anyway...this Robespierre guy?"

Marie sighed, caving to my persistence at last. "In short? He was an instrument of the Revolution. He and his cronies published all sorts of outrageous claims about the aristocracy."

"Such as?" Gazing back at her, I gestured for her to continue.

She gave me a sidelong glance, then said, "Aside from the claims we were all vampires?"

My mouth dropped open. "He said that? Like to normal people?"

Laughing bitterly, she nodded. "He said it every chance he got to anyone who would listen. And the people were gullible enough to believe his lies."

"Well, but you were actually vampires, so that's not actually a lie."

"True," she said. "But so was he. And not all of us were vampires. But regardless, he should have been keeping our secret."

"You're telling there's some kind of vampire rule about it? Like Fight Club?" I laughed at the thought.

She blinked and shook her head in confusion. "Excuse me?"

It was my turn to look at her with shock at her confusion. "You know. 'First rule of Vampire Club, don't talk about vampire club.'"

"I have no idea what you are talking about," she said.

I gaped openly at her. "How can you not have seen that movie? Like, everyone has seen it. Everyone."

Marie frowned in annoyance. "Did you want to hear the story or not?"

"Yes, okay," I said. "But when all this is over, we're watching that movie."

"Fine." She rolled her eyes.

"Right. So he told your secrets and basically was a hypocrite, is that right?"

Settling back against the wall, she smoothed her skirts. "He was in league with the Marquis. He is the one who sent the order to have him released from prison. There were others as well, but Robespierre was vicious in his campaign against me. Still, eventually, he was found out. And when the people realized that he was a monster too, they hunted him down. I thought he had been beheaded, but apparently he was able to escape just as I was. I do not know where he has been hiding all this time. The Marquis must have orchestrated it somehow."

"So you're certain they were working together?"

"Well, they certainly were back in my day, and it appears he has been looking for me all this time."

"What the hell did you do to make so many people hate you?" She looked stricken at my question, and I immediately regretted my words. "I didn't mean it like that. I just don't understand why they're all still holding onto so much hate. It's been two hundred years. Why don't they get a hobby or something?"

"Did it ever occur to you that perhaps I did not have to do anything for them to hate me? I was simply the face they put on an anger and dissatisfaction they felt. They needed someone to blame. I was a convenient scapegoat."

"It can't be that simple."

"No? Believe what you like, then." She gave a deep sigh. "I am too tired to debate this further. Dawn is nearly here. I can feel it. We need to sleep."

"What if this place isn't light tight?"

"Stick to the shadows. Pull your dress up over your head and arms, tuck your feet inside your petticoats, and pray that any light that does come in does not hit you."

"Will I catch fire?"

"No. But you will blister badly. It is like the worst sunburn you have ever seen. It will take weeks to heal, and in the meantime it will be obvious what you are."

I began taking her advice, following her example. It took several minutes to get bundled up under all those clothes, and I lay there, curled uncomfortably, hoping it would be all right.

"Marie?" My voice was muffled under my skirt. "What if someone finds us?"

"Hush, Sybill. Just sleep."

"But –"

"No. Close your eyes and sleep."

"Byron will be here tomorrow, right?" I said.

"I hope so."

"That's not comforting."

She didn't answer me again. I realized she was probably just as frightened and unsure as I was. All I was doing was making it worse. There were no words of comfort she could give me that weren't lies. I stopped talking and shut my eyes. The morning birds began making their sounds of waking, and I drifted off at last, hoping that Byron's plan would keep us from being caught and praying that he was someplace safe.

Sleeping in the mausoleum proved even more uncomfortable than we had anticipated. Though neither of us were burned, the sun crept under the door and around the edges, so we weren't able to relax, always shifting and readjusting to stay out of its beams. Also, a few mice had made a home in one corner, and we could hear them squeaking and scampering around. Periodic gusts of wind whistled under the gap in the door, and while the cold didn't bother us, the dust did. Stirred up from the chat paths in the cemetery, the dust spun in eddies across the stone floor, coating our skin, clothes, and hair in a fine patina of grit that irritated our eyes. Constantly, we wondered if we would be discovered. Each footstep outside made us freeze in place like the marble figures on the tombs outside, and we waited in heavy stillness until they passed.

At last, the sun began to drop low on the horizon, and we could see the shadows grow long and gray through the crack beneath the door. We relaxed a little, relieved we had survived the day without detection.

Once we knew we were alone in the cemetery at last, Marie and I began a game to pass the time. "I'll flip a coin to start. Heads or tails?"

"Heads," said Marie. She had a dubious expression on her face, but we had to do something to keep from going nuts with worry.

I tossed the coin in the air, caught it, then uncovered it on top of my hand. "Tails. That means I go first. Okay, I'll give a topic, and we have to take turns singing a song that includes that topic idea in the lyric. First person to run out of songs is the loser. Winner gets to pick the next topic. Got it?"

She raised an eyebrow. "This is a child's game."

"Would you rather we stare at one another for the rest of the night?"

Her gaze narrowed. "Pick the topic."

"All right. I'll give you an easy one first. Birds."

With only a moment's hesitation, Marie nodded and then began singing. "Oh skylark, have you anything to say to me?"

"Good one! My turn." I grinned and snapped my fingers to set the tempo. "Rockin' Robin tweet! Tweedle-e-dee. Rockin' Robin."

"That cannot be a real song. You are making that up."

"It is so a real song. It's even an old one."

"Define old."

"1950s?"

She rolled her eyes. "That explains it."

"Explains what?"

"I spent that decade in Indochina. Until the war broke out, that is."

It was my turn to look confused. "Indochina?"

"You call it Vietnam now." She rolled her eyes. "I do not know why countries have to keep changing names."

"Okay. Whatever. Your turn again. And stop trying to distract me."

We kept on for an hour or more. I told her songs in French didn't count since I would have to take her word for it the lyrics included something relevant to the topic. She didn't like it, but agreed anyway in order to keep the game going. For all her teasing about my 'childish' game, she became invested and wanted to win.

During one of our debates over the lyrics, we heard footsteps on the gravel path outside. Both of us fell silent with fear, not knowing if it was friend or foe. How many feet? Six? No. Four. Two people? Were there more?

The feet stopped directly outside the crypt. Marie grabbed my hand and squeezed it hard. Suddenly, someone cursed outside. "Damn!"

Marie let go of her grasp and stood up. "Albé?"

There was a scuffling sound and then the lock rattled. "I've lost that hairpin. You wouldn't happen to have another one, would you?"

"You lost it?" I rose and dusted myself off, picking up Byron's cane as I did so. "How did you manage that?"

"Long story. Just pass me another one under the door, would you?" I reached over to search Marie's hair. She flinched and scowled at me. "Unhand me."

"Fine." I crossed my arms over my chest and sighed. "You get it."

She put one hand up and pulled out a hairpin. Stooping by the door, she pushed the pin under the door. We could see fingers reach down to pick it up, and then there was a scratching and rattling of the padlock. "Son of a —"

"Here. Let me try." I recognized the second voice. Polidori. He was here.

"I've got this." Byron sounded annoyed and perhaps a little embarrassed. I could almost hear his eyebrows move together into a frown like two storm fronts colliding. But before lightning struck between them, there came a resounding click as the lock mechanism opened.

When that door creaked wide, I took an involuntary gasp. I hadn't realized just how claustrophobic I had felt until we were freed from that place. Byron stood holding the door, looking in expectantly. Behind him, Polidori stood, clutching a duffel bag, trying not to look at either of us.

"Thank goodness. What took you so long?" It was Marie who broke the silence and tension, stepping out into the starlight to put her arms around both men simultaneously. Startled by her unexpected outpouring of motherly affection, the two of them hugged her back while I stood in the shadows alone. I looked down at myself, feeling suddenly embarrassed by my disheveled and dirty appearance, knowing I must seem even more of a mess than I felt.

I reached a hand up self-consciously and touched my hair. It was standing in all directions, and I remembered Byron teasing me about it when we had first met. That seemed so long ago, though only a few weeks had passed.

Uncharacteristic shyness came over me, and I wanted to shrink back into the corner. So much had changed. Once we found him, how would I ever explain to Raul what I had been through? And how was I going to talk to him about Byron? My feelings were so conflicted. I didn't even know what to say to myself about it. I didn't know how to face the enormity of the changes that had happened since I left St. Louis with Marie. It was a conversation I wasn't ready to face, and I was seized with terror at the prospect.

Polidori pulled away from their group hug and cleared his throat. I realized he must feel nearly as awkward as I did.

I realized I'd been standing there, holding Byron's cane as though waiting for him to say something. Not knowing what else to do or say, I simply held it out quietly, and Polidori took it from me with a little nod of acknowledgement.

"Where is Wolfie?" Marie said, stepping back to look Byron in the eye.

The question had been on my mind too, though I hadn't wanted to voice it, and I turned to look at him directly.

Byron frowned, then said simply, "He couldn't come with us. Don't worry about him. I'll talk to you about all that later."

Marie opened her mouth to say something more, but Polidori stepped forward, holding out the duffel, and said, "We brought you a change of clothes."

Despite his stiff awkwardness, there was a gentleness in the way he spoke, and his words broke my immobility. I reached to take the bag from his outstretched hand. "Thank you. That was thoughtful."

Shifting on his feet, he looked down, but I saw a small smile on his lips. "It was nothing. You might want to change before we leave this place."

Marie pulled back from Byron and nodded in acknowledgement. "Of course. We will just be a moment." Taking my arm, she whirled on her heel and paraded me back inside the crypt, shutting the door behind us. We stripped quickly. I wished the men had thought to bring us something to wash ourselves with, but there was no hope for it. They had, however, brought a hairbrush, and we took turns trying to make ourselves look presentable. It was so good to get into those modern clothes. I sighed happily as I stepped into the jeans they had brought.

"Thank god I'm done with that corset! "I said.

Marie raised a critical eyebrow. "It helped your figure. It was not all bad."

"Helped my figure? What is that supposed to mean? Are you saying I'm fat?"

"I am saying you could benefit from a more ladylike deportment."

"Ladylike deportment, my ass!"

"Charming." She picked up the dirty remnants of her costume and walked to the door. I could feel her disdain hanging in the air, and I balled my fists with fury, imagining the satisfaction I would feel to punch her in the face. "Do bring your things so we can dispose of them, won't you dear?"

My mind was so enraged, I couldn't speak. Instead, I did as she asked, telling myself it wasn't worth starting a fight with her. Eventually, there would be a day when we weren't in mortal terror, and then she was going to get an earful.

Byron stood next to Polidori, leaning on his cane as I had become used to seeing him, and at the hopeful look on his face, all my petty annoyance at Marie melted away, replaced by an uncharacteristic shyness I didn't understand.

I wasn't the same girl I was when Raul and I had met. Certainly, he wouldn't see me the same way anymore. How different I was since Marie gave me her blood, even I didn't know for sure. Raul loved me as a human, perhaps because I was human. Now that I was like him, could he love me any more? I didn't know, and I wasn't sure I would feel the same way about him either. I also wasn't sure how to feel about the change. I should be sad, shouldn't I? I should be upset. But I wasn't. Maybe it was just the shock of our situation, something that would fade. Then again, maybe I was letting go of Raul altogether.

Looking at Byron, those blue eyes met mine with a warmth and tenderness that made my heart squeeze. Something more than friendship had grown between the two of us, and even if I could go back to being the girl I used to be, I wasn't sure I wanted to.

"Can I...help you with that?" He looked down at the bundle of clothes in my arms, and before I could answer, he stepped forward and took them. "We need to get out of here."

He tossed the clothes to Polidori, and then walked brusquely over to the crypt door and shut it, locking it tight once more. "Pity we don't have a way to hide your footprints in the dust. We can only hope if the caretakers notice it, they put it down to tourists."

"Where do we go?" Marie gave her bundle to Polidori, and he staggered a bit, weighed down by the petticoats. "To hear you tell it, we are nearly out of options."

"For tonight? I found us rooms in a hotel. We can shower and change, and then go into the city to gather some things and some information. I don't know about you, but I wouldn't mind a nice bath. I still smell like seaweed." Picking up the empty duffel bag, he began shoving as much of the costume inside as would fit. There wasn't nearly enough room, however, and the zipper would not close. Polidori was still left holding my dress, and he stood stiffly, like a valet in one of those PBS historical dramas.

Marie frowned, placing her hands on her hips. "A hotel? Where? And with what money? Everything I had was back at the monastery."

He smiled at her, placing one hand on her cheek. "Not to worry, old girl. I have it all taken care of. And your money is safe as houses. Just trust me."

She breathed a sigh of relief, putting her hand on top of his and closing her eyes for a moment. "You are a good man, Albé. You always were."

Chuckling, he stepped forward to kiss her brow. "No, but I do have my moments. Come. We can't keep standing here."

With a little wave, he gestured us all to follow him as he turned and began walking back toward the main gates of the graveyard. We made a strange parade, Polidori bringing up the rear. Byron walked beside me, but we didn't look at one another.

After a moment or two, he reached inside his jacket pocket, withdrawing something which he held out to me. "I believe this is yours," he said.

I wrapped my fingers around it and instantly realized it was my .38. The one my father had given me as self defense. That seemed like a lifetime ago. Nodding, I glanced over at him gratefully, and then discreetly tucked the gun in the back waistband of my jeans.

Marie kept talking in low whispers. "So what is it you propose we do once we leave this hotel of yours? Will we not look suspicious if we are all together?"

He nodded. "That's why I propose we break up into teams. Sybill will go with Polly to get phones for us all to use. The untraceable kind. Sybill knows about these things, yes?"

He looked back at me, and I nodded. "Sure. Burners. I got you covered."

"Good." Turning back to Marie, he smiled a little grimly. "You and I will go to find out what we can about Casanova. I'm hoping they won't recognize us in more modern clothes. And your red hair will be unexpected. The wig you were wearing kept it hidden, and I'm counting on that fact to help disguise your identity."

We were close to the iron gates, and as we paused for Byron to open them, I had a flash of an idea. "If you want, I can also find us a place to stay that's more permanent. A house to rent or something. There's got to be a ton of internet cafes. I can look it up."

Byron raised a thoughtful eyebrow. "Will it take long?"

"Nah. I can find listings online really easily. That's a piece of cake."

"Very well. I'll leave that to you. But do not tarry over it."

"You're the ones I'm worried about," I said. "No one knows who I am, really. The pictures of me they showed on the news had my old hair color. This is a long way from Saint Louis. I think I'm pretty incognito."

"I'll be going with you," Polidori said. I'd almost forgotten him, and I felt a little guilty for leaving him out. "I can be inconspicuous as well."

Byron choked back a laugh. "Yes, I am sure you can manage to keep people from noticing you, Polly. I have every confidence in that." His face managed to squeeze itself back into a serious expression. "I'm trusting you to be her guide and get her in and out of the city safely and undetected. Can I count on you for that?"

Puffing up his chest, Polidori nodded. "It would be my honor."

"Good man."

We walked through the gate and out onto the pier. Byron shut the gate behind us with a clang, and I suddenly felt exposed, as though our enemies might see us and swoop in at any moment. That high wall had been keeping us in, but it also kept them out. Now, we had no protection at all, and I felt a chill at that realization. Everyone else must have felt it too, because we wasted no more time talking, hurrying to climb aboard the small boat that was waiting there for us.

We each took a seat, and Polidori set the clothes down on the floor by his feet. Byron took the pilot's seat while I cast off the lines.

"Hang on," Byron said, and we roared away into the night.

Beauty Of A Thousand Stars

Casanova

I had just collapsed back on the bed, such as it was, to contemplate an eternity being forgotten in here with Kit when suddenly, Jenny's voice came from beyond the door. "Psst! Boss? You in there?"

My feet hit the floor immediately as my hope renewed, and I raced to the door in jubilation, lacing my fingers with hers through the bars. "Jenny! Oh god, I had given myself up to be lost and alone forever down here."

"Oi," said Kit. "Alone? What am I? Bloody invisible?"

"I wish," I muttered in an annoyed singsong.

"Now that is just hurtful," he said. "Who's the bird?"

"Nobody you need to know," I said, blocking his view of her with my body.

He clicked his tongue. "Tsk. Rude."

"Hush," I said, giving Jenny a tight smile as I turned all my attention back to her. "Have they found her yet?"

Jenny shook her head. "No, but man, they are hoppin' mad, let me tell ya. They're all runnin' around like a bunch of fire ants who got their ant hill stepped on. It was a bitch sneaking my way in here. They got signs posted everywhere sayin' this area of the building is under construction. Under construction, my butt. To me, that was like a big flashin' neon sign that said 'Casanova's right here.' Who do they think they're foolin'?"

"You shouldn't be here," I said. "It's too dangerous."

She waved a dismissive hand. "Pshh. They got you in custody. I think they figure you aren't goin' anywhere, so there's not as much attention on his place yet. It's everywhere else I gotta be afraid of. They're lookin' all over the city. Anyway, they don't know about me, and I aim to keep it that way. I'm not even on their radar. You were right when you told me to stay clear of all their politics and schemes. If I'd stuck my nose in where it didn't belong, I'd be in here right along with you."

"I wouldn't complain," said Kit, interjecting himself in an undertone.

"You smell like road kill possum," said Jenny, wrinkling her nose. "When's the last time you had a shower?"

"I've forgotten," he said with a shrug. "What year is it?"

"Year?" she said, eyes boggling.

"Don't answer that," I said, shifting to stand between them once again.

"Who is that guy?" she asked. "Friend of yours?"

"Not since he put me here," said Kit.

She raised a brow, looking back at me with wide eyes. "What the hell'd he do?"

"Doesn't matter," I said. "Ignore him. We have more important things to talk about. Tell me what you heard. Is there to be a trial?"

Her mouth twisted to the side, and she shrugged. "Well, I mean, they think you killed that guy, Robes-whatever..."

I winced. "Robespierre."

"You killed Robespierre?" Kit said. "Are you insane?"

Jenny scowled. "Hey, pipe down, mister. What's it to you?"

He snorted. "Even I'm not that foolish, and I've done some fairly wild things in my time."

"Nobody cares," I said, pointedly refusing to look back over my shoulder in his direction, though I knew that's what he wanted.

He laughed. "Yes, well, you would say that. You killed him. They'll execute you for it, you know?"

I gritted my teeth and counted to three. "I didn't kill him. Someone else did, and it was self defense."

"Humph. I've heard that line before. It's less believable the second time round."

"Who are you?" Jenny said again, leaning to one side to peer around me and get a better look.

"No one," I insisted, though my confidence was slipping by the second. "Darling girl, please, we don't have much time."

She sighed, nodding her agreement, and then reached into the inside pocket of her coat. She brought out a plastic sack, handing it to me through the bars. "Here. Brought you some blood bags. Figured you might not get enough while you're in here."

Kit scrambled to his feet and before I could even pull the sack completely through into the cell, he'd taken one of the blood bags and bitten into it hungrily, groaning with pleasure as the crimson liquid poured down his throat.

"Jesus, mister," Jenny said, her eyes round as she stared openly past me at my companion. "When'd they feed you last?"

I could hear him gulping, and when at last the bag was empty, he gave her a wistful smile, a bead of blood dripping from his lip and down his chin. "I don't remember that either."

A look of pity shone in her eyes. "Well, don't drink it all, okay? It's got to last you both until I can get back, and I don't know how soon that will be. I promise I'll try to bring more next time."

"I like this girl of yours, Gio," said Kit. "Pretty thing too."

"You're not," she said, matter-of-factly.

He stood up a little straighter. "You haven't had a proper look at me yet."

She looked him up and down. "I think I've seen enough."

"Never mind. I see the family resemblance now," Kit said, sighing as he settled back down into his spot on the floor.

Jenny looked back at me with a frown. "I'll figure out a way to get you out of here, boss."

"Oh thank god," said Kit, "because all his efforts on that front have been an enormous disappointment. Gio Casanova, the only man to have escaped this very cell, and yet here we are, still."

I bit my tongue before speaking. "It's not my fault they fixed the weak spot in the roof."

"Actually, it is your fault. Because of the giant you-shaped hole you made when you scarpered, they fixed it with sterner stuff so no one else could get out the same way. Not to mention writing about it and gloating afterward in those memoirs of yours. On behalf of everyone who's been chucked in here afterward, I want to express my sincerest fuck you."

"I'll get you out, boss," said Jenny once more, her words stopping me before I turned and launched myself at Kit in a fit of pique.

"Thank you, my dear," I said. "For everything. I don't deserve your kindness."

"He really doesn't," said Kit in an undertone.

"Hush," Jenny and I said in unison, and then we looked at one another and laughed in surprise.

"You'd better go, Jenny, dear," I said. "I need you to run the business in my absence. If anyone asks where I am, tell them I'm taking care of some personal business. No sense alarming anyone. In a couple of days, once the excitement has died down a little, do your best to try to find Marie before they catch up to her, would you? She and her companions will need your help, and perhaps with their assistance, you can find a way to free me from this place."

"I hate leaving you here," she said.

"Just be safe," I said, reaching through the bars to touch her cheek. "That's all I ask."

"I promise," she said with a little nod. "I'll see you soon."

Taking her hand in mine, I pulled it to the bars and kissed the fingers gently. "Go. Before they find you."

"Take care, boss," she said.

With that, she backed away, and then she turned and ran the way she'd come, leaving me standing there clutching the plastic sack she'd given me.

"You think she liked me?" Kit said. "I think she liked me."

Ignoring his question entirely, I stared down the empty hallway in silent despondence. Several moments passed by while the memories of my earlier incarceration in this awful place came crashing in all around me. Long years had passed, and yet the place still smelled and felt the same.

"If you're not going to drink all of that, could I have another?" said Kit at last.

I sighed, reached into the sack to pull out another blood bag, and tossed it over in his direction without looking. "Just stop talking, Kit. Please. For five minutes, just stop talking."

The Game's Afoot

Ernestine

If Mozart had followed my orders, traveling to the coven headquarters should not have taken him more than a couple of hours. I gave him five, not because he deserved it but because I wanted to prove I had been right about him.

When I called Robespierre's phone number to talk to his replacements and was told Mozart had not yet arrived, I smiled, though my inner glee did not reveal itself as I spoke to the harried woman on the other line. "Missing, you say? And you still haven't found the fugitive either? Trace his phone, idiot. Honestly, you people are useless. Must I do everything?"

She spluttered, and I could hear papers rustling on her end as though she were frantically shuffling them in search of information. "Forgive me, madame. I only just arrived. I will have a report for you within an hour."

"You do that," I said. "Don't call me until you have something useful to say. No excuses. I don't have time for patience while you catch up. They're on the move but can't have gotten far. Do the job you're paid for or get someone who can. Now."

"Understood. Yes, madame." Her voice trembled. She was frightened. Good. Fear meant she would obey.

Before she could say any more, I hung up, then sighed heavily, touching my fingers to my forehead.

As I had expected, the man had been too cowardly and self-serving to follow my orders. Still, I needed to find out what he knew all the same. He would have valuable insight into where Marie and her entourage might have gone, and that information would be vitally important if I hoped to capture her and return her to the Master for justice. Bringing the man back for questioning would remind the Master of the reasons why I deserved my position.

With this in mind, I went to his study to ask for permission to pursue Mozart.

"You believe he will divulge greater intelligence than Raul is able to provide into the mindset of our quarry," said the Marquis, looking at me over the top of his desk as I stood before him, hands clasped behind my back in deference. His words were a statement, not a question.

"I do, Master," I said, bowing my head to him.

"Despite the fact he has only been at her side for a short time rather than the decades Raul spent as her closest confidant." He raised an eyebrow. Again, he was observing, not asking,

"Indeed," I said.

He tilted his head slightly to one side, eyes narrowing. "Explain your reasoning."

This had always been the way between us. Cool logic and reasoning were what he prized more than anything, and as a result I had learned to hone my scientific rational mind.

"I don't believe Raul has ever truly been her confidant," I said. "He was not privy to many of her secrets, despite their years together. She treated him more like a child than a friend or an equal. Herr Mozart, on the other hand, was able to gain her trust on the basis of their childhood friendship, and

I believe she may have let her guard down in his presence. He will have more relevant and recent information on her current whereabouts and associates. Information which will be more useful in the present situation."

Tapping a finger on his lips as I spoke, his brow furrowed pensively. He stood in silence for a moment while he contemplated my assessment. At last, he nodded. "Very well. We shall see what he knows."

He didn't ask how I would accomplish this task. My success was a matter of course. However, there was also an implication that failure was not an option, and while I was proud of his trust in me, I felt a twinge of anxiety, though I did not allow that worry to show.

Instead, I bowed my head again and smiled. "Thank you, Master."

As I left the room, I swelled with pride at having convinced him to see things my way. I was determined not to fail. I would bring Mozart back and wring our answers from him. He would pay dearly for his disloyalty, and I would prove my value to the Master beyond any doubt.

Luck Be A Lady

Mozart

Escape had been my focus as I sat on the train departing for Milan. Milan was not my intended destination. It was merely the first city on the train departures list, and I knew I would have time to think about my next move once I was aboard.

As we sped through the Italian countryside, however, I had no idea where to go for safety.

Returning to Chicago was out of the question. Vince was dead, and even if he weren't, I had burned that bridge the moment I left with Marie. Moreover, all my other contacts were associated with the Marquis, so there was no question of relying on them for help.

Venice was ruined for me, and as a consequence, Casanova was of no assistance either. I had been absent from Vienna too long to return there. And France was too near the Marquis' grasp. I was persona non grata in Germany after accruing debts with several associates.

That left only one possible place to turn, though I had avoided it for decades. Monaco.

It was too close to the Marquis for comfort, but with dwindling options, I didn't see much choice.

I had sworn off gambling after it had lead to my entanglement with the Marquis. Unfortunately, all my acquaintances were in the casino business. That's what I get for living a dissolute life.

Stepping in through the front doors of the casino, bag in hand, I was greeted by the familiar hubbub of slot machines. Beyond that, I could hear the call of the staff at the roulette wheel and the craps table, and at the rear, the sound of shuffled cards over all the rest. I stopped in my tracks and closed my eyes, drinking in the cacophony of sound. I heard order in the seeming chaos. Mathematics in every clink of coin. A kind of music. To me, it was a siren song. Despite all my admonitions from the past, I was helpless to its call. Before I could stop myself, I had exchanged all my cash, such as it was, for a stack of chips.

I slid into a seat at the blackjack table, and it felt like home.

"Deal me in," I said, nodding to the dealer like an old friend.

They say luck is a lady. This is too gentle a term. She is fickle and cruel. She takes no prisoners. But oh, how she shines. And when she is on your side, there is nothing better than that rush.

One last hand, I told myself. But there is always one more to follow. Hours went by before I realized I had not yet found a room in the hotel. Another hour more passed before I decided it didn't matter to me anymore.

Presumed Guilty

Casanova

The intermittent tapping of my feet on the stone floor was the only sound in that dark place. I had paced ever since Jenny left, hoping for a burst of inspiration to help in my escape.

Unfortunately, Kit wasn't wrong about the reinforcements that were made to the cell in the intervening centuries since my daring escape. Cursing myself for having detailed the room's weaknesses, I assessed the situation with frustration.

The ceiling was now rendered impervious, steel gage bars covered with sheets of lead and then clay tile roofing lain atop it. Even with my immortal strength, I was not capable of breaking through all three layers in order to escape upwards once more.

The walls were thick stone. Even if by some miracle I could chisel or chip my way through to the outside, I could hardly hide my activities. It would be impossible to create a hole wide enough to pass through, and even if I could, the wall was a sheer drop to the walled courtyard below.

All of these obstacles were ones I had contemplated long ago during my imprisonment. It had taken me a year to escape then, and I doubted I would have so long to work on solving the puzzle this time.

My companion had gone silent. I wasn't sure whether he slept or was merely so used to being alone that the quiet didn't bother him. Either way, I found it unsettling.

No sooner had I thought this, however, than I heard his rasping voice break the silence.

"Afraid of me, are you," he said. "I suppose I ought to be flattered."

I whirled to look at him, stopping my pacing. "Whatever gave you that idea?"

"You did," he said.

"I beg your pardon?"

He laughed, shaking his head. "No need to apologize. I find this development rather comical, given our history."

My eyes narrowed. "I wasn't apologizing."

"You just begged my pardon."

"I meant it as a question, asking how you came to such a conclusion."

Gazing back at me directly, he raised a brow. "You're not sorry, then?"

"No," I said insistently. "I'm not. I want to understand why you thought I was afraid of you."

Again, he snorted a laugh. "You said it. Out loud."

"I beg your pardon?"

With finger upraised, he rolled his eyes. "Oh, I'm not falling for that again."

I sighed heavily, glaring down at him. "Why are you like this?"

"Like what?"

"Like this," I said, my voice betraying my annoyance. "I can't tell if you're actually obtuse or if you're making fun of me."

He grinned then. "When in doubt, most likely the latter, my boy."

I glared.

"Well, you did ask," he said, looking down to examine his nails as if suddenly bored with our conversation. "If you didn't want me to know what you were thinking, you shouldn't have been muttering to yourself. Perhaps you didn't realize you talk to yourself, but that internal dialogue you thought you were having was spoken aloud."

"How long?" I said.

"How long have I been able to hear your mumbling?" Lifting his gaze back in my direction, he gave a long suffering sigh. "Hours. At first, I thought it was important, but then I realized it was a conversation for one. I managed to ignore most of what you said, but once I heard my name, it spurred my attention."

Ordinarily, this information would have made me concerned about having made a social faux pas, but under the circumstances, I simply shook my head and sighed once more. "It helps me to think aloud."

"Mmm," he said. "Rather unsubtly. Yes, I gathered that."

"You might have said something before."

"And interrupt the genius at work? Not a chance." Sarcasm dripped from every word he spoke in a deliberate effort to provoke me.

My brows knit as I scowled. I opened my mouth to make a retort, but before I could do so, I heard footsteps coming down the dark corridor, and I fell silent, turning toward the door to see who was approaching our cell.

The face that came into view through the bars belonged to coven member Signore Barbaro, a man I had worked beside for years. I rushed forward, heart full of hope. "Oh thank goodness, Antonio. I thought it was one of them come to torture me. Get me out of here, would you? I need to get back to work. This is all a huge misunderstanding."

But he didn't smile, nor did he move to unlock the cell. I saw his lips press into a line, and he looked on me as though he didn't recognize me, though we had worked side-by-side for over a century. "I cannot do that, Signore Casanova."

No apology. And he called me 'Signore Casanova' rather than the familiar 'Gio' I had grown used to hearing from his lips. I blinked, and then swallowed hard. "You cannot mean to leave me here, Antonio. We are friends, you and I."

"Are we?" he said. "I think not."

Startled, I stared at him blankly and then addressed him more formally. "Signore, what is wrong with you? We've worked together these many years."

He scoffed. "Perhaps you should have considered that before you betrayed us."

"Betrayed?" I said, shaking my head. "I never did anything to dishonor or endanger the coven. You know me. I would never do such a thing."

"There are serious charges brought against you, Signore. Very serious."

I stepped closer, straining at the end of the chains that bound me. "Well, don't leave me in suspense. Spit it out, man."

"In a word? Treason," he said.

My jaw dropped open, and I stared at him for a long moment. "I never."

"There are a dozen or more witnesses who would argue the contrary."

The chains rattled as I gestured wildly, frustration and fury setting a fire in my soul. "Which witnesses are those? Agents of the Marquis? If you're looking for traitors, I suggest you start there."

"You sided with an enemy state," he said. "Over your own people's best interests."

"Says who?"

"Says an overwhelming preponderance of evidence."

I shook my head, glaring. "Says people who would like to see us align ourselves with the Marquis. If we do that, we lose our sovereignty."

Beneath dark brows, he glared right back. "You are the one on trial, not the Marquis or anyone who agrees with his views."

"I'm on trial, am I?" I said, full of disbelief. "Is this the trial? Hardly just. I deserve the right to face my accusers and to speak in my own defense."

"A tribunal," he said. "Three days from now. You'll get your day in court soon enough, though it won't do you much good."

I tilted my head, frowning. "You speak as though the outcome were already settled."

He shook his head and scowled. "Unfortunately no."

"That's a matter of perspective."

Raising a hand, he held up three fingers at me in emphasis. "Three days, Signore."

I pursed my lips, full of rage. "Not much time to gather my defense."

At this pronouncement, he laughed aloud. "You have no defense."

"I might," I said, "if given time to prepare."

"No," said Signore Barbaro. "You might have time to concoct a beautiful fiction which might convince some who don't know you well."

I sighed, turning slightly away and then glancing back over at him sidelong. "At least I know where you stand."

He made a little bow, a tense smile quirking the corner of his mouth. "Good day to you, Signore."

"Doubtful," muttered Kit from his dark corner.

He had been silent during my entire exchange, and at this pronouncement, both Signore Barbaro and I turned to look at him with a narrowed gaze. But Kit was through talking. Ignoring us completely, he drew up his knees to his chest, wrapped his arms around his legs, and tucked his forehead against against his knees. I had the sudden impression of a turtle who had retreated into his shell to avoid a perceived danger. For a moment, I was struck with a sense of pity for him. He had put on brave face in the time we had been cell mates, but perhaps he was only doing so as an act of self-preservation.

I was the first to speak, turning my gaze back on Signore Barbaro. "I will be ready. Never you fear."

Looking back at me, he scoffed, and then turned away with a shake of his head, walking to the door without another word.

Confessions and Regret

Marie

Albé was true to his word. Not only did he evade our enemies, but he saved our little family too. I didn't know how to thank him for giving me such a precious gift. Even after all these years apart, he still loved me, and I was overwhelmed with gratitude.

He had found temporary lodgings for us in a hotel hidden in the heart of Lido. The rooms were simple, but after the Spartan chambers of the monastery, we did not mind. The showers were large, and the water was hot, which were the only concerns occupying my immediate thoughts. Byron saw to everything, and it was not long before new clothes were brought up to us. I don't know where they came from, and the fit and style was not perfect, but after a long night of dirt and dank, it was heavenly to be clean once more.

As I dressed, I thought over all of the people who had been lost or put in danger over the last few months because of me – Raul, Crystal, Sybill, Vince, Wolfie, Gio, Albé, Doctor Polidori, Casanova's assistant Jenny, and even the monks who had given us shelter. Every one of them was now a target for my enemies because of having come into contact with me. Though I was not responsible for the lengths the Marquis was willing to go in order to capture me, the safety of my companions and acquaintances was my responsibility, and that burden sat heavily on my shoulders. Sinking onto the bed, I sat staring down at my hands, clasping them on my lap.

I did not have long to ruminate over my guilt, however, because a few minutes later, a knock came at the door. I opened it to find the others waiting in the hall together, Sybill standing next to Albé and the doctor a little behind them and off to one side.

Once the door was closed behind them, Albé looked at me seriously, gesturing for us all to have a seat. "I thought it would be wise for us to discuss a few things in private while we have a chance."

"Of course," I said, seeing the sense of such advice.

I sat on the bed once again, Sybill following suit, and Polidori and Albé each took one of the straight-backed chairs next to the window. Albé's face was uncharacteristically solemn, and I felt a deep sense of foreboding seep into the pit of my stomach.

"What is it?" I said. "Where is Wolfie? Something has happened. Something awful."

Without answering, Albé reached into the inside pocket of his jacket and pulled out a crumpled envelope, holding it out to me. It was still sealed shut, my name scrawled across the front in Wolfie's cramped lettering. I willed myself to take the letter, knowing I was not going to like what I found inside.

I tore open the envelope, feeling the others' eyes on me as I withdrew the letter and unfolded it to read aloud. After all, the others had a right to know what the letter contained since he had been their companion as well.

> *My dear girl,*
>
> *I know how close you and Gio have become these last few weeks. I can't pretend it didn't make me jealous. You both hurt me.*

Yet I know what he is like, and I could have forgiven the two of you in time.

Fate took away any chance of that, however, and I fear when you learn the truth of what I have done, it is you who will never forgive me. Indeed, I would not blame you. I cannot continue to let you believe a lie. My conscience won't allow it. I swear, I never intended things to be this way.

There is no time to couch this confession in gentle terms, and so I will be brief and straightforward.

Years ago, the Marquis sent me to America with the express purpose of seeking you out. I ingratiated myself with Vincent, begging for employment, which he gave to me. Do not blame him for my transgressions, my sweet. He believed I earnestly sought a new life, while all the time I had secret intentions to locate you.

Please believe, I would not have stooped so low were I not in the most dire of circumstances. I never learned to be a frugal man. I like gambling and living in comfort, things my human life denied me. The Marquis promised to pay my creditors if I would do this thing for him, and I agreed. I have been consumed with regret ever since.

When you walked in the door of Vincent's hotel suite, I wanted to warn you, but I never knew if Vincent worked as one of the Marquis's agents as well. You expressed your feelings for me, feelings I had always shared but thought were beyond my reach. I saw the potential to escape from under the Marquis's influence and save you at the same time. I believed if I could stay close to you and provide the Marquis just enough information yet still throw him off our trail, he would be satisfied.

First, he only wanted information. I thought I could give him something without putting you in danger. However, the information I provided never sufficed. He always wanted more.

My instructions from the Marquis made it clear if I did not find a way soon to hold you prisoner until they could arrive and take you into their custody, then they would do the job for me.For the longest time, I have wanted to tell you the truth, but there has never been an opportunity. Now I see my remaining with you will only lead them closer until you are caught. I could not live with that on my conscience. The Marquis and his coterie of vampires are weary of waiting for me to do their bidding. They will track my whereabouts in the hopes of finding you if I stay any longer. Therefore, I am leaving you in order to draw them off the trail and to regain whatever shreds of my dignity and honor remain.

You may never forgive me for what I have done. I had hoped to make a confession to you in person, but the time never seemed right. Now it is far too late. I was a selfish coward, but I hope my final act on this day will make up in some small part for the wrongs I have done you.

Always your affectionate,

Wolfgang

P.S. – Tell the good doctor I am sorry. I took his vaccine as insurance in case I am captured.

As I read, I heard gasps all around, and when Polidori heard the postscript addressed to him, he leapt to his feet. "There! What did I tell you? I knew it. That bastard! We have to stop him. We have to find him right away."

"Polly," said Albé, "we have too much to worry about. There's no time to go galavanting off to satisfy a personal vendetta."

"Vendetta?" said the doctor, his nostrils flared and his hands shaking with trembling rage. "This isn't about me or my research. I am insulted, yes, but as a physician, I must set that aside when there is a risk to the general public."

"Dude, calm down. People are going to hear you," Sybill said.

He rounded on her with a withering gaze. "You are the last person in this room with the authority to tell me to calm down. Compared to the rest of us, you're a baby, and you don't know the first thing about our condition or anything else for that matter. You have no wisdom to share, so kindly keep your instructions and opinions to yourself, you ridiculous chit!"

"I'm a...what am I?" Sybill rose to her feet, planting them in a fighting stance, visibly seething. "Look, I don't know what your problem is, and I don't care right now. I've been nothing but nice to you. I may not know a lot about being a vampire, but I sure as hell know more than you do about how to treat other people."

Albé and I got to our feet simultaneously, pushing them both back from one another.

"Stop this," I said. "We have enough enemies. We cannot afford to start fighting amongst ourselves."

"Yeah? And whose fault is that, huh?" Sybill said, rounding on me. "None of us would be in this mess if it wasn't for you. I wish I'd never met you. I wish I could just go back home and pretend none of this ever happened. But I can't. You ruined my life. You ruined all our lives. You can't act like my best friend all of a sudden. I shouldn't be here. None of us should."

I staggered back as if I had been struck, sitting heavily on the bed.

"Sybill, stop," Byron said.

Tears streamed down her cheeks, and her words choked with emotion. "Why should I? Why does she get a pass for all the shit she's done? Because she's the queen? That's bullshit, and you know it. In case you haven't noticed, she's queen of fuck all now, so spare me the lecture on courtly manners. The world has moved on, and she's a relic. I'm not coddling her feelings anymore. I'm done. I want to go home and have a normal life and be left alone."

With this last, she sobbed, sinking to her knees and covering her face in her hands.

During her tirade, Polidori had stood stiffly, staring as though she were a wild creature he was studying under glass, and once she had dissolved into tears, his lip curled in a sneer.

Albé, however, moved swiftly to her side, removing his jacket and draping it around her shoulders protectively. "Shh, lass. Shh, now."

She leaned against him and wrapped her arms around his neck, clinging and weeping as if her heart would break.

All the while, I was immobilized while her words sliced through me again and again like so many shards of glass. She was right. I deserved everything she had said and more. Because of me, she had lost her family and her future. I had done nothing but compound one selfish, careless mistake on top of another, and she had paid the price.

"I am sorry," I whispered. "I am so sorry."

Sybill said nothing, only cried a little harder. I bowed my head and closed my eyes, hands clasped as if in prayer, though I knew it was futile to expect heaven to answer me.

Crossing the room, Polidori went to stand by the window, arms crossed, looking out into the darkened night. Fog had risen on the water, and a cold misting rain was beginning to fall.

"Marie is right," he said quietly at last. "We don't have the luxury of petty melodrama. Like it or not, our only hope of survival right now is to work together. We need one another. We don't have to like it, but if we want to live, we have to set all these personal grievances aside."

Sniffling, Sybill looked over at him, pulling back from Albé and wiping her eyes with the back of her hand.

"Thank you, Polly," said Byron, his voice soft and tender.

"This is all my fault," I said. "I am the reason you are all in danger."

Standing once more, Byron reached out to take my hand, squeezing it gently. "Nonsense. The Marquis is a madman. There is no reasoning with a monster like that. His obsession knows no bounds. You couldn't have predicted his every action."

"No. But I did not have to bring anyone else into this. Sybill is right. I should just turn myself in and bring an end to it once and for all."

"It's too late for that," said Polidori, turning to look at me. "We are all in this now. If you hand yourself over to him, we are all accomplices to the crimes for which he deems you guilty. Every one of us is complicit in hiding you. Punishing you...even killing you...won't satisfy his need for vengeance. He will see us all as part of the same conspiracy, and I have no doubt we will be next on his list to find and destroy."

Those words sent a chill through the room, and for a moment, no one spoke.

"Then what do we do?" I asked at last, feeling helpless and small.

"We fight," said Sybill, a note of certainty and determination rising in her voice once more. "We fight like hell. And we make sure we end this thing. After that, we'll deal with the leftover baggage."

Glancing around the room at one another, we each nodded and murmured our agreement.

Byron held out a hand to Sybill and helped her to her feet, then laced their fingers together. "Stick to the plan. Marie and I go to find out what's happened to Casanova. We need to help him if we can, agreed?"

Inwardly, I breathed a sigh of relief that the worst seemed over, at least for now, and I smiled tentatively. "Agreed."

"All right," said Sybill. "And the doc and me? I'm not staying behind while you're out risking your necks."

Polidori made no such statement, but he did not disagree with her sentiment either, and I took that as a positive, however small a step forward it might be.

"We stick to the plan. The two of you are going to work on the technical aspects of what happens next. I want you to figure out how we can avoid being detected for however long we still need to stay in the area. First, we need a way to communicate with one another."

Sybill nodded. "Got it."

"There's also the financial issues to settle. My assets are not currently accessible in our current situation, and Marie has a limited amount of cash on hand. I have no doubt any attempts to use credit cards will set them on our trail. We need some alternatives, and we need them fast. Something that doesn't involve murdering someone wealthy." Byron turned to Polidori, reaching out to touch his shoulder. "That's where you come in."

"Me?" said Polidori with a raised brow. "I fail to see the connection between our financial situation and my set of skills."

"You know the area," Byron said. "You speak the language. You have lived here almost as long as I have. You need to find Sybill an internet cafe where she can use my laptop and help her locate and gather the supplies we will need. And I want you to do one thing more for me."

Polidori glared, fiddling with his cufflinks. "And what is that?"

"If you can't locate a safe place for us to stay in the next twenty-four hours," said Byron, "someplace our enemies won't look, then I want you to agree to take us to the facility."

He said the final word with special emphasis, and it sent a chill through me, though I did not know what he meant.

"The what?" said Sybill, and her tone of concern made it clear she'd also felt the same sense of dread.

"No," Polidori said, his voice cold and flat. "Absolutely not. It's completely inappropriate, and you know all the reasons why."

Byron didn't break his gaze, keeping his eyes fixed on Polidori's. "I know we can't afford not to consider it. Swear to me, if all else fails, you'll allow it."

"You're mad," Polidori said, but a tone of defeat was in his voice, and it was clear he had given in, though he had not said so aloud.

"Takes one to know one," said Byron, his tight smile an

acknowledgement of Polidori's agreement, though without a hint of gloating.

"Whatever this place is," I said, "I will go there. I will do anything you ask. I want to make this right."

"Oh, the ship has long since sailed on that one," said Sybill. "How about you just stop making things worse from here on out, huh?"

"Sybill…" said Albé.

She sighed. "Fine. I'm sorry. That was uncalled for."

"No," I said. "I earned that. I have given you every reason to be angry with me and no reason to trust me. I want to change that, but I know I have to earn it. Please, let me try. I want to try."

Gazing back at me, I saw her consider what I'd said, and after several uncomfortable moments, she nodded finally. "All right. I'm not giving you a clean slate, but I'll give you the chance to prove you mean what you say."

"Thank you," I said, a ghost of a smile on my lips.

"Good," said Albé, smiling broadly. "Then it's settled. We'd better get to it. We have a long night ahead of us."

As a group, we walked out of the building, stopping only once we were well away from well-trafficked areas.

"This is where we part," Byron said, all business now. "Everyone know what their job is?"

Polidori looked up with a smirk. "Yes. We know. Don't get caught."

Byron glared at him, moving in close to poke his chest with a finger. "You think this is a joke, right now?"

He looked at Byron, a cold challenge in his eyes. "No. I think we are wasting time talking."

Sybill reached in and pushed them apart. "Hey! Enough. This is not a pissing contest. Let's just go do this thing and get back. All right?"

Straightening the lapels on his coat, Byron nodded curtly, then held out an arm to me. "Give us a good fifteen minutes head start before you leave. That way we aren't seen together as a group. Less conspicuous."

Polidori rolled his eyes, pushing his hair back from his face with one hand. "You don't have to micromanage everything."

The muscle in Byron's cheek clenched, and I saw his eyes narrow. I squeezed his arm. "Albé, enough."

He looked at me and nodded. His nostrils were flared with anger, but he turned, and we walked away without another word, leaving Sybill and Polidori behind in the shadows.

We walked to the water taxi area, and Byron engaged us a conveyance to the city. During the ride, I sat with my head on his shoulder, hoping my presence would be a calming influence. He stared out over the water, and I wondered what exactly it was that made him so bristling and sharp. Was it jealousy at being separated from Sybill? Anger at Polidori's words? Or something else? A lingering fear of capture, perhaps. All I could do was be present and hope his mood would change. Sulking broodiness made me sad, and I knew on either side lay self-loathing and rage, both equally possible outcomes of his current mood. His emotions were often volatile, and while he did his best to keep them in check, sometimes they overflowed and could not be contained. I had seen these moods before, and I knew the cycles they could take. The warning signs were as plain to me as if they had been painted on his face.

Throughout the journey, he did not speak. I allowed him that silence, simply letting him know I cared without pressure or expectation. He did not need me to express those feelings aloud. My touch on his arm was enough to convey all that went unsaid.

Only when we drew near to the city did he finally break his silence. We talked in hushed tones to ensure we both understood our roles and agenda for the mission. His voice was tense and matter of fact, and I knew from the businesslike manner of his speech that he was far less calm than he was willing to acknowledge aloud.

We approached the Casanova Disco arm-in-arm like lovers. I knew because he was distinctive-looking, my presence needed to hide his identity. He could not disguise those piercing blue eyes of his, so unsettlingly vivid. His limp also was a telltale giveaway. It was, therefore, my responsibility to be distracting enough to draw attention away from it.

As we approached the main doors of the Casanova Disco, I was struck by the mundane mood of the crowd gathered in the queue. After all we had experienced over the last few days, and knowing Casanova himself had been taken away by the vampire coven of Venice, it seemed incongruous and jarring to find these people behaving as though nothing had changed at all. They stood chatting and texting, their breath steaming in the cold night air, oblivious to the fact their host was being subjected to who knew what torture.

I shivered, though not with chill, clutching Byron's arm a little tighter as we walked past the waiting humans and stopped in front of the man working security at the entrance.

"We are here to see Jenny," I said, tossing my long red locks with a smile. The man looked us up and down for a split second, and then opened the rope to let us pass. A few of the people waiting in line grumbled, but when the man turned a baleful eye in their direction, complaints were quickly silenced once more, and we walked through the doors with heads held high.

The music throbbed on the air like a living thing, its pulse sounding heavy and driving the crowd to the dance floor under the flashing lights. We paused on the edge of that space, and I searched the room, looking for the familiar sight of that young woman from Iowa.

It suddenly occurred to me she might have been captured too. For all we knew, my enemies were lying in wait for me to arrive.

"Do you see her?" Byron said, pressing his lips to my ear so he could be heard over the frenetic din.

I shook my head as he pulled away, a frown furrowing my brow as I pondered what to do next. I did not know what I had expected, but we had come with a very simple idea in mind, only half-developed, and I was uncertain how to proceed. Clearly, no one working here knew their boss was in danger, or if they did, they had no intention of giving away their concern.

Just then, I felt someone grasp my elbow, and I jerked it back instinctively, whirling away in self defense as if I had been burned. But it was only Jenny, her hands upraised, and I felt relief flood through me like water on a fire. Pressing my palm to my chest as if to still my heart, despite the fact it no longer beat, I let out a sigh.

"Sorry! It's just me," she said. "Didn't mean to startle you."

Only then did I realize that Byron had pulled his sword from his cane and taken a fighting stance, ready to come to my aid once more. I placed my hand on his arm, and he slowly lowered the blade. "Jenny, I presume," he said, though he did not apologize for his actions.

She nodded, keeping her eyes on the business end of the sword until it was safely stowed away once more. "I don't blame you for being jumpy. I didn't expect to see you here. Not after...well...you know. When you didn't answer my phone calls and I found out you'd left the monastery, I figured you'd have skipped town by now."

Brow furrowed with worry, I shook my head, biting my lip for a moment as I scanned the bar. Anyone here could be an enemy, and I felt the urge to run begin to rise.

Seeing my unspoken concern, she nodded her head toward a door on the far end of the bar marked "Privato," and without saying another word, she began walking toward it, beckoning us to follow. My fingers clutching Byron's arm, the two of us hastily made our way toward the door and walked through it behind her. Only when the heavy metal door closed behind us, muffling the music, did I realize how truly frightened and vulnerable I had felt while we were in that crowd.

The narrow hallway was dark and smelled slightly musty. Ahead of us was a darkened store room where bottles of liquor lined a series of wooden shelves that appeared to have been used for a century or more. Jenny led us inside, and then she walked toward one of the shelves and pulled a cleverly disguised lever. The shelving unit swung outward, revealing a hidden room beyond. "In here," she said, flipping a light switch just inside and then stepping back to allow us through.

Byron and I walked in to find a cozy office space. A large, ornately carved wooden desk stood to one side, papers in cascading piles on its surface. There was a gold brocade-covered couch with matching armchairs in the other half of the room. Rich carpets covered the stone floors, softening our footfalls. An antique crystal chandelier hung from the ceiling, refitted to use modern electric lights. Books lay in haphazard stacks on tables, but none of them were dusty, obviously in the midst of being used. This was his office and private sanctuary from the modern world, and I couldn't help the little smile that tugged at my lips as I looked around. This was the scholarly side of him few others saw, and it delighted and surprised me. Casanova may have perfected the appearance of a playboy for those people out there on the dance floor, and he was equally adept at the role of statesman and courtier when necessary, but this room was a reflection of who he really was. A persona without artifice. A man of curiosity and internal passions.

Jenny closed the door behind us, and the last sound of the thrumming music was silenced.

"The boss would kill me if he knew I brought you back here and let you see all this mess. He hired me as his librarian. I'm supposed to get all this stuff straightened up, but I haven't had a chance yet with all that's been going on," she said, stepping toward one of the armchairs and gesturing toward the sofa. "Please, have a seat."

Byron and I sat side-by-side, and he rested his cane against the arm of the sofa, still within ready arm's reach if needed. "I regret we haven't been properly introduced," he said. "You may call me George Gordon."

"I am sorry. I thought the two of you were acquainted or I should have said something at the first. Albé, this is Jenny..." I paused, blinking. "Do you know, I don't remember your last name? I'm so sorry."

She laughed, and the sound was a relief from the strain we were all under. I felt the tension ease, and gave her a smile that she returned. "I'm pretty sure I never said it. It's Jenny. Jenny Herveaux," she said, then she turned to look at Byron, holding out her hand to shake his. "We never met, but I know who you are. Gio made sure to fill me in. I figured we might run into one another one of these days. I sure wish it hadn't been like this."

"As do I," said Byron, his voice low and resolute. "How is our mutual friend?"

All the light went out of her smile then, and her brow furrowed with deep concern. "Well, it isn't good, I can tell you. I just came from where they've got him locked up in that old prison."

"Prison?" I said, sitting forward with my hands on my knees. "Where are they holding him? At the coven headquarters?"

She shook her head. "No. I guess they figured he knew too many of the secret ways in and out of that place. He'd have escaped from there in a jiffy. They've got him in one of the old cells in the Doge's Palace. Same place he was held before, as a matter of fact, but this time they've made sure he can't escape through the roof again. Only way he's getting out of there is if they let him out, and something tells me that's not too likely."

My hand flew up to cover my mouth and stifle my gasp of horror. Byron clasped the handle of his cane, and I could see he was twitching to pull out the sword once more.

"How could they put him back in that place," he said. I saw the muscle in his jaw pulse as he ground his teeth in anger. "It's not a fit place for anyone, no matter what their transgression."

Jenny shrugged, then heaved a heavy sigh. "I dunno. They put him in there with some other guy they had a beef with. Who knows how long he's been in there."

"Some other guy," Byron repeated. "What was his name?"

"I dunno," she said, "but he's sure got a mouth on him. Wouldn't shut up so Gio and I could talk. He kept on butting in where he didn't belong. So annoying. I wouldn't be surprised if that's what got him put away in the first place."

"Hmm," said Byron, and he frowned thoughtfully, pursing his lips. "I thought the whole area was open to tourists. How are they keeping people from finding the two of them?"

Jenny looked back at him steadily. "They had signs up saying something about construction, and they roped that section of the building off with yellow caution tape. I managed to sneak my way in there, but I think that's only because they had all hands on deck trying to find you all. I doubt I'm gonna be that lucky again."

"Have they hurt him," I asked, finally willing to allow for that possibility. I had been shoving down the thought he might be hurt or killed, focusing instead on the safety of my little family, but now that I knew where he was and that he was not killed, I was forced to face what his capture might mean.

"Not yet," she said, but her words were of little comfort. "Who knows what they've got planned? Honestly, I think they'd be happy just leaving him there to be forgotten. Let him starve. I gave him a little blood from our storage, but I don't know how long that will hold out or when they'll give him any more. The guy who was in that cell with him looked like he hadn't had any blood in forever. He was white as a ghost and skinny, like a dried up skeleton covered in skin. I don't want to see the boss like that."

"Oh god," I said with a little gasp, feeling my throat tighten until I was unable to speak anymore.

"We'll get him out of there," said Byron, patting my knee with his free hand.

"Yeah, well if you've got a plan, I want in," Jenny said. "It makes me sick seeing him like that. They've got him chained up like some kind of medieval dungeon or something. It's crazy."

I made a strangled sound, covering my face with both hands.

"Shh," Byron said, placing an arm around me. "He's not hurt yet. That's good news. We will think of something. I swear to you."

"How?" Peering over the tops of my fingers, my voice muffled behind my hands, I stared at him with eyes wide. "You heard what she said. Guards. Chains. A locked cell. We had no success finding Raul's whereabouts. How are we possibly going to manage an escape from someplace so public and heavily guarded?"

"Hey," Jenny said, leaning forward to touch my arm. "Don't you worry, all right? He wouldn't want that. I'll find out what I can, and we can work up a plan. If there's one thing I've learned being around the boss man, it's that no situation is ever hopeless. He's been in more scrapes than anyone else I ever met, and he's managed to get out of every one. They're not gonna be able to hold him in there forever. You'll see. We'll think of something. Heck, maybe he'll have a plan of his own. Either way, we're going to spring him out of there. You've just gotta have faith."

Faith. That was something I'd forgotten about over the course of my long life. Too many things had gone wrong over the years for me to have faith in anything, including myself. I had learned the only thing I could count on was an unrelenting drive for self-preservation. Long ago, I had stopped praying. If there was a higher power, it was not listening. It let my husband die, allowed my babies to be taken, ignored the pleas of hundreds who bled for faith and freedom and family. There was no fate, as far as I could see. Life was chaos and disorder, and though I trusted my family not to betray me, I knew that we could be parted at a moment's notice, and once again I would have only myself to depend upon. The two of them were asking me to believe in a child's fantasy of happy endings.

Byron, I knew, would do his best. He was honorable, even after all the intervening years of separation in our past. He had gone to Greece just before we parted, determined to play the hero. I knew his heart. Though he played the role of disaffected cad with a practiced air, he had always been an optimist in the deepest part of his soul. He believed in the power of the human spirit to overcome every obstacle. For me, he would fight to the death, even if he knew the battle was hopeless. Life may have given him little cause for hope, but still he nurtured it in the most secret depths of his soul.

As for Jenny, she was too young to know the cruelty of the universe. She was new to immortality and the pains we must endure to maintain it. Faith is easy when you have never experienced loss like mine. I envied her certainty, but I also pitied her, for I knew the eventual disillusionment she would face. Casanova might yet survive this ordeal, but she would be foolish to assume her faith had anything to do with his having done so. If he made it out of that prison, it would be more due to luck than to anything else.

Both of them had spoken words they thought would be comforting, but they filled me with despair. If we needed faith to guide our actions, I knew we were truly doomed. We had no plan. No clear enemy to fight. No place of refuge and safety at mission's end. No weapons for defense. The best we could do was huddle together and wait for the inevitable.

All of this I knew. Yet as I searched their faces, I could not speak the truth aloud. Though I had no faith left, I could not bear to destroy theirs. Let them have their delusions, then, I decided, for if I spoke what was in my heart, what would we have left but defeat? I had no faith left, so theirs would have to bear me forward until the end came at last. Whatever happened, at least I would know I had not broken their will or taken away the one thing that kept them fighting, however futile that misplaced hope might be.

Thus, I simply nodded, taking their hands in mine and squeezing hard, my face resolute.

Jenny squeezed back, then glanced between Byron and myself. "Do you all have a place to stay? Someplace safe?"

"For now," said Byron. "We're looking for someplace more permanent, but where we are will serve for the time being."

"Good," she said. "Just don't tell me where it is. If I'm brought in for questioning, I don't want any information they might be able to torture or starve out of me. It's safer for all of us that way. For the same reason, I don't want to meet the others you've got with you until we're ready to put our plan into action."

"Agreed," Byron said. "We will contact you here when the time is right. For now, we need to find out more about who is holding Casanova and what they plan to do to him. If it's the coven, there will be rules and procedures in place, and we can perhaps work within their system to free him."

"And if it is not the coven?" I said, forcing my voice to sound calm, though inside I was anything but.

"Then we do whatever we have to. We find out who the enemy is and we fight," he said with a note of finality.

Jenny nodded, her lips forming a tight smile, and while I mirrored her expression, I was far from comforted by his words.

"All right." Slapping her hands on her thighs, she stood to rummage on the desk. She found a business card for Casanova Disco with her name at the bottom and, stepping over toward us, held the card out to me. "Here. You can reach me at this number any time. Day or night. I'll find out what I can and wait to hear from you. You'd better go out the back way, though. Too many people out there. Never know who might see you and tell the wrong folks."

Rising beside Byron, I looked around the room. "The back way?"

She laughed. "Casanova's always got a secret way out. I asked him about it one time. He said he'd learned his lesson. 'Always have an escape plan, Jenny,' he said. 'Even if you think you'll never need it.' Looks like today's that day, huh? C'mon. I'll show you."

She walked over to the desk and pulled out the right hand drawer. Inside was a remote control, and she pushed a button on it. A section of the brick wall behind her swung inward, revealing an ancient wooden door with a very modern looking locking mechanism on it. Walking across the room to the door, she pressed a series of buttons on a keypad and the lock disengaged. She turned the handle and opened the door. Beyond was a narrow passage between buildings, just enough room for us to walk out single file. She stepped aside for us to walk out ahead of her, and then she moved to stand in the open doorway.

The night air was cool, and despite the closeness of the buildings, a breeze stirred, bringing with it the scent of the sea. I could hear the music from the bar beating faintly again, like a pulse, and in the distance was the cry of seagulls and the sound of motorboats and human chatter. While we were in Casanova's study, I almost forgot the world outside, but now it came rushing in with all its raucous vivacity.

Turning to look at Byron, she narrowed her gaze. "You know your way around Venice, right? I mean, you've lived here long enough to know the maze?"

He nodded. "I've been here off and on for more than one hundred years."

"Awesome. Okay. If you go down that way," she said, pointing, "you'll come out onto a little private courtyard between all these buildings. Make a right, and you'll see a metal gate. It opens from the inside, but it'll lock behind you. Go through that, and you'll be close to the train station. You should be able to find your way from there."

Byron took her hand and lifted it to his lips, kissing it softly. "Thank you, Jenny. It has been a pleasure meeting you. I look forward to seeing you once more under better circumstances."

"Oh," she said, startled by his old fashioned gesture. "I...yes. Pleasure. Hmm."

It was my turn to make my goodbyes then, and I leaned in to kiss her cheeks. "We will speak soon, my dear," I said. "Please be careful."

"You too," she said. "And don't you worry about Gio. He'll be all right."

I smiled at her then, though I knew there was no guarantee she was right about Casanova's safety.

"Now go," she said. "Before anyone sees."

"Farewell," I said, and with that Byron and I turned and walked away. I heard the door close and lock behind us.

He led me from that place, following her directions easily. The courtyard was small, with clotheslines strung overhead from one building to another, shirts and sheets alike flapping in the breeze like multicolored flags. We walked beneath in the dark, hurrying past like shades. I could feel the thrum of humanity behind every window, the blood of each inhabitant within those walls calling to me. Never had I felt more like the skulking monster of legend than at that moment. Those people went about their lives according to routine, oblivious to the danger passing so near. Above, the light of a flickering television shone from one window. A child's cry came from another. A couple was arguing somewhere. Ordinary lives. Brief as a candle compared to mine. The recognition made me feel cold and alone. I envied their ignorance and simplicity, but at the same time, I knew I would never want to change places with any one of them. We were surrounded by life, but we would never again be a part of it.

I said nothing of these thoughts, simply following Byron in silence. Perhaps he felt something similar, for he was subdued too, and as we stepped out onto the main avenue and heard the clank of the iron gate as it closed behind us, he took my hand and led me away wordlessly. Indeed, we did not speak until we reached our little boat, and then his words were spoken in a whispered hush, focused only on the task at hand, bidding me step aboard while he loosed the lines and started the motor.

We were well away into the lagoon before I trusted myself to break the spell of quiet that had fallen over us. "It is going to be all right, yes, Albé?"

He kept his eyes fixed on the shore in the distance. "Hmm? Of course it will, old girl."

I knew he could never promise such a thing, but hearing him say it gave me comfort all the same. I settled back into my seat, wrapping my arms around me as he pushed the throttle down and we sped away.

The lights of Lido glittered on the water. When we ducked back into the narrow canal in front of our hotel, I felt the now-familiar anxiety begin to rise. What if Sybill and Polidori had been captured? Killed? What if our enemies were waiting for us on the shore? What if, what if, what if…so many rolled around in my head, I was practically crushed under the weight of them. And yet

I knew if I spoke my fears aloud, Byron would dismiss them as foolish. There is nothing less comforting to a person who is filled with anxiety than to tell them to stop worrying. If doing so were simple, I would have done it long ago. Instead of telling him why my hand trembled, therefore, I stiffened my spine and did my best to hide my internal struggle. My grandmother raised me to be queen, after all, and queens never show the strain, no matter how great the burdens they bear.

Of course, much to my chagrin, Polidori and Sybill were waiting for us inside the hotel room Sybill and I were to share. I had so much pent up fear, I found it difficult to say much to either of them, letting Byron take the lead instead.

He leaned in to kiss Sybill's cheek, placing his hands on her shoulders, and I looked away as he began whispering to her. Their body language was intimate, and it felt intrusive to watch them. I did not know how close they had gotten physically, but it was clear their relationship was more than friendship.

My eyes fell on Polidori who stood watching on with a mixture of fascination and horror. He envied Sybill, though if confronted I knew he would deny it vehemently. I was not sure he even realized the truth of his own feelings. For a moment, I considered speaking to him in order to distract his attention, but then I thought better of it. He might settle his resentment on me instead, thinking I had seen what he would rather bury and ignore.

The moment was brief, and then it was gone. Byron stepped back from Sybill and glanced over in Polidori's direction, reaching out to clap him on the shoulder.

"Well," he said. "How was it? Did you accomplish what you set out to do?"

Sybill grinned proudly, picking up a plastic bag from the bed. "Yep. Well, not the new digs just yet, but we handled the most important part, anyway. I come bearing gifts. Phones all around."

Reaching into the sack, she began distributing them amongst us. "Only use them in case of emergency. Keep it short. Never make a call longer than two minutes. As soon as you hang up, take out the SIM card and replace it with a new one.”

“The what card?” I asked, feeling out of my depth as I held the device in my palm.

She struggled not to roll her eyes, turning instead to look in my direction and answer in a curt but matter-of-fact way. “SIM card. Memory card. You open the back like this, take out the card, and then trade it for a different one. I got a batch of them. Paid in cash. Each time you change the card, you’ll change the phone number as well.”

My brow furrowed, watching her demonstrate the process as she spoke. It seemed simple enough, but I still didn’t understand how these devices would be useful. “Then how do we contact one another if the numbers are constantly changing?”

“Simple,” she said. “I wrote a list of the alternate numbers down for you on these little cards. Keep trying until you reach the person you’re trying to call. Ditch the list if you’re captured.”

She proffered a small slip of paper, and I squinted down at the minuscule writing on it with brows furrowed.

“So it’s a shell game,” said Byron. “They’ll have difficulty tracking us if the numbers keep changing.

“Yeah,” she said, smiling at him. “That’s a good analogy. Oh, and never ever turn on the WiFi. You want the internet, don’t do it on your phone. Internet cafe only, and make sure to wear a disguise. Video surveillance is everywhere. All it takes is someone using facial recognition and they’ll nab us all.”

I blinked slowly, staring at her. “I hid from these people for two centuries. I can do perfectly well without this item.”

With a withering stare, Sybill turned to face me. “You may have been able to stay hidden up to now, but you don’t know the first thing about the modern world and the way these people can track your every move without ever having boots on the ground. You want to stay off their radar and keep that head on your shoulders, you're going to have to do what I tell you. I've been watching my father do business my entire life, business which had to be secret if he wanted to stay alive and out of federal prison. When I was old enough, I learned all the tricks of the trade. When it comes to avoiding modern methods of surveillance, I know what I'm talking about."

My nostrils flared at her tone, but I bit my tongue. She was right, even though I hated to admit it, and I certainly was not going to say so out loud.

She held my gaze for a long moment, then a smirk of triumph crept across her lips. "You're welcome."

I clicked my tongue, then clenched my teeth and sat down on my side of the bed to indicate I was through discussing the matter.

"So," she said, turning away once more to look at Byron. "How about you guys? Find out anything about Casanova?"

Grateful for the change in topic, Byron smiled and relayed the gist of our conversation with Jenny. All the while, I saw Polidori's expression of sympathy at Gio's plight, and I knew he was already pondering our next moves.

I began to feel less useful to the situation, however, and I sat on the edge of the bed in silence while they talked about the situation. I felt irrelevant in the scheme of things. I was brought up to be served. To be the queen. To give orders and be pampered. Those expectations came with a certain noblesse oblige, a sense I was responsible to care for them in a global way, but taking an active personal role in catering to their needs was not only deemed ridiculous, it was against every social rule of protocol. Yet here I was with a nagging desire to be useful dogging me at every turn. I had no idea how I was going to accomplish it. None of my skills seemed relevant in our current situation, and it was clear to me, though none of them said it, the very nature of who I was made me a liability to the others. I was a catalyst for our current circumstances, and I couldn't shake the sense of being on the outside of their conversation.

At long last, their talk wound down, and Byron rose to his feet. "It will be dawn soon. We should rest while we can. Tomorrow we need to start looking for a more permanent residence. If we stay in these cramped quarters too long, we are likely to be found out."

I wanted to add that staying here longer would likely lead to open warfare between us all, but I thought better of it, and instead murmured my agreement, clasping my hands in my lap as I perched there on the edge of the bed.

Albé stepped over to me, stooping to kiss my cheek and whisper goodnight. He smoothed my hair back with a fondness he had not shown in ages. Grateful, I smiled, watching as he turned to go.

Polidori took his cue as well, opting to bow to us both in his own stilted way, murmuring, "Good evening to you both."

Sybill followed the two men to the door and locked it behind them before turning back to look at me. For a moment, I thought she might break the ice so we could go back to that easy camaraderie we had together in the crypt. But too much had been said between the cemetery and the hotel room, and it was not so easy to forget about it or pretend it had not happened.

If we were ever going to heal the wounds between us, I was going to have to be the one to initiate that change. "Sybill, I –"

"Stop," she said, cutting me off. "Don't. I just want to go to bed and be silent."

"All right," I said. "Whatever you want."

"No," she said. "I don't get whatever I want. That's not how this works. I only get what I'm allowed to want, so just save your speeches and excuses and anything else you thought you'd say to me right now. I'm not in the mood to let you make my pain and loss about you again. You don't like it when people don't adore you? Well, that's too damned bad. You don't get to tell me when my emotions are appropriate or how I'm allowed to express them, and you sure as hell don't get to play victim. That may work with everyone else, but not with me. Not after everything you've done. I don't want to hear about how any of what I said tonight makes you feel or anything else, for that matter. I don't care. Just pull your fucking weight until this is over, and I'll do the same. After that, you can find someone else to save your ass because it won't be me."

I stared at her, stunned to silence.

Seeing my shock, she laughed, but it was cold and mirthless. "Finally nothing to say? That's a miracle."

"Come now, dear. Fighting is getting us nowhere."

She shot me a sidelong glance, eyes narrowed. "I'm not your dear. Don't try to pretend you give a damn about me."

"You're my child," I said. "Of course I care."

She rolled her eyes. "Whatever. Let's just sleep."

With that, she turned her back on me, stripped down to her underwear, giving me a good look at those tattoos her clothes covered, and crawled under the covers.

"Get the light, would you?" she said, turning on her side and facing away.

Fighting for control, I stuffed down all the things I might have said and did exactly as she asked. As I lay down on my side of the bed, facing the opposite wall, I forced myself not to cry. I had my dignity, after all, and I didn't want to be accused of trying to rouse her pity. Instead, I stared blankly forward, still and silent, unable to bring myself to rest. While Sybill slept, grief and shame consumed me whole.

In my mind's eye, I kept seeing Gio, bound in chains in his cell, and the thought filled me with pity and fear. I did not know how we were going to get him out of that horrible place any more than I could see how we might recover Raul alive. The possibility of his rescue was also looking more remote by the day, and now, with enemies on all sides, everything seemed hopeless.

On top of everything else, the realization Mozart had kept his true intentions hidden for so long made me feel like a fool. I trusted him blindly, never questioning his loyalty, even though my only knowledge of his character was hopelessly outdated. All I knew of him had come from our childhood together. Yet I had allowed him into my bed and given him a place at my side without question. His betrayal hurt all the more because I should have known better. After my years at court with intrigues and spies on all sides, I was still making the same foolish missteps, and it nearly cost us all our lives.

I hadn't felt shame this deeply since I had lost my children and been forced to bear those unspeakable accusations in open court. I did not want to think about the degradation my enemies had put me through. It was still too painful to contemplate, no matter how many years had passed. My son. My daughter. Gone forever. All my fault. I might be a queen, but I was a mother too, and it was my responsibility to keep them safe. I failed, just as I had failed at everything else. I had avoided the thought of them for so long, hoping the pain would lessen, but regret never quite loosens its grip.

For far too long, I realized, I had let others do all my fighting for me. If I didn't do something this time, history would repeat itself. I couldn't bear the thought of anyone else dying because of my continued failure to act.

Restless, I gave up on sleep, getting up silently to pace the floor in thought.

Suddenly, I had a flash of realization. Here I was, dreading a future that had not yet come to pass. I had thought of myself as a survivor, but this was a fundamentally flawed strategy. I had survived all this time by simply reacting to events after they happened. But this behavior made me an eternal victim, and I was tired of feeling helpless.

I needed to break the cycle if I wanted to ensure a better outcome. I needed to behave like the queen I was, not skulk away into my self-imposed exile once more. I needed to fight for those I held dear.

Full of renewed sense of purpose, I got out the cell phone Sybill had procured for me. To keep from waking her, I carried the phone and my purse into the bathroom. Door closed, I pulled out the card for Casanova Disco, took a deep breath, and then dialed.

Je Te Perdonne

Polidori

Once Milord and the former queen departed for news of Casanova, Sybill turned to me and asked, "So, is it just me, or do you feel like we've been stuck with the stuff they don't want to do too?"

Her question was so unexpected, I couldn't help laughing, the first genuine laugh I'd had in years. "I suppose I am used to playing the servant," I said, shrugging.

She frowned. "Mmm. Well, if it makes you feel any better, I don't think Albé meant it that way."

"Don't you?" I said, pushing my hair back from my forehead with a smirk. "And what gives you that impression?"

Shrugging, she gave me a little smile. "He's just trying to keep the tension between us from turning into World War Three. That's all. In case you hadn't noticed, I'm not very good at keeping my mouth shut when I'm upset."

"You don't say," I said, chuckling once more. It was refreshing to be around someone who could laugh at herself, and her manner put me at ease. "Perhaps you are right."

"Of course I am," said Sybill. "He's actually pretty easy to figure out."

"I have never found him to be so." I said, a note of surprise in my tone.

Not missing a beat, she deadpanned, "Probably because you're listening to his words instead of noticing the things he doesn't say."

I blinked. "I believe I've been around him long enough to know him better than you do."

She shook her head. "It doesn't take any time at all to understand what he's about. He may say harsh things, but that's a defensive mask. He loves you very deeply, John. Maybe not the way you want –"

"I don't believe you know me either," I said, bristling as I cut her off.

Stepping a little closer, she gave me a look that was direct and certain. "Sure I do. You're mad at him because he couldn't give you what you want. And I get it. I do. But expectation is what's wrong with you two. Your expectations don't match up, so you both end up unhappy. But look, he's still here, right? I mean, even though he left his wife and kid, had a string of people he slept with and then left, he's still committed to you. It may not be romantic, but it's still love. Real, true love. I bet his mother was a bitch, so he thinks love means suffering and pain. Verbal abuse maybe too."

"Did he tell you all that?" I said, staring at her with eyes wide.

"Psh. No. I googled him, silly. I quit reading when I got to the stuff about his sister, though." She tucked her hair behind her ear, and her expression softened slightly. "I figure he wouldn't like me knowing all his secrets. Plus, most of the important things aren't written down. They're there in his behavior. I just have to pay attention. Besides, I'd rather wait for him to talk to me about all that stuff when he's ready."

"Talk to you?" I snorted. "Now who's making assumptions?"

"Oh, don't be catty," she said, but she laughed all the same and nudged me good-naturedly. "Don't worry. I'm not taking him away from you."

Raising a brow, I stared at her directly without responding.

"Come on," said Sybill. "We both know you've been worried about it."

My brow raised a little higher. "Do we?"

She laughed again, her eyes crinkling at the corners with mirth. "Of course. It's obvious. But like I said, he's devoted to you. After all, you're the longest relationship he's ever had. It's been what…two hundred years, give or take? If that's not commitment, I don't know what is. And it's love too."

"Do you read palms as well," I said with a sneer, though inside I was still mentally reeling as I contemplated these revelations. She was right about all of it, of course, and I hadn't seen any of it until she spoke the words aloud.

"Ha! Nah. I'm just good at reading people. Helps with my art. I don't just draw or paint someone the way they are. That's what photographs are for. I show what's on the inside. The secret stuff people don't talk about. It's all there if you watch carefully." She paused for a moment, musing, then went on, though she no longer seemed to be addressing me with what she said. "I suppose that's what I found so fascinating about Raul. I couldn't read him. He was an actor, though, so I don't think I ever saw who he truly was. Not really. Maybe he lost himself a long time ago and was just playing a role, you know?"

Her eyes glazed over as she spoke, as though her mind was far away. Then all at once, she shivered, looking up at me with a smile. "Anyway, I just want you to know I get it. You and him. I respect your relationship. Whatever happens between me and him, it's not going to mean he abandons you. I don't want that, and he wouldn't do that to you. He loves you. He always will."

"I wouldn't be so sure," I said, moved by her words to make a confession. "I envy you. The way you are with him. He's different with you. Relaxed. You steady him. I have seen him act this way around a few other people, but it was a long time ago. It bothered me to watch then too, knowing he would never react to me the same way. I think he resigned himself to living unhappily and unromantically ever after with me, but now –"

She reached out and touched my arm. "Hey, John, nothing is different. He's just making room for me to be there too. I don't know if that means as a sister or what, but I think the fact he asked us to team up shows he isn't making this a choice of you versus me. He wants the two of us to get along. He doesn't want to lose you. And he trusts you."

"You don't know that, Sybill," I whispered.

"I do, actually," she said. "If he didn't, he wouldn't rely on you. And he definitely wouldn't leave the two of us alone together when you know all his secrets. He knows you've been jealous. He's worried about it. He wants you to see you matter to him. You're the most important person in his life, John. Don't you get that?"

I was struck dumb by that statement, and when words finally came, they were halting and slow. "I...I have never....felt important to him."

"You are," she said firmly. "He feels responsible for you. He worries about you."

I shook my head. "That's not love."

"It is when it's been two hundred years, and he still does it," she said.

I took a moment to absorb that assessment. She was so certain. Love. I had given up on ever finding that from anyone, and here she was telling me I'd had it all along and simply hadn't recognized it for what it was.

"Why can't he say so?" I said, my voice choking.

Her voice was warm and kind, and she laughed a little to break the tension. "Because he's English and a man. You guys don't talk about feelings. Are you kidding? There's pride involved too, for goodness sakes. I'll bet you haven't told him either for the same reasons. I mean, god forbid, either of you should admit your vulnerabilities. But believe me, he feels it or he wouldn't stay. And he sure as heck wouldn't be working so hard to make sure you and I get along."

I swallowed hard, frozen in place while I tried to absorb her words, looking down at the ground. She stepped a little closer, that gentle hand on my arm squeezing a little. "Hey. It's all right."

Clearing my throat, I looked up at her and smiled weakly, giving a nod of acceptance and understanding.

"C'mon," she said, beaming back at me and winking. "We've given them enough head start. There's stuff to do. We'd better get to it, don't you think?"

I nodded, chuckling softly. "Yes, by all means."

Her words affected me more than I could say, and I knew it was going to take some time for me to let them sink in. All this time, I had looked on her as a temporary interloper, but now I realized this was what family could feel like. True family. Inclusive rather than competitive. A source of trust and support. She was showing compassion and openness to me, and it was almost too much to take in at once. My parents always had such high expectations for me, along with a burden of disappointment and resentment. I had no frame of reference for this sort of easy camaraderie and companionship. My mind found so much positivity anxiety-inducing. After all, if you have something good, it can be taken away. Still, she had given me a kernel of hope. Perhaps with time and patience, it would grow. Until then, at least I had found a friend. Maybe eventually, I would see her as a sister.

As a result of our conversation, rather than approaching our collaboration as a chore to be stoically borne, I was looking forward to the excursion alongside her. We walked to the jetty in a far more congenial manner than I had expected, and my jealousy and resentment began to ease.

"So, how do you want to play this?" she said, glancing over at me sidelong.

With a quizzical brow, I caught her eye. "Hmm? I don't understand the question."

With an almost childlike enthusiasm, she skipped, then turned her face toward me, beaming, her words spilling out rapid-fire as each thought occurred to her. "When we get to the city, I mean. What's our cover story? We can't be ourselves. Too obvious. So...who are we? Students on vacation? A couple on their honeymoon? Or...oh! Can you pull off sounding like a native? Maybe I'm a rich heiress in search of a villa. You could be my decorator. Or...I don't know. You tell me."

"How about a doctor and his sister?" I deadpanned, eyes narrowing.

She made a sour face and shook her head. "Boo. Boring. No one is going to believe we're related. Come on. Would you buy the idea we had the same mother?"

"Half-sister?" I smirked, but under her withering gaze I relented. "Fine. Fiancé, then. Just don't make me do the talking. I don't do well with people, and I am not a very good liar, I'm afraid."

"No?" she teased. "Well, don't worry. I'm good with schmoozing. I'll take care of the idle chit-chat. You just stand there looking handsome and adoring. How's that?"

"I think I can manage that," I said, though my tone was dubious.

She stopped abruptly in the middle of the sidewalk and turned to face me. "All right then. Show me."

I blinked, nearly stumbling on the sidewalk in an effort to avoid tripping over her. "Show you what?"

"The adoring look. Show it to me." She smiled up at me with eyes wide, expectantly.

I tilted my head, one eyebrow raised.

Sighing, she mirrored my expression, crossing her arms over her chest. "It's like you're not even trying."

"Well, you put me on the spot," I said.

"Exactly," said Sybill. "The people who are after us aren't going to come up and say, 'Pardon me, old chap, but would you mind coming along with us? There's a good lad.' You've got to be prepared."

I squinted. "I don't sound like that."

She wrinkled her nose. "A little. Yeah."

With a click of my tongue, I glared. "Maybe this wasn't such a great idea after all."

With a pleading look in her eye, she smiled at me in an almost saccharine way, a wheedling tone in her voice. "Are you kidding? It's the perfect cover. Come on. It'll be easy. Just call me 'Darling' and say 'Yes, dear' a lot, and I'll do the rest of the talking."

I stared at her, sucking my cheeks. "I meant putting us together wasn't a good idea. Perhaps I should go back and leave you to –"

"What?" said Sybill. "No! I need you. I don't know my way around this place. Seriously, you can't abandon me. And it'll be fun. I promise. Didn't you ever play make-believe games when you were a kid?"

"No," I said. "I was busy with school work."

Her jaw dropped. "You're kidding, right?"

Standing still, I stared back at her, lips pressed into a line.

She sighed. "All right. Fine. Half-sister it is. Different fathers. Deal?"

In relief, I nodded, feeling the tension go out of me again. "Deal."

"But I'm the sister you love best," she said quickly, moving in close to place her arm in mine. "Obviously."

The teasing tone in her voice made me laugh, and just like that, she broke through my resistance. We began walking again, and I placed a hand on hers, looking over at her with a rueful smile. "Obviously."

"That's perfect! Look at me just like that," she said, eyes twinkling. "See? Now was that so hard?"

"Excruciating," I said.

She poked me in the ribs. "Rude."

Matching my stride to hers, I laughed. "I did say I'm not a people person."

"True. I'll let it slide this time," she said. "How exactly are we going to get to the city, by the way? Albé and Marie took our boat. I assume we're not attempting a boatjacking. You don't strike me as the criminal type."

I smirked. "You don't know me well enough to make that assessment."

"Point taken," said Sybill. "Still. Boat? What are we doing? I'm not swimming across, thank you very much. The only way I'm getting in that water is if I'm thrown, and then it had better mean I'm being eaten by sharks."

"Is that a request?" I said, and then I winced as she pinched me. "Ow!"

"Boat!" she said. "Focus, here."

"I thought we would take the public water bus," I told her. "Blend in with the crowd."

She blinked. "There's a water bus?"

"You didn't think everyone here is rich enough to own a boat, did you?"

Her forehead furrowed. "I have no idea. I've never been here before."

"Well, trust me," I said. "They're not."

"Is it like a ferry, or what?" she said, and her confused expression was so comical, I laughed aloud.

"You'll see," I said. "We're nearly there."

The public docks were within view, and I stepped up to the ticket window, sliding over a few Euros to the cashier for the fare. I took the tickets, and then Sybill and I walked to the back of the queue of people waiting for the transport. We didn't have to wait long, the large white public transit boat which ferried passengers back and forth between the islands in the lagoon arriving only a few minutes later. A few passengers got off, and then we climbed aboard and took two empty seats near the bow.

"What did Albé mean about the other option we might have to consider moving to?" She leaned against the rail as the boat pulled away from the dock. Her close cropped hair ruffled in the breeze, and she looked the part of a carefree young backpacker on The Grand Tour.

"Hmm?" I turned my head toward her, smiling, one brow raised. "Oh, I shouldn't worry about that. He's only being dramatic."

"It didn't seem that way to me," she said. "What place is he talking about?"

I shrugged noncommittally and stared out across the water. "It's a place I used as a clinic for a while. But the whole thing has been abandoned for years. He knows Marie would never agree to such a thing. It would be impossible to make her comfortable there. The building wasn't designed for comfort, even when it was in use, and now...well...let's try to find something else. He's only mentioned it because he knows it will motivate me to find alternatives."

"Ah," Sybill said. "That makes sense, I guess. Still, the sooner we're out of that hotel, the better, in my opinion. I don't hanker after spending too many nights sharing a room with...her."

The emphasis with which she said this last made me peer at her sharply, eyes narrowed.

"What?" she said. "It's just the truth. I'll bet you feel the same about bunking with Albé. There's such a thing as too much togetherness."

I laughed, then looked down at the waves, feeling a little exposed by the way she saw through me. "Does it bother you being right all the time?"

"Nope," she said, and I could hear from her tone she was smiling even if I didn't look to see it. "I'm used to it. Sure is a pain in the ass to everyone else, though."

With a soft chuckle, I elbowed her jovially, though I didn't tell her she was wrong about her assessment. Though she hadn't said anything aloud, she might not like the idea of Byron sharing a room with me for reasons she wasn't ready to admit. Perhaps I wasn't the only one who felt a twinge of jealousy. I decided to keep my supposition quiet, however. While she was handy at dealing out truths as she saw them, I wasn't sure how well she would handle being on the receiving end. Besides, I liked her letting her think I was a gentleman. She was wrong, of course, but I wasn't ready to break the illusion for her. Not yet.

As the boat neared a docking area in the heart of the old city by the Rialto Bridge, I leaned over and whispered in her ear, "Are you ready to play the tourist?"

Rather than answer, she smiled as we rose to stand together, and arm-in-arm we walked off onto the shore. Small cafes and shops greeted us as I led her away from the Grand Canale. She pointed at some of the quaint buildings, murmuring how she wished she had a camera. I had visited this area so often, the beauty of it was lost on me, but seeing the city from her perspective,

I felt a renewed sense of wonder and appreciation at the engineering feat which allowed this place to rise from the swamp. For a moment, we became the tourists we were impersonating.

I wanted to ask about her family, but I feared the subject would be a somber one, so I set the topic aside for a later date. Still, I was lost in playing the tour guide for her, and only when we passed an electronics store with smartphones on display in the front window did I return to the task we had been sent to accomplish.

As we entered the store, I turned to her and whispered, "I defer to your expertise here. I haven't the first idea of what we need."

"Burner phones, of course," she said, as though the answer was obvious.

Frowning, I shook my head. "And what exactly are those? Do we set fire to them?"

She covered her mouth with her hand to contain her laughter.

"You're so literal. No. They're for temporary use. Cheap phones. No contract. Easily disposable." When I stared at her without comprehension, she whispered, "The kind that drug dealers and assassins use."

"I see," I said.

Snickering, she grinned at me. "You don't, but that's all right. I know what I'm doing. Why don't you go look at the televisions? I've got this handled."

She patted my arm, and then kissed my cheek and walked away, leaving me to fend for myself. I slipped my hands into my pockets and took her advice, making my way to the rear of the store where the more expensive items were on display. A football match was on every screen. I was never given to watching sporting events of any kind, so the rules were foreign to me. Watching the screen studiously, I crossed my arms over my chest, trying to puzzle out what was happening. My eyes followed the action, and there seemed a kind of graceful mathematics to the way the players worked together as a unit. Just as I was beginning to find order in the seeming chaos of the game, I felt a tap on my arm that startled me out of my reverie.

"I'm not interrupting, am I?" said Sybill.

"No no," I said, turning to face her. "That was quick."

She held a paper bag, and she took my arm again, leading me toward the door. "I knew what I was looking for," she said.

"Do you want to show me what you bought?" I asked, holding open the door for her to walk through.

She smirked. "You're just asking to be polite, aren't you?"

"Am I that transparent?" I said.

Laughing, she nudged me. "When we get back to the hotel, I promise to bore you with all the technical details."

"Excellent. I cannot wait."

"Internet cafe?" she said.

"Internet cafe," I agreed, leading her on toward our next stop.

"Have you ever used computers before?"

"For compiling research data," I said. "I don't pretend to be proficient by any means, however. I know enough to do what I need to do, but that is all."

"I'll do our search then," said Sybill, the tone in her voice letting me know the matter was decided. "You're still ahead of Albé, anyway."

I raised a brow. "Whatever reason would he have for using one?"

"Typing up his translation manuscript, of course. He and I bought a laptop and a printer for him not long ago."

"You do realize he will never use it," I said.

With a baleful eye directed at me, she said, "You sound certain."

I snorted a laugh. "I know him."

"I'm going to give him lessons," she said.

"And I wish you the very best of luck with your endeavor."

I would have said more on the subject, but by then we were in front of the Internet cafe, so I dropped the subject and led her on inside.

At tables around the room, business people, students, and vacationers alike sat with laptops and cell phones, staring at illuminated screens without speaking to one another while soft music played through the speakers overhead. Low wattage lights hung on cables suspended from the ceiling. As I looked around, I was relieved to see no one took notice of us. Each person was far too focused on their personal machines to care what anyone else was doing.

To keep up the pretense we were tourists on holiday, I ordered two lattes, knowing we would leave them untouched. Meanwhile, Sybill paid for an hour of computer use, giving a false name to the clerk behind the desk.

A bank of computers ran along the back wall of the cafe, a small wooden divider between the screens providing a modicum of privacy for the users. She took a seat in front of one machine on the end, and I pulled up a stool beside her, effectively blocking the view of the monitor from any prying eyes.

She cracked her knuckles. I winced, but she took no notice.

Her fingers were a blur as she typed. All the while, she mumbled to herself in an undertone so low, I could hardly make out any of what she said.

"Do you know you're talking to yourself?" I said. "It's very distracting."

Eyes still fixed on the screen, she hissed, "Shh. You're the distracting one. Nearly there. Nearly there....here. What do you think about that?"

Abruptly, she sat back, letting her hands rest on the wooden counter.

I narrowed my gaze. "What am I looking at?"

Gesturing toward the computer screen, she pointed at a four bedroom villa on Lido. My eyes widened as soon as I saw the price below the photos. "You must be joking."

She turned her head to face me, scowling. "I am not sharing a room with her. This was the least expensive option for a place with the privacy we need."

"Well, the price..." I said, tapping the screen, "...is absurd."

"You're not going to do the whole 'Back in my day, bread cost a penny,' are you? " she said. "Because inflation is a thing."

I rolled my eyes. "I am simply telling you he won't allow us to spend that much. He won't even want her to see the property. She's likely to say yes, and then they'll argue over money, and let me tell you, no one wants to be in the middle of that storm."

She sighed. "Let me see what I can do."

Leaning forward again, she began tapping furiously, and I took a moment to look around at the other patrons in the place.

A fat man sat in the corner with a small dog on his lap, feeding it bites of a croissant while a young woman at a table opposite him kept glancing over out of the corner of her eye with an expression of annoyance. At a table in the center of the room, a cluster of university students were completing online lessons on their laptops. Their table was littered with napkins and empty coffee cups and dessert plates. Every so often, one would look up and ask the others for help. Near the window, a couple sat together holding hands and sharing a laptop between themselves. Their heads were near one another, and periodically they would kiss or whisper intimately together. One woman sat alone reading an ebook on her tablet while she drank a glass of wine. A group of teenage girls sat taking silly photos of each other with their smartphones, giggling as the images were posted into the ether.

This was a world I didn't comprehend. While the internet supposedly connected the world, these people were intentionally isolating themselves and ignoring their neighbors entirely. Though it was convenient for our purposes that none of these people would have looked up from their screens to notice either of us, I also found this realization terribly sad.

"I don't understand," I said.

"Understand what?" she said, still scowling at the screen.

Turning my head back in her direction, I lowered my voice and whispered. "This century."

"This is not a newsflash," she said. "No offense. I kinda dig the retro thing you've got going on. All you need is some goggles, a top hat, and a few gears sewn onto your clothes, and you'd totally be steampunk."

I paused, then shook my head. "I have no idea what you just said to me."

She laughed. "Shocking."

"Have you found anything yet?" I said, eager to change the subject.

"No," she said, still facing the monitor, "but I did find a way to solve our money problem."

I made a slow blink. "I didn't say we had a money problem."

"Oh? Then what would you call it?"

"We have an access problem. It's going to be difficult to withdraw large amounts of cash from the accounts without drawing unwanted attention, and other methods of payment are all traceable."

"Exactly. So we have a money problem. Except now...we don't." She pointed at the screen with a look of triumph.

I stared, tilting my head to the side, eyes narrowed. "What is a bitcoin? Is that money?"

She pressed her palm to her face with an exasperated sigh. "Oh my god. There's no time to get into all that. Just...trust me. I've solved our problem."

"Where did this...bitcoin come from?"

"I can't actually answer that question here. Sorry."

"Why? Is it illegal?"

Biting her lip, she did some more clicking of keys to log out of that screen. "I'll tell you later.

"Oh my god," I said.

"Hush," she said. "It's fine."

Sarcasm dripped from my lips as I murmured, "Oh, well. If you say it's fine, I feel much safer now."

She elbowed me, still clacking away at the keyboard.

"What are you looking up now?" I said. "That doesn't look like a listing of properties."

"It isn't," she said. "I just want to check something."

Just then, I saw a picture of Sybill flash up on the screen. The hair was different, but it was very definitely her face. "What are you doing?"

"I just want to see if my parents are all right. I can't call home, so...oh Jesus." The change in her tone made me instantly anxious. I leaned in to see what she was looking at, but she had already logged off and was pushing back her stool to stand. "We have to go."

"What? Wait." Hastily, I stood and followed her awkwardly as she walked toward the front of the cafe. "We haven't been here ten minutes. We don't have a place to stay yet."

But she didn't stop walking, so I had no choice but to scurry along behind. "Please, let's just get out of here," she said. "I can't. Not here."

"You can't what?" I said. "I don't understand."

We turned a corner and found ourselves in an empty passageway between buildings. I reached out to clasp her elbow and force her to stop. "Talk to me. Please. What happened?"

She rounded on me with eyes rimmed with red. "My mother is in the hospital, okay? She's had a heart attack from the stress of my...my disappearance. The police told her they thought I was dead, and she had a heart attack."

"I am so very sorry," I said after a moment's pause. "That's not your fault, though, Sybill. You mustn't blame yourself."

"I don't," she said. Her hands trembled with emotion, and she swiped away a tear from her cheek, words spilling out in a torrent. "I blame Marie. If she had just left me alone, none of this would have happened. I'd be home, eating my father's leftover birthday cake and playing Jenga with my Nanna. Instead, I'm here, playing hide-and-seek, monster edition. My mother might be dying, and there's not a damn thing I can do about it. I'm so angry. I didn't ask for any of this. I never wanted it. But Marie didn't care. She didn't ask me. She made me this...thing...and expected I'd accept it and not complain. We're all supposed to just give up our whole lives for her. 'Oh no. Poor Marie. No one has any more cake or diamonds for her. What a tragedy.' Ugh. It's ridiculous. She's not queen anymore, goddammit. She's just this totally oblivious narcissist who has ruined everything for all of us, and she's not even sorry. I hate her. God, I hate her."

With that, she flung her arms around my neck and clung tight, sobbing against my shoulder. It was all I could do to simply stand, awkwardly patting her shoulder. "There, there," I said.

She laughed through her tears, and then pulled back to look at me. "I didn't think people actually said that out loud."

"Crying women make me very nervous," I said, too anxious to be anything but brutally honest. I reached into my pocket to pull out a handkerchief. "Please don't take it personally."

"I don't," she said, taking the handkerchief from me with another laugh. "You really aren't from this century, are you?"

"I'm really not," I said, a crooked smile pulling at my lips.

She dabbed at her eyes, then folded it up and handed it back. "Thank you."

I nodded. "It's my pleasure."

"Please don't tell them I went looking for news about my old life. I don't want to hear about how dangerous it is and blah, blah, blah. Can we just keep this between us?"

There was so much hope in her sad eyes, I couldn't bear to disagree. "Of course," I said.

"You're a very nice man," she said, taking hold of my arm again and beginning to walk back toward the public docks again.

"I am decidedly not," I said. "You haven't seen my bad side yet. I pray you never do."

She raised a brow. "Now I'm curious."

"You know what happened to the curious cat."

"Yes," she said. "But I'm your favorite sister, remember? You wouldn't."

I didn't answer her, just patting her arm and leading her quietly back to the boat that would take us back to Lido. The ride was more crowded with tourists and locals alike, and we couldn't get enough privacy to talk. Instead, she sat with her head on my shoulder, staring pensively into the middle distance.

We returned to the hotel in a more subdued and somber mood than when we had left. Nonetheless, the activities of the evening had bonded the two of us, establishing a base upon which we might become friends. For that, I was grateful. I also felt protective of her as Marie and Byron joined us not long after.

I let Sybill do the talking for the two of us. After all, it had been she who knew the details of the phones she had procured, and it seemed only right for her to be given credit for what she had done.

As I watched on from the sidelines, I watched the interplay between the two women. I couldn't help thinking of all Sybill had said before, and the self-centeredness of which she had spoken was suddenly quite clear to me. It was all I could do not to cheer when Sybill snapped at Marie for her complaints. I knew better than to impose myself between them. However, if Marie had pressed her case, I might have felt obligated to choose a side, and I knew where my loyalties would lie. It didn't do to speak such things aloud, but I found her candor refreshing. I wondered whether perhaps straightforwardness might be the answer to the rift that stood between Lord Byron and myself. No raised voices. No arguments. Simple honesty for once.

When at last the time came for us to leave Sybill and Marie alone, I wished both women goodnight and walked with him to the door. He and I returned to our room. I locked the door before I turned to face him, pausing for a moment to gather my thoughts. He walked across the room and sat on the edge of the bed to remove his boots. My jaw clenched.

"You going to stand there all night," he said, "or are you coming to bed?"

Brows furrowed, I shook my head. "No," I said simply. "I will not lie down and pretend everything is fine. Now that we're alone, I must tell you how completely baffled I am by this entire situation. Yet again, you allowed Marie to make everything revolve around her. Do you truly not see how utterly ridiculous this entire situation is? We were fine all these years, but since they arrived, everything is upended. We've lost everything – our home, our peace, years of work – and for what? To protect Marie?"

His brows shot up, but his mouth quirked with sly amusement. "This isn't about Marie. You're jealous of Sybill. Listen, I know you're disappointed I care for the girl, Polly, but honestly you and I were never good for one another romantically. It's been almost two centuries now. You have to stop trying to force this to be anything more than it is."

"For the love of…I am not jealous!" My voice rose until I was practically shrieking with fury, my fists clenched until the knuckles were white.

"Yes, obviously," he said, sitting up on the side of the bed and smirking. "What was I thinking? Clearly, no jealousy whatsoever is going on. Silly me."

"You're impossible," I said, reaching up to loosen my tie and unbutton my collar. "You really are."

His expression turned serious then. He rose and stepped forward to grasp my collar in both hands, tugging me closer, forcing me to stand toe to toe with him as he scowled down at me. "No. That's you. The utter hypocrisy you're demonstrating is absurd. You're upset because Sybill's presence took my focus off you. Am I the only one who sees the irony in that? Not a day in the last two centuries has passed when I haven't been forced to hear your whining, Polly. If you don't like her, fine. I won't require you to be her new best friend, but that girl has been through hell, and I won't have you treat her with disrespect or unkindness. This is all new to her, for god's sake. She's frightened. She's been chased and threatened continuously ever since she was turned. She lost the man she thought she loved. She lost her family. She lost her entire life. I know it's a stretch, but try to dig down deep and find an ounce of compassion."

I clenched my teeth throughout this speech. "Oh, that is rich, coming from you. You speak of all her loss and of treating her with compassion? Where was that compassion for me, I'd like to know?"

He rolled his eyes and turned away. "Polly, don't start."

"Fine. After all, I'm used to having my feelings ignored and pushed aside. I've dealt with the same thing all these years. What's one more day?"

Rubbing his hands over his face, he groaned. "Jesus, Polly. Give it a rest. Mea culpa. Mea maxima culpa. Okay? You happy now? Or do I need to wear a hair shirt? Maybe let you give me fifty lashes?"

"Sometimes, I think I really hate you," I said under my breath.

He sighed, shoulders sagging. "I know. You've made that abundantly clear. Can we just sleep and have this argument later, please? I don't have the energy for it now."

"And when exactly is this 'later' you're talking about? When does it get to be my turn to talk?"

"Fine," he said abruptly, turning to look at me with world-weary blue eyes. "You win. Talk."

I blinked. I'd expected him to continue disagreeing with me, and his sudden surrender caught me off guard. All my thoughts scattered, and I hesitated, unsure where to begin.

"Well?" he said. "Don't leave me in suspense."

"This has nothing to do with Sybill at all," I said. "In fact, though it surprises even me to say so, I like the girl. I think she might actually be good for you."

He blinked. "If you're not upset about her, what is it then?"

"I am still upset because you didn't listen to me when we were packing to leave," I said, removing my cufflinks so I had something to focus on while I gathered my thoughts. "I was trying to explain about the missing vaccine...why it's important...and you cut me off completely."

He placed his hands on his hips as if bracing himself. "So you're upset because even though we were in imminent danger, I wouldn't stop everything and listen to you witter on. I see."

I placed the cufflinks on the bedside table, not taking my eyes off him all the while. "I don't think you understand how serious it is."

"How...how serious what is? My interrupting you?" He raised a brow as if he were gearing up to argue, but then he shook his head and began unbuttoning his shirt. "All right then. Point taken. I apologize. Are we done?"

"No!" I said, glaring. "That's not what I meant."

Untucking his shirt tail, he looked rumpled and tired. "Then what is it?"

"The vaccine. I don't think you understand the serious possible consequences of it being stolen."

He paused, gazing back at me for a moment, and then he sighed.

"Look, Polly, I understand your frustration. Losing all your work. It's years of effort, and you're back to square one. I'm sorry I didn't take the time to express my condolences. You're right. I should have." He reached out then, eyebrows raised in an expression of hope and conciliation. "I am sorry. Truly. I wish things were different. I wish I could get it back. But right now, with all our lives in danger, it's just not possible. I hate that, but it can't be helped. I will help you rebuild your lab. I will give you whatever you need."

I stared at his hand and didn't take it. "You still don't understand."

He dropped his hand, and sat heavily on the bed, hitting the mattress with his open palms as he leaned forward and groaned.

"What the hell do you want from me, Polly? A pound of flesh? Fine. Take it. It's yours." Looking up at me, he pulled open his shirt, baring his chest. "Just fucking do it. I'm so tired."

Eyes wide, I stared, realizing he was asking me to stake him. "I just want you to listen for once. Stop trying to solve things or make me be quiet and just listen."

Closing his eyes, he bent his head forward, covering his face with his hands. He sat like that for a moment or two, before letting his hands fall to his side. He looked up in defeat, whispering, "I'm listening."

In the past, I might have backed down, but instead I planted my feet, slipping my hands into my pockets, and gazed back at him somberly. "That vaccine isn't a favorite toy I've lost. It's a deadly disease in a tube. One without a cure and the results of which are unpredictable. I don't know how it will affect normal humans if they become infected. I don't know how it will affect any vampires who might be injected with it. I don't know what vectors the disease might take if it mutates. It could remain a blood-borne illness, or it might become airborne. There's no way of knowing. I hadn't had time to test it for any of these things. We both know the results of my previous experiments. I don't need to explain to you the potential for catastrophe if the vaccine falls into the wrong hands."

He frowned for a moment, pausing to think about what I said. "Mozart has no interest in science, Polly. He couldn't use the vaccine as a weapon even if he wanted to. He wouldn't know how to even begin."

I shook my head again. "His interest in science is irrelevant. What if he decides to sell it to the Marquis? What if he hands it over to our enemies? And even if he doesn't do so willingly, he may not have much choice. You know what he and his minions are capable of. How long could anyone hold out before giving up everything to the Marquis?"

At last, I saw a flicker of doubt in his eyes, and he whispered in horror, "Jesus."

"And I haven't even talked about the worst case scenario," I said.

His eyes widened, and he gaped at me in disbelief. "There's worse?"

I nodded. "Oh yes. What if Mozart handles the vaccine improperly and becomes infected? He could inadvertently spread the contagion to who knows how many others he'll come in contact with. There's no way of containing this. It could potentially become an epidemic we can't stop."

He blew out a puff of air, and then blinked. "Jesus."

Smirking, I snorted softly. "You said that."

"Yes, well, it needed saying again," he said, but his voice had lost all of its usual edge.

"If you say so. I don't think calling on a higher power to save us is a useful strategy, however." I crossed my arms over my chest. "Now do you understand why I might have been upset about the vaccine going missing when we were back at the monastery? My concern isn't about me and my work, though those issues are a nuisance, I grant you. This is about preventing a potential epidemic."

He nodded. "I get it. Yes. I understand."

"Good," I said, giving a tightlipped smile. "Then you'll help me try to get it back."

He bit his lip and then shook his head. "No."

It was my turn to be shocked. "What? What do you mean 'no'? How can you say you understand and not want to do something to stop it?"

"Because there's nothing we can do now to stop it," he said. "For all we know, the Marquis already has Mozart in custody. Hell, unlikely as it seems, Mozart might have gone straight to him and offered the vaccine by choice. We don't know. Regardless, there's no getting the vaccine back at this point. I'm sorry. I really am. I agree every one of the things you mentioned could happen. But that's why I can't abandon our family. Marie and Sybill, they need me. Need us. I know you don't think of them as family, but they are whether you acknowledge it or not. If you want to go off after Mozart on your own, I won't stop you. But I can't help you if you do. And if things go south with you, there won't be any way for me to stop it. Not this time."

"Jesus," I said, covering my face with one hand.

He laughed, and I knew it was to relieve the strain he felt. "Is there an echo in here?"

With a sigh, I let my hand fall to my side. "I have to do something. I'm a doctor. I took an oath to do no harm. You may not think I'm a good doctor, and I know I have made mistakes in the past, but I take my role seriously. I am trying to do the right thing. The vaccine is my responsibility. I'm the only one who really understands what it could do. I have to do something."

"I don't think you're a bad doctor, Polly," he said. "You're highly skilled and knowledgeable. I just don't think you can undo what you created now.

You're going to have to wait like the rest of us and deal with the consequences, the same way you've done before. You've been conducting these experiments for decades now, and the risks you're talking about have always been there. Things have gone wrong before. This isn't the first time."

His words stung me deeply, and I stood very still, staring back at him, my hands trembling.

"I'm not blaming you, Polly," he said, his voice softening as he rose and moved toward me. "I know you've ever only done what you thought you had to. You've always hoped for a cure, and that is truly admirable. I know I've teased you about your work, but I never thought you didn't know what you were doing. I know your heart is in the right place. I know your dedication. I have protected you, haven't I? Hate me if you will, but I have never tried to stop you or questioned your motives. You and I both know science can't advance without trial and error. Failure is part of the process. So when I say things have gone wrong, I don't mean to blame you or put you down. I admire you for your determination and drive. I, myself, may not want to be cured, but I know countless others feel as you do, and you owe it to them to continue what you started. But you can't put the genie back in the bottle, Polly. You have to accept that what you've lost is another error to be dealt with like all the others. I trust you to keep moving forward in the pursuit of knowledge."

After all these years, he finally admitted to respecting what I did. I couldn't help my surprise, and for several moments, I was speechless, torn between throwing my arms around him with gratitude and shouting at him for taking so long to say what I'd longed to hear. And all the while, I still felt overwhelmed with frustration at my inability to control what had happened.

"What do I do?" I said, misery seeping out under the enormity of the pressure I felt to fix the situation.

He smiled, reaching out once more, and this time I stepped closer and took his hand. "You help us here. And when this crisis is over, you get back to work. That's what you do. I swear, I'll help you. I want to see you succeed, Polly. I believe in you. I do."

"Thank you," I whispered, blinking back tears, and I looked down to keep from letting my emotions get the better of me.

"You don't need to thank me," he said. "Just stop blaming yourself for what happened. You couldn't have foreseen Mozart's actions. Let go of thinking you have to carry that burden. It's not your fault."

I nodded, too fragile to speak.

He squeezed my hand and then let go gently.

"She knew," I said. "She was absolutely right about everything."

With a quizzical brow, he gazed at me with those piercing blue eyes, deep as the sea. "Who was right about what?"

"Sybill," I answered simply. "She said you trusted me. That you cared. She said I'd been all wrong about you. She was right."

It was his turn to be speechless for once. He stared at me, and after a long pause, he cleared his throat. "What...what else did she say?"

I smiled, feeling my expression soften. "That she knew I loved you. That you would never return the feeling in the way I had once wanted, but there is love between us all the same. And that she knows you're committed to me in your own way. She said she wouldn't try to get in the way."

"Did she?" he said, and I detected a hint of coldness, even brittleness, in his tone. He was steeling himself for rejection.

I reached to touch his shoulder. "She loves you. More than I ever could. She sees you with all your flaws, and she loves you for them. She isn't afraid to speak her mind, and you need that. You need someone who is your equal. I thought she was a nuisance, but after I have gotten to know her, I see what draws you to her. I won't stand in your way. I couldn't even if I wanted to. She is what you need."

Shifting on his feet, he looked down and shook his head. "I don't...I don't know if she feels that way about me, Polly. She is still holding Raul in her heart."

"That is fear talking," I said.

He met my gaze once more. "Life is not a fairy tale, Polly. You and I are both proof of that."

"She is no princess in need of saving," I said. "You mistake her if you believe yourself to be the prince on his white steed in this scenario. She doesn't need one. You are equals. I have only seen you behave this way with one other person. I was jealous then too, if you recall."

His eyes widened, and again he didn't speak.

"Must I say the name aloud, or are you too afraid to speak it even now?"

"His ghost haunts me," he whispered. "That was a horrible business. It was all my fault, what happened. I sold it to him, you know. The boat that capsized in the storm. He drowned because of me."

"You have to stop blaming yourself for Mister Shelley's death," I said, gathering my courage to say his name. "After two hundred years, you can set your guilt aside. He would want you to."

He shook his head, pulling back and walking toward the window where he stopped and stood, gazing down at the canal below. "No. I should have stopped him going out that day. I should have begged him to stay just one more night in Pisa. I should have insisted."

"You tried. Even Teresa tried."

I saw his reflection in the window panes, his eyes closing with pain at the memory of her.

"My dear Teresa," he said, closing his eyes, his voice tremulous. "She knew, you know. How I felt about him. How I'd felt for years."

"Anyone who saw the two of you together knew. Shelley's wife, Mary, knew. I knew," I said.

"I never told him," he whispered. "It never stops hurting," he said. "I haven't let myself speak of him in all this time, and the pain is just as great as ever."

"I know. I have always known. That is why I never spoke of him. Even when you and I were at our worst, I knew that was a line I could not, and should not, cross."

I heard a shuddering gasp escape his lips, and when at last he turned to face me, I saw his eyes glistening in the dark.

"I know," said Byron. "And I am grateful for it."

"It is time," I said. "Shelley would want you to be happy. After all this time, you have done whatever penance is necessary to mourn him."

Though he didn't wince as I said the name, I knew how it must hurt him.

"Sybill will understand," I went on. "She's intuitive, that one. If you let her in, I think she will show you that you are capable and worthy of love at last. Though you don't need it, I want you to know I give my blessing."

"Polly," he said, speaking my name in a low intimate murmur like a plea.

I shook my head, stepping closer again. "No. You need to hear this. Don't make the same mistake again. Don't wait until it is too late. Let go of your regrets. Please."

He knew what it cost me to say such a thing.

"She is so young," he whispered. "I don't deserve someone so innocent."

"Geordie," I said, stepping close and reaching out to touch his hand. I hadn't used the name in two centuries. The word was filled with the love I had felt during that beautiful brief moment when I had believed I was his in all the ways I had dreamed. It was a name I had held in secret longing, but now I could finally use it again with gentle affection.

He froze, staring at me with a look of boyish surprise.

"Don't close off your heart," I said, smiling at him gently, my voice low and intimate.

He squeezed my hand then, nodding at last. Though the gesture was small, I knew what a great turmoil he was undergoing internally. I nodded back, for once being the strong one in our relationship.

"Come on," he said, clearing his throat. "Let's get some rest. We have a lot to do tomorrow."

I nodded again, pulling away slowly, letting my hand fall to my side. The enormity of what I had started began to settle on me. My relationship with Byron was about to change drastically in ways I couldn't predict. Uncertainty made me feel unsteady, though I knew there was no stopping the things in motion. Something new was developing, and I only hoped it would bring about positive change for us both.

"Are we good now?" he said, brows raised as he saw me retreating internally once more.

"We're good," I said, mustering a small smile.

He flashed a brilliant grin, eyes crinkling at the corners. "All right then."

The two of us exchanged warm looks in silence, and then went about the business of preparing to rest. My heart felt lighter than it had in almost a century, and at last it seemed we were reaching a new level of understanding between us.

Mousetrap

Ernestine

While I knew he was predictable, I didn't realize just how easy it would be for me to track Mozart down. I checked all his usual haunts, looking for his known aliases. In Monaco, I found him at the blackjack table. His back was to the door, but I could see from the chips in front of him, his luck had not improved since the last time he had been here.

"Mister Wolf, I presume," I said, taking a seat beside him with a smirk.

He flinched, but didn't try to run, reaching instinctively to guard his chips.

"Oh, now don't pretend you're surprised to see me. You made this far too easy." I crossed my legs, leaning one elbow on the blackjack table.

Making a half-turn in his chair, he faced me with a crooked smile. "Did I? Well, I shall have to try to be a little more unpredictable next time."

"Mmm. One might think you almost wanted to be caught."

With a wink, he grinned a little more, showing his fangs. "Oh, now don't go getting romantic on me."

I laughed and shook my head. "You are charming. I will give you that."

"That's what your mother said."

Anger flashed through me, though I guarded my expression so it wouldn't betray me.

"Enough." Uncrossing my legs, I stood, gazing down at him. "You know what happens next, I suppose?"

He looked me up and down and licked his lips. "Oh, I'm counting on it. Mind if I cash in before we begin?"

"You're out of time. But I'm sure these nice gentlemen won't mind holding onto your chips for you." I gestured toward the casino security guards who had flanked me.

"Pity. My luck was just about to turn." Pouting, he looked down at his chips and sighed.

"Isn't it always." My smile disappeared, lips tightening into a line. "Come. I have some questions that need answers."

He shook his head as he looked at me shrewdly. "I can think of some other things you need."

Glaring, I wiped all expression from my face. "We are leaving. Get up."

"I love a take-charge kind of woman." He hopped off the stool. I towered over him in my heels, and he looked up with a lascivious leer. "Tell me there's a spanking involved."

"Out. Now." I grabbed his elbow and began dragging him toward the doors, not slowing down despite his stumbling to keep up. He tried to pull his arm free, but I maintained an iron grip. I brought him through the front doors and out to my car, shoving him against it while I unlocked the door and opened it. I gripped him again and pushed him toward the opening.

He spread his hands on the roof of the car, bracing himself against me. "Did anyone ever tell you, you're a bit too intense sometimes?"

I pulled his arms down behind him and zip-tied them together. "Only clowns like you."

"Oh, now that hurts."

I took him by the hair and yanked. "Get in the car."

"Now I know you really are flirting. You naughty girl, you."

"Shut up." I smashed his head into the frame of the car. This time, he crumpled into submission. Once he was in his seat, I glared at him. "Try anything, and I kill you."

He gave me a broad grin, licking a trickle of blood from his lips and running his gaze up my long legs. "Promises, promises."

I slammed the car door in his face, and then walked around to get behind the wheel.

He bit his lip and fluttered his eyelashes. "Is this the part where you take me back to your place and have your way with me? Please say you want to be on top, mistress."

Ignoring him, I reached into the glove box, pulled out a roll of duct tape, and tore off a long strip. I put the roll away and removed a handkerchief from my purse with my free hand, shoved the handkerchief into his mouth, and then sealed it shut with the duct tape, smiling at my handiwork when it was done. "That's better. We have a drive ahead of us. I'd hate to spoil it with talking."

He flared his nostrils and scowled but didn't fight any more, and I drove away from there with a smile. Once I had him back in my father's castle, he would tell me everything I wanted to know.

Parting of the Waves

Sybill

I left the hotel room as soon as Marie went into the bathroom to shower. It had taken a long time for me to realize just how much bottled up anger and frustration I'd been carrying. Now that my unacknowledged rage had finally come to the surface, I had to get out of there before my mouth made an unpleasant situation even worse.

From the moment I'd met Raul, even before I knew her name, Marie had overshadowed more and more of my life. I finally realized how much she had taken from me. She seemed oblivious to the loss she brought to others. As far as I could tell, she saw it as a necessary sacrifice others made on her behalf. She believed her own needs were more important.

Though objectively, I could understand the reasons why she behaved that way, being the person who is directly affected by those circumstances made me realize though she used to be a queen, she was no longer entitled to the same sort of deferential behavior she was given two and a half centuries ago. History had moved on, and it was long past time for her to realize no one owed her obedience or self-sacrifice.

The only logical place I could go was to the room occupied by Byron and Polidori. Though my conversation the day before made me feel more at ease with Polidori, I still worried he resented my presence. I tried to put myself in his shoes. I would have trouble accepting someone new in the middle of a relationship that had been going on so long. Though he'd never shown direct jealousy to me, I had no doubt he'd felt it at some point. How could he not? Whether he liked me or not, I was still intruding, and he must be harboring at least some frustration, I was certain, no matter what he said.

Biting my lip, I knocked at their door and stood rocking on my heels while I waited for one of them to answer.

Polidori opened the door, and contrary to my expectations, his face lit up when he saw me. He reached out to take my hand in his. Since he almost never touched anyone, this behavior took me completely by surprise, though I did my best not to let it show.

"Sybill! Come in," he said. "We were just talking about you."

"Oh?" I said, raising my brows as I walked into the room.

"All good things, I assure you," he said. "I was just off to do a little skullduggery."

I stared at him in confusion, and the look on my face made him laugh out loud.

"Not literally, I hope," I said.

He laughed a little more at me, giving a sly wink. "That remains to be seen," he said.

"Come now, Polly," said Albé, walking in from the bathroom. "There's no need for theatricality."

Polidori scoffed and shook his head. "Don't spoil my fun," he said, and then he turned back to face me once more. "I'll return later, and hopefully, I will have some good news."

"Well, that's cryptic," I said.

Byron snorted with laughter. "You don't know the half of it."

"Why do I feel like there's an inside joke I'm not getting?" I said, my forehead furrowed.

"Don't worry, lass," he said. "The joke wasn't at your expense."

"I wasn't worried," I said.

Laughing softly, Polidori stepped past me, waved, and went out the door.

As Polidori had walked away from us, I had watched Byron's expression. So much repressed emotion there. Once we were alone, he sat on the bed, and I suddenly realized Byron and I had only really spoken about their past relationship in a very general way. Was he afraid of what I might think? Was he deliberately avoiding the topic because of me? Had I given him the impression he couldn't talk about it? That I didn't want to know?

I frowned, biting my lip thoughtfully. As he settled back into a more relaxed position in his seat, I took a deep breath, leaned forward, and said, "When did you first know you were —"

Immediately, his body tensed. He turned his face toward me, one eyebrow raised in warning. "No."

"What? I was just —"

"No, you weren't."

I leaned back with surprise at his reaction. "I asked because I just wanted you to know it doesn't bother me, and we can talk about it if you —"

"Look," he said, "is this a conversation you regularly have with your straight friends, acquaintances, potential lovers? Is this your usual way of getting to know someone? Asking them about their sexuality?"

I stared at him, mouth agape. "I just —"

"Lass, believe it or not, my sexuality is the least interesting thing about me. You're not going to learn anything about me by asking those sorts of questions. Ask me my favorite season. How I began writing poetry. When I fell in love for the first time."

"But you just said not to ask about your love life."

He shook his head, his gaze narrowing. "No. I didn't. I said don't ask about my sexuality. My love life is quite another thing entirely. That's about people. I'm interested in talking about people. I'm even interested in talking about sex, if you like. That's a subject upon which I'm quite well-versed. But talking about my sexuality...asking me to label and quantify it or to describe myself as though I were part of some social experiment....I find the entire prospect boring and frankly not worth my time. I have never been interested in what society has to say on the subject of who I shag. Besides, my preferences have very little to do with what's between someone's legs. It's what's up here –" he said, tapping the side of his head, "– that matters. If you want to understand me, ask about art, music, theatre, any of a million other things that make human life worth living."

Tilting my head, I gazed back at him directly. "Head rather than heart? I thought you were a romantic."

Chuckling, he smiled, all the tension gone out of him once more. "Ah, lass. Don't you know? A brilliant mind is the way to my heart. The two are intricately entwined."

"Ohh. You're sapiosexual," I said with a broad grin. "Now I get it."

"Don't label me, woman," he said, his words emphatic, though he snorted with laughter as he spoke. "Besides, you made that word up."

"It's totally a real thing. Google it, smarty pants." The dumbfounded expression on his face at this instruction had me rolling my eyes and laughing harder still. "Oh my god. You have got to learn how to use your computer."

I couldn't pinpoint the precise way in which it occurred. Everything happened in a blur. Suddenly, he was on his feet, his arms around me, his hands pulling me close, and his mouth was making my knees weak. I clutched his collar, clinging to him as though he were the only source of oxygen in the room. The kiss lasted simultaneously forever and mere moments.

When as last our lips parted and I touched back down on my heels, my head swam a little, the taste of him still on my tongue. "Oh."

He opened his eyes slowly, gazing back at me with darkened wonder. "Mmm."

There was an implied answer buried in that simple sound. It was an answer I liked very much.

I smiled, nodding as I bit my lower lip. "That was –" I said, my eyes fixed on his, hands still clutching his collar.

"It was," he said, nodding, his voice an intimate whisper. "It definitely was."

A crooked smile tugged at the corner of his mouth. All traces of his usual sardonic sneer had been replaced by an almost vulnerable look of tenderness, warmth, and surprise. As I gazed back at him, I felt like I was seeing something few people had ever witnessed. He'd dropped his facade, and I was seeing the genuine face of the man he normally kept hidden away.

I lifted a hand to brush the curls back from his forehead. He allowed me that, not moving away, but instead leaning closer. His voice was soft and low as he whispered, lips brushing mine, "Sybill…"

But before he could finish what he wanted to say, Marie burst into the room without knocking. "Albé, I…oh."

We both blinked and stepped back from one another as if we'd been caught doing something naughty, turning to face her. Byron slipped his hands into his pockets, and I crossed my arms over my chest.

"Yes?" he said coolly, and as he spoke, I glanced over to see that hard shell drop down over his expression as though a castle gate had dropped closed with a resounding clang.

"Where's the fire this time?" I said, glaring at her balefully.

She didn't respond to this or even look in my direction. Keeping her eyes fixed on Byron, she went on as if I hadn't spoken. "I have spoken to Jenny, Casanova's assistant," she said. "There is to be a tribunal in three days time. If he is convicted, the punishment is death."

"Convicted?" he said. "Of what crime?"

She flinched slightly, and then she said flatly, "Aiding and abetting me, a wanted fugitive. Conspiracy and contravening coven law. Ceding to the will of a foreign power against the best interests of the coven."

"Treason, then," he said simply.

She nodded. The only visible signs of her distress were her hands, twisting a small piece of fabric in her fingers.

"I see," he said. He took a breath and then squared his shoulders. "Very well. There's nothing for it, then. We must leave here."

"We can't," Marie and I both said simultaneously. I scowled at her, and she mirrored the expression back at me.

"What do you propose we do?" he said, turning to look at me with a furrowed brow. "We have no army. How do you plan to take on the entire Venice coven? They greatly outnumber us, and this is their home territory. Every part of the city will be on alert, looking for us. We cannot hope to evade them. If we stay here, we might as well surrender to them and be done with it. We will be found out. I prefer to keep my head firmly attached, thank you very much."

"He's in that situation because of us," I said. "We can't just leave him to die."

Marie's brow raised. "Now you speak of 'us'? I thought you said everything was my fault?"

That stung. Jaw clenched, I placed my hands on my hips. "And it is, but if we abandon him, we're just as guilty."

"Agreed. I refuse to endure the guilt of causing an innocent man's death," said Marie.

"Oh, like that would be a first for you," I said waspishly.

"Sybill..." said Byron with a tone of warning in his voice.

"What?" I said. "You know I'm right. She'd sacrifice us both to save her own skin."

"That's enough," he said, his eyes flashing as he gazed at me sharply. "If we are busy fighting each other, we might as well give ourselves up."

I seethed, but he was right. Snapping at Marie was wasting time. Much as I hated to admit it, I was going to have to put away my anger so we could focus on the task at hand. "Fine," I said. "But when this is over –"

"Then you can say what you like to me," said Marie, finishing my sentence. "We will sit down for a long talk."

I had no intention of sitting down for any sort of talk with her, long or short, but there seemed no point in saying so when there was so much to do. Instead, I simply nodded curtly before looking back toward Byron again. "What do we have to do?"

Marie stepped forward, placing her hand on Byron's forearm. "Casanova wouldn't be in this situation if it were not for me. I feel obligated to help him, Albé. After all, he is the one who brought me back to you."

I could see the warring emotions on Byron's face. On the one hand, bringing us together meant the two of them were reunited, and as a consequence, I had been introduced into his life. However, Byron's life had been peaceful and settled before our arrival. A part of him had to resent the turmoil her arrival had brought.

There was a long moment when I wasn't sure how he would respond, but at last I saw him grow resolute, and his spine straightened as though he was a soldier in a war he was obligated to fight, no matter the odds. He nodded, a stony stoicism settling on his face. "All right. We fight, then."

Marie shook her head, her hand reaching up to touch his cheek. "No. I won't put you both at risk. This is something I need to do myself."

Byron and I both stared at her. I was struck speechless for once, and Byron was uncharacteristically flustered, stammering, "Wh-huh...how do you propose to accomplish that?"

"I don't know just yet. Jenny has suggested that I go to Casanova Disco so the two of us can make a plan. Either she and I will help Casanova escape, or we will speak on his behalf at the tribunal."

"But that's what they want," I said. "You'd be giving yourself up to them."

"Only as a last resort," she said softly, smiling at me as though touched by my show of concern for her. "I can't keep letting other people risk their lives for me. You were right about that. This has gone on long enough. It's time for me to take the fight to them. Gio is in danger. That is the only issue of importance right now. Any inconvenience I might be forced to undergo is slight in comparison to his suffering."

"So be it," Byron said quietly.

"No. You can't let her do this," I said, turning to face him. "They'll kill her."

"Not if Jenny and I succeed," she said, moving toward the door. "Take care of each other. Find someplace safe and wait to hear from me. I'll come to you as soon as I can."

Byron reached to take my hand, pulling me close by his side. "I will."

She nodded, and then turned and walked out, head held high, leaving the two of us alone once more.

I didn't know whether we would see her again. However angry I had been before, the prospect of losing her filled me with a sense of dread. I couldn't admit that, though, so I turned my focus to our other concerns.

"What about Polidori," I said, my eyes searching his. "How will we find him?"

"I know where he is. Don't worry, lass. I have an alternative place for us to stay." A tight-lipped smile came across his lips. "It will be unpleasant, however. You won't like it."

"More unpleasant than being locked in a dusty tomb with Marie?" I said.

He shrugged, laughing a little bitterly. "I can't make any promises."

I frowned. "I don't like the sound of that."

"It is a last resort, but as uncomfortable the place might be, we will be safe there. I wouldn't mention an alternative if I didn't believe we could withstand it."

My heart sank. "Where is this place?"

"You'll find out soon enough," he said, squeezing my hand. "Polidori won't like it either. He's going to hate it, in fact, though his discomfort will be different from yours or mine. But it can't be helped. Meet me here as quickly as possible, and I'll take us where we have to go."

A chill ran through me. Wherever we were going, Byron obviously didn't want to go there either, and a feeling of dread came over me.

For a fleeting moment, I desperately wanted to beg him to run away with me. The two of us could just leave Venice for good, travel the world, and never look back. We could even take Polidori with us, though I suspected the doctor would refuse. I just wanted all this fear to be over with. I wanted peace and stability. I wanted to find it with him.

However tempting it might seem, though, escaping meant abandoning Marie and walking away from the only chance we had of rescuing Raul. It felt cowardly and wrong. How could I make such a suggestion after scolding Marie for running away from her problems in order to save her own skin? I would be no better than she was. I might be angry with her, but I couldn't cut and run the way Mozart had.

Taking a deep breath, I swallowed down my wishes and nodded. "All right," I said, letting go of his hands to step away from him.

He stopped me, reaching out to take my face in his hands. "Sybill, wait."

Gazing up into those mesmerizing blue eyes, I whispered, "Yes?"

"It's going to be all right. I promise. One day, it's going to be all right."

"You can't actually promise that," I said, nuzzling my face into one of his hands.

"So stubborn," he said with a laugh.

I dusted a kiss over his palm, laughing with him. "Mmm. You knew that before."

Leaning in, he smiled, caressing my lips with his thumb. "True."

I moved in closer, placed my palms against his chest, and then slid them up slowly to wrap around the nape of his neck. My fingertips brushed into his hair. He licked his lips.

"Sooner or later, we're going to have to talk about this," I said.

He raised a brow. "Mmm?"

"This," I said, one hand reaching up to touch the curls over his forehead.

"Mmm," he said. "I suppose we will, yes."

But talking wasn't what he did. Instead, he bent closer still and kissed me again, slowly this time, lips full of longing. My fingers twined in his hair and tugged a little, and I stretched up on my toes.

At last, he broke the kiss and pressed his forehead to mine, whispering, "We have to go."

"Mmm," I said, eyes closed, breathing him in. "Okay. Five minutes."

"Five minutes," he repeated.

Before I let myself kiss him again, I pulled away reluctantly and walked out to gather my things. As the door was closing, I heard him sigh audibly. Perhaps I wasn't the only one who wanted to run away.

Marie was gone by the time I reached our room. Frustrated as I was with her and all she'd done to me, the place felt strange and empty without her. I hoped things would go well for her, not just for her sake but all of us, including Casanova.

I could still feel the press of Byron's lips on mine as I packed, and in spite of all my fears, I smiled, repeating his words back over in my mind. *It's going to be all right. One day, it's going to be all right.*

GAMBIT

Mozart

"Tell me again why you disobeyed my direct order," said Ernestine.

"Order?" I said, forcing my voice to sound lighthearted. "I took it as a suggestion. One I was disinclined to oblige."

"I fail to see how such a misunderstanding is possible," she said. "Play the conversation back for me, please."

This instruction was given to a young man dressed all in black who stood beside her. He pulled out a small hand-held recorder and pushed the play button.

Her voice, slightly tinny through the small speaker on the device, was nevertheless clear and direct:

> *"Don't play dumb. I don't have time for games. Get a boat. Go now. I need you at the Palazzo Ducale now."*

He clicked the button once more, and the recording stopped.

"You didn't say 'please,'" I said with a cheeky grin.

Suddenly, I was struck hard across the jaw. The young man drew back his fist once more and was about to hit me a second time, but Ernestine caught his wrist and held him back from swinging.

I spat blood onto the floor and looked up again, chuckling low. "Always knew you had a soft spot for me. So did she, you know. Lips sweet and soft as a virgin, but the things she could do with that tongue would make even the devil cry for mercy."

"You son of a bitch." The young man's feet scuffled on the stones as he wrested free of her grasp with a growl and punched me again.

This time, Ernestine made no move to stop him, and his fists connected with my cheek, then my nose, and then with my ribcage.

Though the chair was bolted to the floor, the bolts gave, and with the third blow they pried loose with a screech of metal, sending me and the chair tipping backward. I crashed to the floor with a clatter and a thud, skull smacking the stone hard enough to rattle my jaw. I grunted and groaned, seeing stars.

He was cursing, fangs bared and lips curled back in a feral snarl. I had just enough presence of mind to refrain from crying out when the pointed toe of his shiny boot made contact with my midsection. Before he could kick me a second time, I heard a voice I had been dreading. The Marquis.

"That's enough, son." His voice was soft, but commanding.

All the fight went out of the young man, then, and he stepped back, head bowed, tugging down his sweater and then smoothing over his slicked down hair. "Yes, Master," he said.

At his command, Ernestine righted my chair. I sat for a moment, blinking rapidly, trying to clear my vision and to regain my equilibrium. I saw the Marquis lean in to whisper in Ernestine's ear. She nodded, and then Ernestine wrapped an arm around the young man's shoulders and escorted him out.

Being left alone with the Marquis was a dreadful prospect. I wasn't sure whether he was here to play "good cop" or if he was planning to torture or kill me as punishment for not cooperating. Given his reputation, I thought the latter was the more likely scenario.

The Marquis turned his full attention toward me, gazing down with a benign smile that would have seemed almost kind, if I didn't know who he was. On his face, the expression felt ominous, and it was all I could do not to shudder and scream for help.

In a tone that was terrifyingly calm, he said, "You've broken our agreement, Wolfgang. I am disappointed."

The statement was open ended. I wasn't sure how he expected me to respond. Did he want an apology? His entire demeanor seemed poised for one. I couldn't say I was sorry. I wasn't sorry at all. But he knew that, surely. So if he wasn't expecting me to apologize, was he wanting me to beg? I couldn't do that either. I might be a self-serving coward, but I was a long way from being desperate enough to ask for mercy from him, and I knew he would never give it, regardless. Begging was an exercise in futility. There was no mercy in that man. Thus, I simply sat, gazing up at him in silence.

After a moment, he smiled again, as though he were indulging me. "You've made my daughter very upset. And my adopted son...well...he is still young, but you can understand why he might be angry with you too. After all, he is Marie's progeny. He is bound to have some lingering feelings for her, deep down, no matter how he despises what she's done to him."

So that's who the young man was. Raul. Her child who had been missing. All this time, she'd been trying to find a way to rescue him, and he'd joined the other side instead.

Chuckling darkly, I shook my head, licking blood from the corner of my mouth, pondering this new information.

"You're amused? Pray, tell me what you find so humorous." His voice had an edge, suddenly.

I had one last gambit to make. I didn't know whether it would save my life or not. Survival seemed like a lost cause at this point. I hoped, however,

I might save Marie, at any rate.

"She doesn't need him anymore," I said. "You've put all your efforts into a person she doesn't care about."

He tilted his head, peering at me with a narrowed gaze. "I doubt that. She may be self-centered and shallow, but blood matters, even to her."

I shook my head, laughing scornfully. "She has other family now. Family that is far more trustworthy than this disloyal boy of yours. How long has he been working for you? Was he a spy like me? Or do you think you've turned him into your own good little soldier? If he was willing to betray her, you can't trust him not to do the same to you, if he thinks it's to his advantage."

"Oh, I doubt that very much. Raul knows now who his true family is." The way the Marquis spoke his name made my skin crawl. There was a note of praise that chilled me to the bone. He paced before me for a moment, tapping his finger on his lips, and then he stopped, turning to face me with a shrewd glare. "But I am curious about this 'other family' you mentioned. The young woman –"

"Sybill. Her name is Sybill."

"Yes. Sybill. Raul has been quite distressed over her death."

"She isn't dead," I said flatly. "But you knew that, surely."

"I had my suspicions," he said. "Thank you for confirming them."

"She isn't the only one," I said. I knew telling the Marquis about the others was a betrayal, but I hoped it would buy me some time.

His eyebrows rose. So he hadn't known about Byron. "If you think you have something to gain by feeding me false information –"

"It's not false. Why do you think she went to Venice in the first place? It wasn't just to hide from you. She was looking for someone. Her other progeny. She thought he could offer her protection. He did."

"Oh? I thought that was coming from Signore Casanova. Are you telling me my information was wrong?"

I smiled, though not with mirth. "Casanova was her pawn, just like all the others. She didn't care for him any more than she did for me or that boy you've got in here or even Vincent DeLuca. She has left a trail of lovers, men she used and discarded when she grew bored."

"You sound bitter."

Shaking my head, I chuffed a bitter laugh. "I am a realist. I never expected her to treat me any differently."

"So you say. And this other family you speak of?"

"I want a guarantee of safety before I give you their names."

"Names? Plural?" His eyes widened for a split second. Then, quicker than I would have believed possible, he was in my face, fangs bared, all pretense of kindness or benevolence gone. "You get no guarantees. You deserve none. But you will give me those names."

He grasped my lapels in both hands to pull me forward fiercely, and as he did so, the glass vials in my pocket clinked. Eyes darting downward, I pulled back, struggling to get free. "Let go of me."

His gaze followed mine, and I saw a wicked smile stretch his mouth wide. "What have we here," he said, reaching in to pluck the vials from my coat pocket. Six glass vials clutched in his hand, he let them rest in his palm while he plucked one out to examine it more closely.

"No!" I said. "Give that back!"

"Oh, I think not," he said, peering at the label. "Tell me what this contains. Now."

"Insurance," I said quietly, shoulders sagging in defeat.

"Enough of your games!" he roared. All at once, he was on me, clasping my throat in his free hand and squeezing savagely. He lifted me from the seat, and I gagged, feet kicking, my hands struggling to loosen his grip, but to no avail. I squeaked helplessly as he shook me like I weighed no more than a child, and then he tossed me back into the chair. "Answer me."

His hand let go once more, and I coughed, leaning forward for a moment, reeling in pain. Then I looked up, wincing, and croaked, "It's a vaccine. Developed by a Doctor John Polidori. He was turned by Marie's first progeny, the poet George Gordon, Lord Byron, and he's been working to perfect it for two hundred years."

He took in this information with only the slightest narrowing of his eyes to indicate his surprise. "And what is the purpose of this vaccine?"

"I don't know," I said, coughing once more. "But they were determined to keep you from getting it. The doctor called it a secret weapon. I believe it is a serum that will make them invincible."

The opposite was true, I knew. I remembered back to the conversation we'd had when we first arrived at the monastery. Polidori had talked to us then about his research. This vaccine, he'd said, was intended to be a cure for vampirism, but his testing of the serum was incomplete. But the Marquis had no way to know any of that. I knew he would think I was backed into a corner. I had stuck to the truth as nearly as I could, praying it would sell the lie.

"I took the vaccine as insurance," I said. "I knew it was only a matter of time before you caught me. I thought it might buy my freedom from you."

"How many of those around her have taken this?" He lifted one of the vials and shook it experimentally. "Is she creating an army?"

I couldn't help laughing, though it was a bitter sound. "An army? Marie? She's far too interested in saving herself to share this with anyone else."

He sneered, placing the vial back among the others in his other hand. "She's taken it, then? Foolish if she thinks she can fight me. I have hundreds under my command."

"She doesn't think of fighting," I said. "Only of her own survival. No different than she's always been. She wouldn't have shared this vaccine with me, and I doubt she'd have allowed the others to take it either. It was intended for her alone."

This was playing into his suspicious nature. He already believed she was selfish and greedy. I let my words hang there, full of recrimination.

"Mmm. Perhaps you are right. This seems like an insufficient amount if she is intending to create an army," he said. "How much of this vaccine does she still have in her possession?"

"None," I answered honestly. "Or at least none that I am aware of. I stole all that was available in the doctor's laboratory. If he has another stock of the serum, I didn't see it."

He turned his predatory gaze on me once more, studying my expression. "If this was insurance, why did you not give it to Ernestine right away and save yourself all this unpleasantness?"

"Because I had hoped to take it myself," I said, looking down with a sigh, as though he had forced me to show my hand. "Give myself an edge over all of you."

I looked back up with an expression of resigned defeat. Regarding me in silence for a long moment, he pondered that statement. I was making a dangerous bluff, and I wasn't at all sure he would buy it. I kept my eyes fixed on him, but my body language was fatalistic. I knew better than to ask him to believe me. That would be overkill and raise immediate suspicion. Instead, I let my words stand as they were. The truth doesn't need protestations.

"And the dosage?" he said.

I sighed and shook my head, answering truthfully, "I don't know. I stole one of the syringes from the box nearby, however. It's in my other pocket. I had intended to fill it and then inject myself in increasing increments. I assumed that through trial and error I would find the right amount."

He searched me quickly and found the syringe. His eyes narrowed thoughtfully. "If you have held anything else back from me, I will know it."

"I can give you names," I said with another sigh, looking down dejectedly.

His brow raised in suspicion. "What other names are these? Are there more conspirators? Or are you attempting to delay the inevitable?"

"The inevitable?" It was my turn to look surprised.

He smiled slowly. "You didn't truly think you would make it out of this room, did you?"

I stammered, eyes wide. "I...I hoped...that is, I thought once I told you what I knew —"

Laughing, he placed all but one of the vials in his pocket, and then filled the syringe with great deliberation, making me wait and watch. He placed the empty vial in his pocket, and then tapped the side of the syringe while he pressed in the plunger just enough to remove the air. A tiny jet of the serum sprayed in an arch from the needle. He turned to look at me with the syringe in his hand, and I stared at it with wide eyes.

"Don't," I said, shaking my head, recoiling. "Don't. Please."

"Don't what? Give it to you?" He laughed again, and the sound sent a chill right through me. "I have no intention of it."

His grin spread wide once more, sharp fangs glinting wickedly. I watched on in horror as he pushed up his own sleeve and inserted the needle into the blue vein in the crook of his elbow. He injected himself with the entire contents of the syringe and then pulled the needle back out again. He looked up at me, and for a moment nothing happened. I had a fleeting thought that perhaps I had stolen the wrong vials or that the serum was ineffective. Perhaps all this effort had been for naught.

Our eyes met. He chuckled ominously.

All at once, his smile became a grimace. He groaned, hunching his shoulders, his fists clenched. He dropped the syringe to the stone floor. It shattered, small shards of glass scattering. The Marquis fell forward then, leaning toward me, his hands reaching out to grip my lapels again. I scooted my chair back, the metal scraping and screeching across the floor under my weight. His fingers lost their hold, and he slid face first onto the cold grey stone with a guttural cry.

"Help!" I said, though I didn't know if anyone could hear me.

The door flew open, and Ernestine and the young man I now knew was Raul came rushing in, kneeling beside the Marquis' writhing form.

"What the hell have you done?" Raul was screaming at me, but Ernestine stepped between us and held him back from me.

"Raul, no," she said, her voice firm despite her own obvious fear. "We're going to need him."

More of their servants flooded the room, and the Marquis was carried away in a rush. I heard his cries as he was moved down the hall.

"I will kill you," Raul shrieked over and over at me, even as the servants pulled him to the door. "I will fucking kill you!"

The cell door was slammed shut, and I was left there alone in that place, certain I had signed my own death warrant. Silence descended, but I knew it wouldn't last long. Eventually, they'd be coming for me, and death would be a blessing by the time they were through with me.

PART II

Study of Revenge

Ernestine

Suspended animation. That is what they called it. The clinicians who worked for my father had put him into suspended animation to keep his brain alive while the rest of his body recuperated.

Whatever was in that vaccine was not a poison as we initially feared. The doctors struggled to identify the problem, and each test result was more baffling than the one before.

The word "recovery" had lost its meaning.

He was undergoing some sort of transformation. That much was clear. Though he hadn't regained consciousness, his skin, which had sloughed off, was slowly growing back. The new skin was strange, slightly see-through in places, and shiny like the skin on a burn victim. His nails and hair lengthened, and his gums receded until every tooth was elongated.

The influx of blood through his IV was also having an effect. He seemed slightly swollen, his face fuller. I couldn't help seeing a resemblance to a well-fed tick as I stared through the glass.

I saw him fall. The Master. My father. The Marquis de Sade. The man who made me what I was. I thought he was invincible. I was wrong.

Standing in his room, I gazed down at his face through the coffin-like glass case where his body lay. Machines beeped. Monitors displayed sensor results. Blood dripped from a bag on a hook. He looked like death.

I should have been shaking with rage, tearing the earth and sun apart to avenge him and bring justice to his enemies. Instead, I stood there, numb and frozen, like a little girl waiting for her papa to come back home. I wanted to be there when he opened his eyes. I wanted to hold his hand and tell him all the things I never took the time to say. Most of all, I wanted to help him get his revenge. I lingered in his room, sitting by his side. I found myself talking to him, telling him stories, reminding him of our past, and saying how much I needed him to wake up.

He didn't. He lay there immobile and unresponsive. I was helpless and alone. My frustration was boundless. I had never been so frightened.

Dozing by the side of the hyperbaric chamber that housed my father's body, I was awakened by a hand shaking my shoulder. It was one of the doctors in charge of his case. She was smiling at me, and I could see a glint of excitement in her eyes. "Ma'am, we have something we need you to see."

I shook my head, trying to shake the sleep from my mind. "I can't leave him."

"You are going to want to see this," she said, and something in her expression made me get up to follow her.

She led me out of the room and down the hall to a laboratory. Inside, three white-coated assistants were hovering around a computer screen with interest. When they heard us approach, they moved away to make room for us. The woman gestured for me to have a seat in the office chair in front of the desk.

"What am I supposed to be looking at?" I said. "All I see is some sort of line graph."

Taking hold of the computer mouse, she scrolled backward along a graph. "We have been monitoring brainwave activity with deep sensors inserted directly into the skull at key points. Since the night of the incident, there has been very little happening, as you can see from this relatively straight line.

We could tell that he was still technically not deceased, but that was all."

She scrolled forward. "This happened just about twenty minutes ago."

Leaning forward, she pointed at the screen which showed a graph with a series of zigzagging vertical spikes.

Fully awake, I turned to look at her in astonishment. "What does that mean, exactly? Is he waking up?"

"It's too soon to tell," she said. "He has a definite increase in electrical impulses in the brain. So far, these impulses are centered mostly in the midbrain, which means that his vision, hearing, and other basic functions are recovering. He has a long way to go, but this is an important first step."

"So it's promising, then?"

"It gives us a good deal of encouragement, yes." She smiled, and I looked back at the screen, feeling hope for the first time in days.

Just then, alarms started sounding, and the lines on the graph went completely flat. I turned to ask "What happened?" but the doctor and lab assistants were already rushing from the room, barking orders down the hall. I ran after them, trying to stay out of the way, but terrified of what had gone wrong.

The doctor turned to look at me over her shoulder. "Stay back!"

A pair of orderlies came to block me from moving forward in the corridor. "It's under control, ma'am."

"What's under control," I said, struggling to see around them.

There were crashes and screams and the sound of glass breaking. The noises were coming from his room. Out in the hall, a group of doctors, assistants, and scientists, stood staring into the room with wide-eyed panic. "Oh Jesus," said a young man, falling backward against the wall, scrambling to get away.

"Lock the door, dammit!" said the doctor I had just been talking to.

An orderly in blue scrubs pressed a button, and the steel door slammed shut. I heard several bolts slide into place.

With varying expressions of horror, they were all staring into the room through the observation window. One man fainted. Another turned and ran.

I shoved my way past the orderlies and pushed through the crowd until I was able to see into the room.

Broken glass was scattered on the floor. The hyperbaric chamber was broken open from the inside. Medical instruments lay strewn all over, and the fluorescent light fixture flickered overhead, sparking and partially torn from the ceiling.

A dark figure stood over a body which lay in a pool of blood on the floor. The thing was naked, leaning over the chest of the corpse. I couldn't tell if the dead person had been a woman or a man. As for the creature, its skin was black and blue all over and swollen. Its nails were like talons, and it was using them to rip into the body before burying its face in the gash and drinking the blood. A hideous gurgling sound came from the thing as it slaked its thirst. Blood was not all that it was after, however. Once the body was drained, it began tearing the skin away and biting off the flesh in hunks, swallowing it down. I could hear it gulping with hungry pleasure as it filled its gullet with one mouthful after another. The body was quickly dismantled, marrow sucked from the bones.

Its meal finished, the creature turned slowly to look toward the observation window. The pupils had swallowed the eyes in darkness. Mouth dripping gore, the thing dropped the shattered bone it was holding and rose to its full height. Its lips parted, revealing a mouth full of razor sharp teeth, and then it made a ghastly inhuman sound like the screech of an enormous bat. I shuddered, staring, as a pair of wings unfurled from its back. Despite the surreal and terrifying nature of the thing's appearance, there was something familiar in its features. I stared for a long moment before gasping.

"Oh my god." I said. "Father?"

At that word, it looked up at me, and I reeled with the impossibility of what I saw in that expression.

Staring at the creature that used to be my father, I saw nothing left of the man I used to know. He moved in a strange, sinewy way, eyes soulless as though all human thought were gone and he was moving based on pure instinct alone.

I pressed my palm flat against the glass. His eyes narrowed and suddenly he was up against it, sniffing like a predator, fangs bared.

Could he smell me through the glass? Did he recognize me?

There was no comprehension in his eyes. Only emptiness and hunger and fathomless darkness.

"What happened to him?" I said, my voice a hoarse whisper.

The doctor shook her head. "I have no idea." Her words were a confession. "He is not like anything I have seen before. This is something entirely new."

My jaw set, I felt myself fill with a newfound strength and determination. "Doctor," I said, "can you help him?"

She said nothing, her round eyes frozen in a look of horror.

"Doctor," I said again, shaking her.

"Not without knowing what we are dealing with," she said, though her eyes never left the horror inside that room. "The best I can do is keep him sedated."

The creature roared and flexed its wings experimentally, eyeing the ceiling.

"Do it now. I will get you answers."

She nodded. "The sooner the better. I don't know if this is the end of his transformation or only the beginning.

Without waiting for a reply, she turned away and began barking orders.

I turned back to look at what used to be my father. "I will fix this. I promise you."

He turned his head sharply toward me and roared once more, and I almost thought it was in answer. Then the room filled with a cloud of smoke until I could only see a dim shadow of his figure. I heard another strange and unnerving sound, followed by a thump as a clawed hand hit the window. For one second, I thought he would hit it again. Maybe even break it. Instead, the hand relaxed and slid down the glass. His body fell to the floor in a heap, smoke moving in whorls in his wake.

Poveglia

Sybill

Byron sped the boat's motor up and banked hard to the right.

I had returned to his room with bag in hand, and he'd been all business once again. The tenderness between us had ebbed in those few moments apart, and he was focussed on the urgency of the situation. His stiff posture, clipped speech, hurried step, and brusk manner as we checked out of our rooms told me more about his anxiety than any words he could have said. I didn't push the issue. Calling attention to his shift in mood would only cause tension, so instead I let him take charge. I'd been around him long enough to know he had to be active so he didn't buckle under the pressure. He needed me to be quiet for a while, so I settled into the seat beside him and kept my gaze fixed on the water ahead.

After a few minutes, an island came into view. It was silent, dark, and overgrown, with no lights anywhere except on a few posts to keep boats from running aground. Heavy fog hung low, vegetation like black smudges in the mist. Everything was damp, and there was a cloying scent of decay.

An irrational sense of being watched came over me, and I broke my silence, whispering, "Are you sure about this?"

He looked at me askance, but didn't answer. Instead, he cut the motor and ran alongside the decrepit dock. "Help me offload our things. Quickly. I need to stow the boat out of sight."

I obeyed, carrying his computer and my bag in either hand. Once I was a few yards onto the shore, I turned back to look at Byron. He was standing on the dock, gripping the small boat firmly with both hands, and struggling to lift it up onto the dock.

"Here, let me help you with that," I said, setting my burdens down on the ground and walking toward him with a determined set to my jaw.

Brow raised, he looked at me. I knew he was debating telling me no. Byron was old fashioned enough to think he should be a gentleman, but he was modern enough not to think men were superior. He was aware I wouldn't take it well if he treated me that way. He'd also been around me long enough to know I was both stubborn and capable.

"All right," he said finally, making room for me to take the other side.

With considerable effort, the two of us were able to hoist the small boat upside down over our heads. We carried the boat onto the shore of the little island. Clearly, no one had been here in a long time. Byron led us deep into the scrubby brush and waist-high weeds to an area beneath a tree with low hanging branches, and then the two of us set the boat down on the ground.

He did his best to cover the hull with fallen limbs, and then stepped back to look at his handiwork with the boat, tilting his head to one side to examine it carefully. "I think that's pretty well hidden now, don't you?"

I nodded, raking a hand through my hair to calm my nerves. "Yeah. Looks good to me."

"Right then. Let's go. We need to hurry before daylight." We walked back to gather our things, and then he led me through the brush with sure feet. "Watch your step. There are sinkholes in a few places. Hard to see them in the dark, even for us."

"Sinkholes?" Alarmed by the thought, I pushed a tree limb out of my way and then let it swing back behind me with a whipping sound. "Where are we going?"

"Up there." He pointed toward a brick building in the distance ahead, the top of which was just starting to emerge from the dense vegetation. "Hurry. We need to get moving."

"What is this place?"

He heaved a sigh. "Poveglia."

"I don't know what that is."

"I'll explain once we're inside. Come on. There's a way in over by the tower." He turned and walked away. There was broken concrete here, and weeds were growing up through the cracks. "Trust me."

I'd felt reassured until he said 'trust me.' In my experience, that phrase generally meant something was wrong, and the other person didn't want you to know the truth.

Frowning, I looked around us, trying to make out details of our surroundings. There was a high vine-covered wall around one side of the building. It looked more like a compound than a refuge, and the crumbling state of things didn't inspire confidence. "Was this a prison or something?" I said.

"Not exactly."

"Not exactly? What's that supposed to mean?" Just then, I heard a long low moan on the wind. "What was that?"

He didn't answer. Instead, he picked up the pace, and I stumbled along behind. "Albé? Wait!"

"Shh," he said. "They'll hear you."

I looked around us, but couldn't see anything but trees and scrub. Anything could be hiding out there. I hurried to catch up, lowering my voice to a loud whisper. "Who will hear me?"

A rustling came from several yards away, and I turned to look in alarm. "Who's out there?"

Fast as lightning, Byron's hands gripped me tightly, one covering my mouth, the other holding me against him. He gave me a serious look before his glance darted around to scan the bushes. In a barely audible voice, he whispered, "No talking."

Eyes wide, I nodded and tried to keep my hands from trembling. He was frightened. And if he was letting me see his fear, whatever or whoever was out there must truly be a threat.

The rustling sound came again, a little closer this time. I jumped.

"Dammit," he said. Without warning, he let me go and, taking my hand, began running toward the building, tugging me along behind. Byron called over his shoulder, "Don't stop running, no matter what you hear. And don't turn to look back. Just keep up."

I didn't answer, and I didn't argue. All the fight was out of me. My only goal was to get inside where we'd be safe.

I stumbled but kept running as a chilling cry came from behind us. A rumbling began, and I heard something heavy crashing to the ground. More inhuman cries echoed in the dark. Though I was tempted, I didn't stop to look back. My feet pounded the uneven ground as the trees scratched my face, wet branches reaching out like talons. My whole body was damp from the chill evening mist. I could just see Byron's shadow moving in front of me, and I struggled to keep up. His limp didn't slow him down given this much motivation.

He made an abrupt turn to the left, and I skidded on the uneven ground to follow. As we ran through the trees, my mind was racing as fast as my feet. We shot out of the woods into a clearing, and suddenly a rusted steel door at the base of the tower came into view, cloaked in fog, just as a loud roar sounded behind us.

The uneven ground made me stumble a couple of times, but I kept up with him, a rising anxiety driving me on. Tall grass scratched my calves, but we sprinted to close the distance between us and the door.

Pulling a key from his pocket, Byron quickly unlocked the door. The hinges screeched in protest as he pulled it open to reveal an interior drenched in shadow.

Just then, a horrible, unearthly snarl came from behind us. I tried to look back over my shoulder. Byron stopped me, though, grasping my arm and turning me back toward the open maw of the gaping doorway. "Get in."

Fighting panic, I plunged forward into the darkness. He followed, pulling the steel door shut behind us with a slam of finality which echoed through the building. Squinting in the inky black, I turned and was barely able to make out Byron's figure just as he reached up and lowered a heavy steel bar, barricading the door from the inside.

Once it slid into place, I finally felt safe to speak. "What the hell was that?"

He shook his head and grabbed my arm in silence, dragging me away. We stopped in a small vestibule with stairs leading up and down. He paused briefly, looking in each direction as though trying to remember which way to go. Only a second later, he made a decision and started up the stairs, pulling me behind.

As we reached the top of the landing, the door below us rattled, and then I heard a long wail of frustration. That sound was enough to make my guts shake, and though I knew whatever was behind us couldn't get through, I stumbled over my feet in an effort to hurry away from there.

My eyes slowly adjusted to the dark, but what I saw did not comfort me.

Greenish paint the color of decay flaked from the walls, and everything was covered with streaks of black mildew and dust. The stairwell was covered with tiles the same color as the walls, all of it coated in a patina of mold. Plaster had fallen in chunks from the ceilings, crunching underfoot as we walked. The musty scent of damp, disuse, and dirt was overwhelming. Our feet echoed in the empty space despite our every effort at stealth.

We kept going up and up till we reached the top floor landing. Byron opened the door just enough to put his head and shoulders through. He peered in both directions before he pushed it wide and pulled me through.

Hurrying to keep up, what I saw in this new space made me even more anxious. The ceilings were worse here, and electric light fixtures were hanging lopsidedly, wires draping loose. I couldn't tell whether they had fallen or been ripped down, but clearly any hope of switching them on was futile.

At the end of the hallway, Byron paused by a pair of double doors. A rusted metal gurney lay turned over on its side on the floor, and I skirted it carefully to reach Byron's side. "Is this an old hospital?"

Without answering, he pushed experimentally on the doors. The left side was locked, but the right one opened with a squeak of effort. He shoved his way in, and I followed close behind. No sooner was I in the room, than Byron reached up to bar the door with a latch that pushed up into the doorframe. We were bolted inside.

Byron leaned his forehead against the door, eyes closed for several moments, taking deep breaths. Finally, he turned to look at me and nodded. "Yes, this was a hospital once. A mental hospital."

I stood still and stared at him. "You're kidding, right? Tell me you're kidding."

He looked down into my eyes. "I wouldn't joke about that."

"Why did you bring us here? And what was chasing us outside?"

"I brought us here because I had no choice," he said. "No one will look for us here. They wouldn't dare. And no one would believe we came here by choice. I told you before you wouldn't like it, lass. Stay here a moment."

With that, he let go of my hand and strode away into the gloom. I heard a match strike. There was a sudden tiny flash of light. He stood beside an electrical panel, illuminated by a halo of flickering flame. Reaching up, he took hold of a large antique breaker switch just as he shook the match light out. We were plunged into darkness again briefly, though it was long enough to make my skin crawl with panic. Then I heard a loud snap as he turned on the breaker, and all at once the room roared into bright florescent light. What I saw was not comforting.

We were standing in an operating room. Unlike the rest of the building, this space was clean and modern with no signs of the decay so readily apparent elsewhere.

"As for what was outside," Byron said, "you are right in asking 'what' rather than 'who.' Those poor creatures haunt this place. Alone. Unwanted. Feared. Dangerous." He paused for a moment. "The doctor who used to run this place conducted experiments on his patients. Unnatural experiments. In this very room, in fact. Afterward, he set them loose on the island to fend for themselves. Just before leaping off the top of this tower, that is. Only the strongest of his creatures survived. They killed the weaker others."

I didn't reply. I couldn't. I was frozen in place. My mind was numb.

Byron walked over and took my bag from me, and the action jarred me out of my stunned stupor. My stomach gave a lurch. "I think I'm going to be sick."

"Just be glad you haven't seen what's out there yet. Then you really will be sick."

I looked at the door behind us, then back at Byron. "Won't they know we're up here? With the lights on and everything, I mean?"

He gave a soft sardonic snort. "They knew the moment we stepped foot on the island. They were watching when we hid the boat."

With rising panic, I stared at him with wide eyes. "Can they get in?"

"I hope not," he said.

My hand flew over my mouth in an effort to keep from screaming. I swallowed hard and then whispered. "Why did you bring us here? If you knew about those...things."

He reached out then, his palm pressing to my cheek in an effort to calm me. "Lass, no one will dare to look here. And if they do, they won't get far. Those creatures are just as dangerous to the people who are looking for us. Maybe more so."

"So you're using them as guard dogs."

"Basically, yes." He nodded, but the thought didn't make me feel any better.

I bit my lip for a moment, glanced toward the door again, and then said, "And what about Polidori and Marie? Are they coming here? Or are we going to leave and find them?"

He smiled, pulling me close to kiss my forehead. "We'll figure it out, lass."

Placing my palms against his chest, I pushed him back just a little, gazing up with a furrowed brow. "That's not an answer."

He laughed. "I don't know yet, Sybill. Don't be so impatient. Let's take problems one at a time, shall we?"

With a sigh, I pursed my lips, but I nodded. He was right. There was a limit to even his abilities to problem solve. I gave in then, wrapping my arms around him and burying my head on his chest. He held me close, and I could feel the tension going out of us both. We were alive. We had each other. For now, it was enough.

He had done everything he could to keep us safe. However harrowing it had been to get here, we were together. I trusted him. The way he held me told me he felt the same way. I had no doubt he would die for me, if it came to it. And as I clung to him, I knew I would do the same for him.

At last, I pulled back to look around the room, though I still held his hand to remind me I was safe.

The only thing resembling a bed was an operating table in the center of the room, and that didn't look appealing, especially after the chilling story Byron had told me. "We're not sleeping in here, are we?"

"Well, you can if you want, but I was thinking the doctor's apartment might be more comfortable." His mouth curled into a crooked smile, and he led me purposefully across the room toward a door in the corner. He turned the knob and pushed.

Through the open doorway, I could see a small apartment. Clearly, the place had been decorated in the seventies, with brown and gold shag carpeting and fake wood paneling on the walls. "It may not be pretty," he said, "but at least it's safe. Those things won't come in here."

"How do you know?" I stepped into the room after him, trying to assimilate the contrast between this room and the others we had walked through.

His laugh was bitter. "They're too afraid. After all, this is where they were made."

Every surface had been recently dusted. A gold glass ashtray stood on top of a rustic wooden coffee table, and there was a dark wooden couch with brown and white woven cushions. On the wall hung a string art portrait of a ship at sea. A burnt orange armchair with a matching square ottoman was beneath it. Opposite these pieces of furniture, a large antique television with a rotary dial for channels stood, rabbit ears akimbo. A yellow and orange lamp hung from a chain in the corner.

"Jesus. I've just been transported into my great-grandfather's living room."

Byron laughed again, and this time he sounded less tense. "I never said the doctor had taste. But it'll do for the night."

He shut the door behind us, cutting off the view of the operating room, and locked it. I breathed a little sigh of relief. "I'd give you the tour," he said, "but it's not really much to look at. Come on in and make yourself at home."

I walked through that small space, taking it all in with wide eyes. The dining area held a small table and a couple of straight backed chairs, and next to it was a kitchenette with avocado green appliances. Down the hallway on the left was a bathroom that sported a gold sink, tub, and toilet. At the end of the hall was the bedroom. I stepped inside and set down my bag in the corner of the bedroom. It was Spartan, with a straight wooden chair in the corner, a small dresser, and a double bed covered in an avocado green blanket. Beside the bed on one side was a nightstand with a wind-up alarm clock and an ugly brass lamp. There were no windows in the entire apartment.

"Guess he didn't entertain much."

"I expect not," Byron said from the doorway. He had followed me in and stood there, watching me. His expression was uncharacteristically uncertain.

I suddenly realized how awkward this situation was. We had never been completely alone, and neither of us was sure exactly what to do. We hadn't discussed sleeping arrangements, and the intimacy of the bed was a symbol of all that remained unsaid between us. I'd be lying if I said I hadn't thought about lying beside him, but I had pictured something very different. After everything we'd been through to get to this place, I was still shaken. For a moment, I contemplated going back into the living room to sleep on the couch, but the thought of being alone in another room, asleep and vulnerable, knowing those things were out there, made me reconsider.

He broke the silence, walking over to switch on the light, as he said, "It's not the Ritz, I know."

"I've never been to the Ritz," I said quietly.

He laughed then, moving in close to touch my cheek. "No need to sound so forlorn, lass. I'll sleep on the sofa."

"No!" I said, and the emphatic tone in my voice made him raise his brows. "I mean…I just…I don't want to be alone. Please. Stay?"

Nodding, he smiled and wrapped his arms around me, tucking my head on his shoulder. "It's all right, lass. I've got you."

The way he said it made my whole body relax. My arms around his waist, I closed my eyes, and held him tight. "Thank you," I whispered.

"Shh," he said, turning his head to kiss my forehead. "No need for thanks."

"There is," I said, eyes still shut. "I feel like such a spoiled brat. I'm sorry."

"Sybill," he said. The way he said my name was like a caress. "You had a horrible fright. There is no shame in admitting that. But you are so brave."

"I'm not," I murmured. "I was terrified."

His hand reached up to cup the back of my head, his lips still brushing my temple. "So was I."

I pulled back to gaze up at him with surprise. "You seemed so calm."

He laughed. "Years of practice, lass. That's all. I was perhaps even more afraid than you were. After all, I know what those creatures are capable of, and I led you through there, fully aware of all the ways things could go wrong. You, on the other hand, didn't have all the facts. I thought maybe if you knew it would be harder for you to agree."

"You thought I'd be stubborn," I said, smiling tentatively. "It's okay. You were right. I'd probably have freaked out and refused."

"I know," he said. "I love that stubborn streak of yours."

"You say that now," I said, nudging him. "Just wait. In a year or so, you'll be sick of it."

He shook his head and whispered, "I don't think even in a hundred years I could ever be sick of anything you do."

If I was still human, I would have been blushing furiously, but doing so wasn't possible anymore. Instead, I smiled shyly, biting my lip. "You shouldn't say stuff like that."

"Oh?" His brows rose. "Why?"

"I'm not...," I began, but I didn't know how to finish the statement, so I simply shrugged and looked down.

"Sybill?" Taking my chin in his hand, he lifted it gently to bring my gaze back to meet his. "You are."

Looking up at him with wonder and surprise, I stood still, basking in the warmth of his affection for a moment. "Can you just hold me?" I whispered at last. "Just that."

"Of course, lass," he said, smiling. "For as long as you want."

He led me to the bed, and when I sat down on the edge of it, he knelt at my feet to help me remove my shoes.

"You don't have to –," I said.

"I know," he said, setting one at the side of the bed, and then reaching for the other tenderly, his hand clasping my ankle. "It's all right to need someone. Let me take care of you. I want to."

Though his words were a statement rather than a question, there was an implicit request in the way he said it. He was asking me to give him permission to be tender. My heart melted. I nodded, sighing a little with relief.

"I do," I said. "Need you."

"I know that too," he said.

The other shoe set beside the first, he rose then and smiled. "Lie down, lass. I've got you."

I nodded again, stretching out on top of the covers, keeping my eyes fixed on him. No one had ever been this gentle with me since I was a very little girl. I hadn't allowed anyone to see me being vulnerable. With anyone else, I'd have been frightened, but with him, it felt right. He made me feel safe. Comforted. Loved. I had never been with a man like him before. He was the first to anticipate my needs. It was a stunning surprise.

He pulled off his boots, setting them beside my shoes, and then he turned out the light and crawled in beside me. Wrapping his arms around me, he pulled me into his embrace. I nestled against his side and rested my head on his shoulder, one hand flat against his chest. He stroked my hair. His lips brushed my forehead in a soft kiss. "Sleep, love."

He'd never called me that before, but it felt right. I sighed and murmured a soft "yes." Though I was sure I couldn't rest after all we had been through to get to this place, I drifted off quickly, and I slept without dreams.

Full Dark

Raul

"What was in the syringe?" I asked for what seemed like the thousandth time.

Mozart gurgled. His mouth was full of his own blood.

"I didn't catch that. Let's try again," I said. "What was in the syringe, you little toad?"

How long had I been in this cell with him? I wasn't sure. Time had slipped sideways and felt irrelevant. I would stay as long as it took. He was going to give me answers.

I picked up one of the knives the Master had given me as thanks for a job well done. Mozart whimpered. Smiling, I brought the knife toward him and drew a long, curving, crimson line over his chest. The edge sliced deeply. I took my time. Mozart made a noise like a wounded animal. I lifted the dripping blade and licked the blood from its flat side.

"Mmm. Still a lot of blood left in you," I said, wiping the corner of my mouth with my thumb. "You might want to rethink your strategy. I can do this for ages."

His eyes were swollen shut and purple where I had punched him repeatedly, but I saw a tear leak out from one all the same. He sobbed and sagged in his seat as it left a wet streak on his cheek.

"No? All right," I said, shrugging. "Guess we'll get back to it."

I moved toward him once more, prepared to make another cut.

"Please," he whispered, trembling. "I can tell you about your girl. About Sybill."

I paused for a moment, knife in hand, to ponder this offer. He must have thought he could play on my sympathies and take advantage of a perceived weakness. The thought was revolting, and my eye twitched with anger.

"Yeah, no," I said. "That's not going to work."

Another slice. His body was covered with them. So far, I had avoided any major arteries. I needed him to be able to talk.

He cried out, wordlessly, gripping the arms of the chair he was chained to.

Annoyed, I flipped the pommel of the blade in my palm and then stabbed quickly downward, impaling his hand through into the wood below.

He screamed.

"Wrong answer." I sighed, touching my forehead with the tips of my bloodstained fingers, closing my eyes for a moment. I counted to ten. Then, calmly and quietly, I looked at him again. "You thirsty? I'm thirsty."

Turning away, I walked over to one side of the cell. A steel cart stood there, containing an array of implements of pain as well as a thermos of warm blood and a cup. I took my time opening the thermos and poured some of it out. The scent filled the room. He groaned. I closed the top of the thermos and then with cup in hand, I moved back to face him.

Sipping deliberately slowly, I regarded him with a raised brow, tapping a finger on the side of the cup.

He lifted his head and sobbed. "Please."

"Hmm. All right. If that's the way you want to play it," I said.

I stretched my free hand out to take hold of the knife. Gritting my teeth, I wiggled the blade back and forth a bit, and then yanked it free with a grunt of effort. He cried out again.

"Here," I said, holding out the blood toward him. "Drink up. You're looking a little pale."

Chains rattling, he took the cup, and as he lifted it to his split and bloody lips, he groaned. The echoes of his gulps reverberated in the stone cell. I curled my lip, looking away with revulsion.

"Thank you," he gasped.

"I didn't do it for you," I said, snatching the empty cup away. "I'll give you ten minutes to heal, and then we'll begin again. I won't be nearly as nice after this. Something to think about."

With that, I turned, set the empty cup on the cart, and stalked out. The sound of his weeping followed me down the hall.

SANCTUARY

Marie

Jenny met me at the back entrance to Casanova Disco, pulling me in from the cold alley and tugging me into a hug the moment the door was closed.

"Oh, thank God," she said, giving me a little squeeze. "I was so afraid they'd catch you."

Her behavior was a stark contrast to the way Sybill and I had parted. For a moment, I just hugged her back and heaved a heavy sigh. "I made it."

This last was more to myself than to her, a recognition of how uncertain I had been about my odds of arriving unscathed or at all.

As she let go and pulled back, she smiled, the expression warm and genuine. "Nobody saw you, did they?"

I shook my head.

She let out a "whew" through pursed lips.

"How is he?" I walked on into the room and set my bag down on the carpet by the desk.

Her brow furrowed. "It's not looking good. I don't know how we could possibly get him out of there before the tribunal. That place is like Fort Knox."

I tilted my head at this description, but though I didn't completely understand her reference, the context was clear. "We will think of something," I said. "I promise you. He will not die on my account."

Her mouth twisted wryly. "I've been tryin' to think of something. I got in there once, but it wasn't easy. They hadn't had time yet to prep for guarding him. Now…well, I'm pretty sure there's no way to avoid the guards anymore."

I bit my lip, frowning as I took a moment to think.

"What if I turned myself in?" I said. "Do you think they would agree to an exchange?"

She stared at me, mouth agape, then she shook her head, with a heavy "Pah" of breath. "I think they'd just want to kill both of you. Maybe at the same time. They're like hornets. Persistent and plain mean."

"I see," I said, sitting in Casanova's chair.

I did see. I had caused an awful tangle, and Gio had been caught in the middle.

Propping my elbows on the desk, I pressed my palms together, fingers peaked and resting against my lips while I pondered.

"You fixin' to pray about this mess?" she asked, studying my body language.

"Hmm?" I said, brow furrowed. "Perhaps."

She shrugged, then took a seat on the edge of the desk. "Might as well. Probably won't do any good, but it can't hurt, right? Besides, there's not much else to do."

"Is he allowed an advocate?"

Looking up at me sharply, she said, "A lawyer, you mean? I don't know."

"That seems as though it might be an inroad to gaining access to his cell."

"I don't know any good vampire lawyers," she said.

I smiled. "Do they know who you are? Would they recognize you on sight?"

She shook her head, picking up one of the pens from his desk and fidgeting with it. "No. Gio always made sure I stayed off their radar. He didn't want me getting involved just in case something went wrong."

"Had he expected something of this nature? A revolt or a coup?"

With a soft laugh, she raised a brow. "Gio always thought something might go sideways. It happened so often in his past, he was always half expecting it."

"Hmm," I said, fingers tapping my lips thoughtfully once more.

"Sounds like you maybe have an idea," said Jenny.

A crooked smile tugged the corner of my mouth. "Just the beginning of one. It might be dangerous, though."

"Lay it on me, sister," she said, setting down the pen with a broad grin.

Her wording made me smirk in spite of the seriousness of the moment. "Prepare to get laid."

The two of us dissolved into raucous peals of laughter. We had both been so tense, we verged on hysteria, and it took several minutes for it to settle down before we were able to talk once more.

"Don't say that ever again," she said once she was through giggling. "Seriously. Just no."

"Noted," I said.

She took a deep breath, letting it out slowly. "Right. Okay. Tell me your idea."

Inheritance

Ernestine

With the Master in stasis, I left the makeshift medical facility which had been set up in the dungeons and headed down the hall to see how Raul's grilling of Mozart was progressing. It was more important than ever to get answers from him, and I was determined to learn everything we could in order to halt and reverse the progression of his transformation.

The moment I entered the cell, however, I was struck with the metallic scent of blood, and I knew the interrogation had gone incredibly wrong.

"What have you done?" I said, stopping in my tracks to stare open-mouthed.

My question was rhetorical, of course. The answer was right in front of me.

Mozart's corpse lay spread-eagled on a wooden table in the center of the cell. His arms and legs were bound. He had been sliced down the middle like a biological specimen, his skin peeled back on either side, his ribs split open wide, and his internal organs on display. Some of them had been removed and were lying on the table beside his body.

Raul stood next to the table like some sort of mad scientist. Blood stained his hands and even his forearms nearly to the elbow. It splattered his cheeks, streaked in places where he had tried unsuccessfully to wipe it away. He held a set of pliers and as I watched, he yanked a tooth from Mozart's mouth, part of it breaking off.

Just then the body on the table groaned, and I realized to my horror that Mozart was still alive.

Raul held the tooth up to examine it more closely. The root on one side was snapped off. "Pity," he said. "I'd hoped to give it to the Master as a get well gift. I thought it would make him smile. Guess I'll have to try again."

"Stop this. Stop at once." Crossing the room, I took the pliers from him, pushing him back. The Master wasn't going to smile. The Master was still heavily sedated, and with good reason. "What is wrong with you?"

Looking back at me like a petulant child, Raul frowned as though he didn't understand my question. "I want answers. Same as you. I want to know about that vaccine. What was in it. What its purpose was. How to undo the damage."

"And you thought this..." I swept a hand over the man laid out on the table for vivisection, "...was the way to accomplish that?"

He shrugged, pursing his lips for a moment. "He was uncooperative."

"Uncooperative," I said, staring at him in disbelief. "Is that what you're calling it? How exactly did you expect this to help?"

"Don't worry," he said cooly. "I'll give him some blood soon. He'll get better, and then I'll start again."

"You'll do no such thing," I said, nostrils flared. "He's no good to us now. What you've done, he can't recover from."

"Sure he can. It'll just take a little while. I remember where most of these parts go. We'll put things back inside. Sew him up. Get him a snack and a nap. Good as new." His casual tone was shocking.

I glared at him, full of revulsion. "This is beyond a snack and a nap, Raul."

With a derisive wave of his hand, he snorted a laugh and shook his head. "Don't be so dramatic. He'll talk sooner or later."

My eyes cast down at the body lying on the table. What I saw made me reel with disgust. "How? You've cut out his tongue."

He scoffed. "Only partially. It can be reattached."

"Get out," I said firmly, shoving him toward the door.

Balking, he pushed my hands away, his expression ominous and determined. "Hey! Don't touch me."

Enraged, I took hold of his shirt in both fists, forcing him toward the door as I practically screamed, "Out!"

The cell door slammed between us, and I leaned forward, head bowed and eyes closed, bracing myself to face this mess.

I was no stranger to the use of torture. That word didn't apply to what Raul had done, however. My methods might have been ruthless, but I never inflicted pain without reason. Without doubt, I wanted answers about the vaccine just as much as Raul did. Clearly in this case, though, he had tortured the prisoner despite knowing nothing would or could come of it. What Raul had done went so far beyond purposeful interrogation, I shuddered.

Of course I knew where this behavior came from. Raul had not become this way on his own. He was imitating techniques he'd been shown. He had learned it from the Master.

What bothered me most, I realized, was not so much the violence itself, though what he'd done was truly horrific. It was the fact that Raul had so readily taken to it despite living so long despising even the most basic urges of his own nature. This wasn't done to get answers or revenge. Not this much extreme violence. The things he'd done to Mozart were cruel in an intimate way. He had taken his time and drawn it out. This was pleasure to him. He'd gone this far simply because he had discovered he enjoyed causing pain. Raul was far more like the Marquis than I had realized. In imitating the Master so closely, he was clearly more an heir to his legacy than I could ever be, despite my long years of dedication. No wonder the Marquis had called him "son."

There was another agonized groan from the table behind me.

"I'm coming," I said quietly, all emotion drained from my voice. "I'm coming."

One last moment to steel myself, and then I turned to face the nightmare that lay spread out before me. He was hideously still alive. It was monstrous. I feared I might be sick.

"I'm coming," I said once more, forcing my feet to move forward until I stood beside his ruined face.

"K-wwghhh unghh," he said.

The words were garbled and guttural, as though he were swallowing them whole and choking on the syllables. It was inarticulate, but I understood all the same.

"Yes," I whispered.

Gritting my teeth, I picked up a scalpel which rested on the far end of the table. It had already been used to remove various appendages and organs. One last one, and his pain would end.

"Goodbye," I said gently. What was left of him quivered with relief. Then I took a deep breath and cut out his heart. I pulled it free, and as I did so, he spasmed once and died. The heart fell from my hand, hitting the floor with a sickening squelch. It was over.

I dropped the scalpel to the stones and leaned against the table heavily, closing my eyes in an attempt to recover from what I had just done. No one should die like that.

Raul needed to be punished for what he'd done. With Mozart gone, we had no way of knowing what had been in that syringe. We didn't know how to fight the change, nor did we know if there were more horrors to come.

How could the Master lead us in the state he was in? Our entire operation would crumble without his leadership.

I might crumble too. He had been my adoptive father and the center of my world. He had taught me everything I knew. He had given me strength and purpose. He guided me and made me feel special. I needed him to live. I needed him to turn back into the man I had known for two centuries. I could not imagine how to go on without hope of his recovery.

Raul's vengeance came at too steep a price. He might have felt satisfaction in what he'd done to Mozart, but in so doing, he had sabotaged any chance of learning any relevant information.

Turning away from the scene, I walked out of the cell, hands still drenched in blood, determined to bring Raul to account. I found him in the medical wing, standing in front of the observation window, gazing at the Master's lifeless body, once more strapped to a bed. Sedative was being continually pumped into the Master in order to keep him under control while the doctors conducted tests.

Striding over, my hands balled into fists, I gritted my teeth and glared at Raul. "There is no excuse for what you did," I said. "Now we have nothing but a mutilated corpse and no answers."

He ignored me entirely, staring through the glass.

"Did you hear me?" I said. "You've ruined any chance we have of finding a cure for the Master."

"Why is he tied down?" Raul was frowning, still looking at the Master's inert form. "What are you doing to him?"

"It's a sedative," I said. "He became combative and out of control."

"He doesn't like it," said Raul.

"What? What are you talking about? He's unconscious. Stop trying to change the subject. I'm talking about –"

"I know what you're talking about," he said. "And I'm telling you, he doesn't want this. He wants to be set free."

I grabbed his arm, trying to force him to look at me. "You're not listening to me. He's not awake."

Wrenching his arm free of my grip, he turned away and headed toward the door of his isolation chamber.

"Raul, stop," I said. "You can't go in there. You didn't see what happened earlier. Raul, come back here!"

But he was already throwing the door open wide and walking inside. As I looked on in horror, cursing, he moved to stand beside the Master, gazing down at him with a smile. Raul leaned in close to his ear and whispered something, his hand reaching to touch the corpselike hand of the Master.

I saw one claw twitch.

Banging on the glass in warning, I shouted at him. "Get out! Get out of there! He's awake!"

My efforts were in vain. No sooner had I said the words than the Master sat up and clamped his fangs into Raul's throat. I could hear the gulping noise as he swallowed deep mouthfuls of blood.

I screamed as his body went limp, anticipating that the Marquis was going to tear Raul apart and eat him, just as he had done with the others previously. I didn't think he was still able to recognize Raul or me. He had become something new and terrifying. Devoid of humanity.

Yet, as I looked on in horror, I saw him pull back and then offer Raul his wrist.

He was turning him. He was making Raul into whatever he was becoming.

Raul accepted what was offered, and I cried out in anguish. "No!"

At the sound of my voice, the thing which had been my father looked at me and made a piercing shriek. The glass of the observation window shattered with the force of it. Backing up as far as possible, I flattened my body back against the wall, unable to look away.

In his arms, Raul was already starting to change. He was shuddering, his body gone rigid. I covered my mouth with my hand to keep from making a sound.

The Master's eyes were still fixed on me as he made the noise again, and this time, there was an answering roar, many voices crying out at once from the dungeons below. It was the revenant army he'd been building. He was speaking to them in a language only they could understand. They were answering his call.

Something instinctive took over my body, and I froze in place, staring in horror as a pair of batlike wings unfurled from the Master's back, impossibly huge. Clasping Raul against his chest, he clambered toward me through the broken window. He stank of rotten flesh and death. My mind was screaming at me to run, but I couldn't move. He came closer still. I could hear him sniffing. His head tilted. At this proximity, I could see the livid hues beneath the surface of Raul's skin were already beginning to match that of the Master's.

People think of vampires as monsters. For the first time, I understood why. Nothing prepared me for the sheer terror his presence evoked. The man I knew was gone. As I stared into those inhuman eyes, the thought of becoming like him filled me with dread.

"Father, please," I breathed, my voice quivering.

He came nose-to-nose with me with predatory appraisal. He sniffed again. I closed my eyes, waiting for the inevitable.

He made another gut-shaking screech, I heard another roar of the revenants in answer, and then suddenly, with a flap of those enormous wings, he flew away through the dungeons, taking Raul with him.

He had spared me, though I didn't know why. Was it the last vestige of his fatherly love? Or had he found me unworthy? Either way, he clearly recognized me. He had left me and taken Raul instead.

I chased after them, panic rising. I wanted to believe some part of him remembered me, loved me. I wanted to believe he could be saved. When I reached the pens where he kept the revenant army, however, I realized it was impossible.

He had brought Raul there, not to literally take him under his wing as I had thought, but for a more sinister purpose.

The blood supply for the revenants came from a central holding tank and from there it was pumped out to feed the creatures from above in the most efficient means possible.

I arrived to find him holding Raul over the top of the tank, one razor sharp talon slicing his neck from one side to the other. With a gurgling gasp, Raul's blood began pouring into the tank while I watched the Master lift his body upside down to let it drain completely. My father had not infected Raul in order to include him in his plans. He had brought him here as a way of infecting and transforming his entire army all at once. Frozen in place, I watched as the rush of blood gradually slowed to a trickle. He then tore Raul's head from his shoulders and tossed his remains to the floor.

Covering my mouth to stifle a scream, I heard the loud buzz that signaled feeding time to the revenants, and then blood rained down from the ceilings of each pen. They looked up, and with hungry moans, they drank. One by one, they each began to change. The transformation was far more rapid than my father's had been, perhaps because of the advanced vampiric state they had already reached. Horror filled my soul as the entire hoard began to turn as batlike and monstrous as he had already become.

In triumph, he faced them, wings open wide, and shrieked. They cried out in response, their voices shattering the glass of their enclosures. Then, like a dark cloud, they rose and followed him as he flew out into the night, disappearing over the ramparts.

My feet moving as fast as they could carry me, I ran out onto the parapet overlooking the valley below. I expected the swarm to fly down into the sleepy little town and decimate the population, but instead they rose higher and flew off toward the east, swooping away like a colony of bats.

Clutching the railing, I stared dumbfounded for a long moment, my hair whipping in the breeze stirred up by their wings. Suddenly, I realized where they had gone. Venice. There was little doubt of it. He was going in pursuit of Marie to get retribution. He was taking his army with him.

How many others would he transform once he arrived? Hundreds? Thousands? I knew how ruthless he could be, and with the last vestiges of his humanity gone, he would decend on the city like a plague. I was the only person he might respond to. The last link to the life he'd once known. I had to follow and try to prevent the worst from happening. If I failed, the thing he had become would be the fate of all vampires.

I raced to my father's helicopter pad on the far side of the castle where the machine stood. Throwing open the door, I climbed aboard and strapped myself in behind the stick. I had flown it on missions before, but I never dreamed I would one day be on the hunt for the Master himself.

As I completed quick engine crosschecks, I pulled out my cell phone and called the coven headquarters, hoping to give them time to prepare. No answer. My call went straight to voicemail.

"Dammit," I said.

I would have to keep trying en route, but there was no more time to waste. Muttering under my breath, I turned the key and flipped some switches.

The engine roared to life, blades swirling and sending dry leaves scattering from the rooftop of the castle. Lifting off, I flew in pursuit, chasing the swarm as it headed off into the distance. I only hoped I wouldn't be too late.

Baying For Blood

Jenny and I walked swiftly across the checkerboard pavement stones of the Piazza San Marco, our high heels clicking. Pigeons scattered in our wake.

"You sure this is gonna work?" she said out of the corner of her mouth.

"I am sure this is the best chance we have," I said.

"That's not reassuring," she said, tugging down the hem of her business suit jacket and shifting her briefcase from one hand to the other.

She might have said more, but by then we were standing at the security check for the entrance of the Doge's Palace, and we had to both play our parts.

The coven couldn't resist pomp and pageantry, and so despite the fact this building was supposed to be strictly for tourists, when it came time for the tribunal of the great Giocomo Casanova, no place else would do. They had reserved the entire palace, and signs had been posted for a "private event."

"Hi there," Jenny said brightly to the guard at the door. "We're here for the tribunal."

He scowled. "This is coven business only. You don't belong here, and neither does she."

At this pronouncement, he pointed a meaty finger in my direction.

"We're with the firm of Gordon and Associates." She flashed a newly printed business card we had made up for just this purpose. "My associate and I are here to represent our client, Signore Casanova."

"This is irregular," he said.

"Yes, well, so is this tribunal, but here we are. Our client has several powerful friends who want to be certain everything remains above board in this proceeding."

"Who sent you?" He bristled at us both suspiciously.

Jenny smiled. "I'm not at liberty to say, but I can tell you they're associates of the late Mister DeLuca. I believe you can understand why they might have a vested interest."

His brows knitted together at the mention of Vince's name. "Just a moment," he said, and then he turned away to stride over to a small office. I could see him pick up a telephone, but I wasn't close enough to overhear what he said.

We had taken a big gamble, Jenny and I. We were counting on her brash American manner to disarm the guard, and the name she had dropped was a risk.

The phone conversation went on far longer than we hoped. I forced myself to stand still, but Jenny began shifting from foot to foot, though she tried her best to hide her agitation.

Everything in me wanted to run. The last time I had been in this place, I had barely escaped with my life, and my clothes had been drenched in blood. But I had to follow through on our plan. It was my only chance to make things right for Casanova. That night had begun so magically and ended in such horror. I was the reason he was in this mess. He didn't deserve to be punished simply for spending time in my company, and no one else ought to die on my account. I held my head high, my back straight, and sent a silent prayer to the heavens we would all come out of this unscathed.

At last, the man hung up the phone and came back to us, moving slowly and deliberately. "Come with me," he said, his voice flat and almost robotic.

I didn't like the sound of that at all. My instincts were screaming for me to get out, to run as far and as fast as my feet could take me and never look back. Centuries of self-preservation made this reaction instinctive. However, I knew if I gave in to that voice, Casanova would die and all the things people had said about me would be true. Sybill was right. I had behaved like a coward, not a queen, and it was time for me to change.

Determined to overcome my baser self, therefore, I stuffed down my misgivings and forced myself to move forward.

We followed the guard onto the colonnade outside the courtyard, then we turned and climbed the stairs to the first floor. He led us along a loggia lined with carved columns that faced out to the courtyard below, and then we made a sharp right to begin climbing a long steep staircase. The walls were decorated with gold leaf, painted with ornate Renaissance frescoes, and carved with intricate designs, the effect of which was clearly intended to impress visitors to the Doge with the wealth and power of this ancient city. Our feet echoed on the stone floors. The space was dimly lit and empty since it had closed to official tourist business. There was an air of secrecy about our presence in this place, once the hub of government for this influential seafaring city state. We reached the first floor and then were led to another flight of stairs, climbing still higher.

At the top, we turned to the right again and entered a room with four doors, one in each corner of the room. Breathtaking frescoes covered the walls. Each doorway had marble pillars and carved lintels above, all created by some of the finest craftsmen and artisans the world has ever known. Having grown up in Austria among a similar opulence and spending my married life at Versailles, I didn't find the palace rooms surprising, but Jenny's jaw dropped, and she stared around in disbelief.

"Holy wow," she said, the words barely audible.

The guard didn't stop for us to admire the room, however. He led us toward the right hand door at the far side of the room and then walked us through a smaller antechamber toward a pair of heavy wooden doors. Two guards stood outside it. They must have been told to expect us because they opened the doors for him, and he led us through into another large chamber.

After the lavish paintings and gold gilt that adorned the walls of the other rooms, this space was spartan. There were still frescoes on the ceilings and the upper portion of the walls, but the majority of the wall space was covered in darkly severe wooden paneling. With mounting dread, I realized we were entering the infamous Sala del Consiglio Dei Dieci, The Chamber of the Council of Ten. They had been the most feared and secretive governmental body in Venice, only hearing cases that dealt with extreme matters of state, including treason. Beyond this room were the torture chambers and the prisons. Somewhere just beyond this room was Casanova, waiting for his case to be heard. I should have been prepared to enter this room. I knew the history of this place. The Council of Ten were a thing of legend. They were the boogymen of the Inquisition. Of course the coven of this city of secrets would still hold to the tradition. I was foolish to have thought it could ever be otherwise.

An assembly sat on a stage at the far end of the room. Every member was dressed in a black robe, symbolizing the seriousness of the charges. The only break from tradition to bring the council into modern times was the inclusion of female coven members in the tribunal.

Every face turned to look at Jenny and me. Their expressions were like the ominous gloom of an impending storm. My heart sank.

Then one member of the council rose to his feet, looking at me directly.

"Hey there, doll," he said. "Well, ain't this a kick in the pants?"

"Vince?" I said, my voice a whisper of surprise.

He smiled. "I told them you couldn't forget me. Didn't I, fellas? I said, 'Not my Marie. No sir. She's loyal as the day is long.'"

There was an edge to his tone, and I knew it was a rebuke.

I stared. "I thought you were dead."

"Don't sound so disappointed."

"I am thrilled," I said. "I just did not expect this. They told me you had been killed."

"Oh, I see. That must be why you threw yourself at my piano player. Only he wasn't useful enough to you once you got to this city, right doll? No sir. You got off the plane, took one look at the man with the power here, and dropped the musician like a hot potato. But I'm sure that was all because you were beside yourself over me. Ain't that how it was? Hmm?" His gaze narrowed, and then without warning he stormed up to me and roared. "Ain't it?"

My knees trembled. I couldn't lie, and it would do no good if I had. So rather than answer his question, I said the only true thing I knew.

"I am glad you are all right," I said. "Truly. I was devastated when I heard about the explosion. I do not know how you survived, but I am happy to see you are still alive."

I saw nothing but contempt and bitterness in his eyes. The Vince that had loved me was long gone, and in his place was a man in search of vindication.

"Save it, sister," he said. "The only thing you were sad about was you couldn't come crawling back begging for any more favors."

His rage knew no bounds, and I realized he must have been waiting for me. He knew I would try to help Casanova. He had counted on it. This was a trap. We were going to die. Jenny, Casanova, and I were doomed, and it was all my fault.

"Vincent, please let them go," I said, willing my weak legs to keep standing, though they felt like water. "You want your revenge. I understand that. You can have it. Take it out on me. But they are innocent. Please just let them go."

"'Let them go,' she says." He scoffed, turning to walk back toward his chair beside the other council members. "You believe that? 'Let them go.' You must really love this guy, huh? No other explanation. I ain't never seen you beg for nobody but yourself. But here you are, fluttering your lashes and asking me to have mercy on the man you took up with once you moved on from me. Do I look like a merciful guy to you? Have I ever? In the whole time you've known me, have you known me to be the type of guy to let bygones be bygones? Huh?"

"No," I said. My voice sounded tiny and insignificant in that room.

He smiled. "No. And that's my answer to you, Marie. You used up all my favors. Ain't a person in this room who doesn't want you dead, except maybe the dame you came in with, though I'm betting she's thinking better of it. Ain't that right, sweetheart?"

Jenny said nothing. She only stood tall and proud, gazing back at him unfazed, as if his angry rant hadn't happened.

"Yeah," he said. "That's what I thought."

I stood a little taller, determined not to let myself seem weak. "Where is Casanova? Have you killed him already? Or have you not begun the tribunal yet? I expected to see him here so he could defend himself."

The entire council laughed at this, and I looked around the room at them in bewilderment. "Does he not even have the chance to speak on his own behalf and answer to the charges?"

"In a word, madam, no," said a man I recognized as Signore Barbaro. He had given me his seat at the coven meeting when Sybill and Mozart and I had just arrived in Venice, but I saw no trace of kindness in his expression anymore. "The Council of Ten conduct their business without such distraction. We have evidence from various witnesses to discuss, and we will reach our verdict afterward."

"What about his rights?" Jenny asked.

The council looked at her with surprise. "Rights? What rights? He forfeited any such rights when he betrayed his own people."

"But he didn't," she said. "And you'd know that if you'd let him defend himself."

The man laughed aloud, shaking his head. "This is the problem with democracy by the masses. Anything he has to say would only delay justice."

"There's no justice in condemning someone when you don't have all the evidence."

"We have all the evidence we need," he said with an icy sneer.

"This is ridiculous," said Jenny. "We aren't living in the Dark Ages."

"We have traditions, madam. Traditions which have sustained us through out the centuries, and –"

But before Signore Barbaro could finish that statement, there was a commotion outside in the corridor. Scuffling and incoherent shouting echoed in the ancient halls.

Vince stood, turning to look in the direction of the outer hall. "What the hell?"

The only answer came in the sounds of gunshots just out of view.

"Bolt the doors!" one member of the council cried.

Jenny and I looked at each other. An unspoken agreement passed between us, and we both kicked off our high heels and ran for the door we knew led to the prisons on the opposite side of the chamber. We had to get to Casanova. Whatever was happening, this was our only chance to save him.

Because the entire building was open to the public as a museum, the rooms were clearly marked, so it was easy for us to find the formerly secret entrance to the prisons. We entered a large room decorated with paintings depicting dire consequences for sinners, went through a small doorway hidden behind decorative paneling, and bolted the door behind us.

All this while, Jenny and I had run without stopping, but I paused in the stairwell before following her up. I had to warn the others. If we were in danger here, I wanted to make sure they got to safety. Pulling out my cell phone, I sent a hasty text to Byron.

Under attack at the Doge's Palace. Gone to get Casanova. Be safe, please. I will find you when I can.

"Better turn your ringer off," whispered Jenny as I was slipping the device back into my pocket. "Don't want someone to hear it accidentally."

She was right. I followed her advice, and then put the phone away inside my jacket.

A guard was talking on a cell phone as we rounded the corner. His eyes were wide. Whatever he was being told was so alarming, he hardly took any notice of us.

More screams came from down below us. The man shrank back, dropping the phone onto his desk. Jenny moved forward and took his arm. "What? What's happening?"

"It's some sort of monster army. And they're killing...they're killing everyone."

"Who are they? Where did they come from? What do they want?"

"It's the Marquis," he said. "The Marquis de Sade."

I froze in horror at that name. "Oh god. No. That's impossible."

The man shook his head, reaching down to touch his keys anxiously, as though he were counting. "His people called to warn us. But it's too late. He's here." We could hear footsteps running on the stones in the stairwell. "I have to get out of here," he said. "I have to get out."

Jenny stepped forward and took ahold of the key ring, saying with the voice of authority. "We'll take it from here. I'll secure the prisoners. You go."

Of course. The guard didn't know we weren't part of the council. Why would he?

The man hesitated for only a moment. Then there were more screams, closer than before. He handed over the keys willingly, nodding as if relieved to relinquish his responsibility. Then he turned away and ran for the stairs.

"You're welcome," said Jenny under her breath.

Panic rising, I got out my phone again and texted a follow up message to Byron.

It's the Marquis. Save yourselves. They brought an army of monsters. Don't try to be a hero, please.

To protect the others in case I was captured, I removed the SIM card just as Sybill had shown me, then stepped to one of the barred windows overlooking the canals and dropped it and the phone to the dark water below. Both disappeared from view, and I knew they would be washed away on the tide.

I turned back just in time to see Jenny heading for one of the cells, keys in hand.

"Hey, boss," she said. "I'm getting you out of here."

Fumbling with the keys, Jenny tried first one and then another and another. At last, the correct key fit into the lock and turned. She pulled open the door to the cell, revealing an interior cloaked in darkness.

"Jenny?" It was his voice. Casanova. "Thank god, it's you. What is happening out there?"

Racing to her side, I peered in to see him standing in chains, moving as close to the door as he could manage. "Oh god, Gio, what have they done to you?"

Before he could answer, Jenny hurried over to him and began frantically trying to find the right key to remove his manacles. "Dammit," she said. "Doesn't anyone have WD-40 around this place? Ugh."

After several failed attempts, the lock clicked, and the chains fell loose. Casanova's wrists and ankles were chafed and bloody from the manacles, but he was free, and that was all that mattered. Jenny hugged him tightly, and then he looked at me with a wan smile, reaching to take my hand. "I can't believe you're here. It's like a dream."

As we started for the door, someone cleared his throat and then said from the corner, "Not to trouble you, but do you think you could see fit to set me free as well? I don't fancy being killed by whoever or whatever has come to take the city either."

Peering into the blackened gloom, I made out the figure of a man, rising to his feet, all rag and bone. Jenny hesitated, looking to Casanova. An unspoken conversation passed between them, and then she stepped over to the thin man to unlock his shackles too. He rubbed his wrists and came forward into the half light, raising a brow. "Thanks for that. Where are we going?"

"You aren't part of 'we,' and I'll thank you to keep quiet," said Casanova, making his way out of the cell and holding hands with Jenny and me.

"Rude," said the man, following close behind. "But I'm sticking with you until we are all free of this place. Besides, I've done a little swashbuckling in my time. I can be useful to you."

"You don't have a sword, idiot," said Casanova, hissing.

"Not yet," he said, raising a finger. "But I do know the fastest route to the armory from here. Those weapons might be used for display now, but they're still sharp, and they'll do the job. What say you?"

Startled, we all turned and looked at him. This was actually a good plan and one none of us had considered.

"He's definitely coming with us, boss," said Jenny, and she reached out a hand toward the man. "Come on. Lead the way."

Casanova sighed, realizing he had no choice but give in. "All right, fine. But keep the talk to a minimum."

Nodding, the man raised finger and thumb to his pressed lips and made a motion as if locking them together. Then he led us toward the stairwell, peering out with caution. The screams had quietened, but in an eerie way that made us all feel unnerved.

With the man leading us forward, we crept as silently as possible down the stairs and around corners to the armory. Most of the collection was displayed inside glass cases.

The guns were all ancient, requiring black powder and steel balls in order to be fired. Useless. I sighed inwardly, as those were the only weapons I might possibly have been able to make use of.

Jenny paused in front of one of the cases, however, looking in. "Ooh! Crossbow," she said.

"Can you use it?" asked the man, but not meanly. He simply wanted to know the answer.

She nodded.

He peered around in all directions, and not seeing any immediate danger, hauled back his arm and then struck the case with his bony elbow. The glass shattered, and he reached in to grab the weapon along with a few arrows also on display, handing them over to her with solemnity. "We don't have any extras of these arrows, so make sure you don't waste them."

She studied the antique firing mechanism for a moment, testing it a couple of times before loading it. Then she stowed the extras in her coat pocket, looked up, and smiled. "I've got this."

The man gave her an approving nod, and then he and Casanova glanced around the room to see what else they could use.

On the far side of the room was a niche in which stood a suit of armor with a sword. Above it, was a carved plaque with the name "Henri IV." The man moved toward it on tiptoes.

"You can't take that," I said in a loud whisper. "That was a gift from the king of France!"

He looked back over his shoulder at me with a wild smirk, then he reached out to take the sword from the display. "He's not using it. And since I'll be defending one of his country's former queens, I'm fairly certain he wouldn't mind."

Casanova took a sword from another display and handed it to me with brows raised with a silent question.

I shook my head. "I don't know how to use it. That sort of training wasn't deemed fitting for me."

With a wink, he pulled two more swords free from the display so he had one in each hand. "Then stand beside me, my dear. I know enough for the both of us."

Best Kept Secrets

Sybill

I awoke to the sound of murmuring from the other room. Two voices, both male, spoke in low tones, clearly having an animated discussion. Sitting up, I ran my fingers through my hair, then swung my legs over the side of the bed and stood. I dug in my bag, removing the .38 and slipping it into the back of my jeans out of habit, and then I followed the sound of the voices down the hall and into the living room. As I stepped around the corner, I saw Byron and Polidori sitting next to one another at the table. Byron's cane was leaning against the table beside him as if waiting for his use. They stopped talking as soon as they saw me, looking toward me with fake smiles.

"Hope we didn't wake you." Byron pushed his chair back and stood.

I blinked at Polidori. "How did you get here?"

Rather than answer right away, Polidori cut his eyes over toward Byron and an unspoken conversation passed between them. He gave a barely perceptible nod, then turned back to look at me. "Byron and I have been here before. He called and told me where you'd gone."

By this time, Byron had crossed the room and taken my hand, giving it a gentle squeeze.

Still looking at Polidori, I tilted my head, brows furrowing. "But how did you get in? The door was barred."

"There is another entrance," he said, as though this answer was obvious.

"Oh," I said, but my eyes narrowed.

Before I could ask any further questions, however, Byron wrapped an arm around me, leaning in to kiss my brow. This display of affection in front of Polidori was a surprise, but one I found comforting. I couldn't help but smile, wrapping an arm around his waist.

"Hi there," I said, my voice much softer than before.

He chuckled a little, nuzzling my cheek in an intimate way.

Polidori didn't seem bothered by this display of affection. In fact, he seemed to find it fascinating and even pleasing, judging by the expression on his face. Though he didn't say so, I could tell he approved of this development by the way his eyes crinkled in the corners, a hint of a smile playing on his lips. I wondered just how long it had been since he'd seen Byron looking happy. I guessed it must have been quite a long time, given what I knew about them both.

"I suppose we should discuss our plans," said Polidori. Though his tone was indifferent, I could tell that he was not, and the fact he used the word 'our' meant he wanted to continue to be part of whatever happened next.

I nodded, reaching out to touch his arm. "Yes, we should. And whatever you were talking about before I got here, you don't have to stop on my account."

The two men exchanged glances. Byron ran a hand through the dark curls that hung down over his forehead. "I told you she would know something was afoot," he said. "She's cleverer than you or I when it comes to ferreting things out."

"Ferreting?" I said with a snort. "They're cute and clever, but I'm not sure I like being compared to a rodent."

Polidori laughed, and whatever tension had been in the room before I arrived dissipated like smoke. "Milord was trying to convince me that staying here was a good idea. I was in the process of explaining all the reasons it was not."

"Pro and con," I said, sitting at the table. "I like it. Should I take notes?"

"Uh well," said Byron, his brow furrowed, "I'm not sure we need to go back over every detail. He and I have had it out between us for quite some time, and I'm not looking forward to doing it all over again just yet."

"That's a fancy way of saying you don't want to talk about it in front of me," I said.

With another sharp laugh, Polidori covered his mouth and closed his eyes. "Oh dear."

"What? It's true. You know it."

"I never said I disagreed," he said.

Just then, Byron's phone, which had been lying on the tabletop, made a pinging sound. He picked it up to check his messages. His expression quickly shifted to one of deep concern, worry lines plain on his forehead. He held the phone out to me, and after I read it, I passed it over to Polidori whose eyes widened with alarm.

"What on earth does that mean?" He looked up at Byron sharply, handing the phone back over to him as he stood, his chair scraping over the tiles. "Under attack? By whom? The coven? How on earth are we to interpret what she's talking about? That woman is infuriating. 'Be safe.' Humph. How, exactly? Text her back. Or call her. We need more information than that."

"No," said Byron. "She will have enough to deal with, whatever is going on. I think we had best remain here and wait for her to contact us. She said she would."

"And if she doesn't? Then what? Do we just wait forever? What if she's been captured? Killed? How would we know? What if they're looking for us?"

"They wouldn't come here," said Byron. "No one would come here."

"Well, we can't stay here forever," I said. "Sooner or later, we will have to leave in order to get fresh blood, and as soon as we do, we're all targets.

Besides, how can we just leave her there to fend for herself? You've met her. Do you honestly think she can use a sword or do anything practical when it comes to a physical fight for her life?"

"I think she is capable of more than she realizes," said Byron. "Besides, if Casanova is there, he can help her far better than we can."

"What if she can't get to him? What if they have her right now? We have to do something! We can't just sit here."

"That will put us all in jeopardy," he said.

"By 'us,' you mean me," I said.

"Yes," Byron said. "I mean you. I won't be responsible for putting you in danger again. It was bad enough coming to this place. Once we leave here, we're vulnerable, just as you surmised. As long as we are inside this building, nothing is getting in except by air, and no one else knows where we are. Even Marie doesn't know. This is the safest place possible."

I crossed my arms over my chest. "You're acting as though I'm a child. I'm not. I know what leaving here means. I don't want to go any more than you do. Those creatures out there may be terrifying, but they're a great defense. You were absolutely right about that. But if we abandon her, we're no better than she is."

Byron leveled his gaze at me. "We aren't abandoning her. She told us to be safe. We're doing exactly that."

Turning my head in Polidori's direction, I raised a brow. "You're awfully quiet. What's your opinion on this? Let's put it to a vote."

"Oh no," he said, hands raised defensively. "I'm not in favor of either of those options. I was in the midst of arguing for leaving this place altogether before you came in the room."

"What? So you want to just leave her behind? Is that it?"

He and Byron exchanged looks. I scowled.

"I can't believe the two of you," I said. "What happened to family being important? You were the ones who didn't want me arguing with her. Now you've changed your minds? What's different?"

Polidori was gearing himself up to respond when Byron's phone beeped again.

"There," he said smugly, picking it up. "I told you. The old girl doesn't need us."

But his expression changed as soon as he read what was on the screen.

"What?" I said as he handed the phone to Polidori. "What's happened?"

Suddenly looking stricken after reading it, Polidori handed the phone over to me. "See for yourself."

Full of trepidation, I took it from his outstretched hand and read the name that we had all come to dread. "The Marquis?"

Byron took the phone back. His blue eyes were dark like a stormy sea. "You saw it. 'Don't be a hero,' she said."

"What are you going to do?" I said, standing and walking to stand beside him, my hand reaching for his and lacing our fingers together.

"I have to be a hero and do something, of course," he said, but his voice was full of dread.

I nodded, squeezing his hand tightly in mine. "All of us. You don't have to go alone."

"I won't risk you," he said. His voice was very quiet, as though he was admitting something he wasn't quite ready to say. "I can't."

"That isn't your decision to make," I said. "It's sweet, but you can't stop me from going. I want to help. I want to do something. I need to. I'm involved in this now, and I have to act, even though I'm still furious for what she did to me. Besides, I'm not going to sit here alone and let you go out there without me. If something happened to you, I couldn't stand it. I'm going, and that's final."

"You are a stubborn little thing," he said, but he smiled with deep affection, reaching out to cup my cheek in his hand.

"Ahem," Polidori coughed. "That goes for me as well."

"I thought you were all for leaving here," I said.

"Yes, well, that was before you decided to be foolish," he said. "I'm going wherever you go. God help me, but someone has to make sure you don't do anything reckless. After all, what sort of family member would I be if I didn't do my best to help?"

I blinked. "Are you saying you're only going because of me?"

He shuffled his feet and then sighed. "Don't get used to it."

With a smile, I leaned in close and kissed his cheek. "Thank you."

Though he stiffened at the kiss, his expression softened, and I knew he was pleased. That expression lasted only a moment, however. He straightened and pulled away, his face growing cold and distant.

"You'd better go," he said. "The two of you head for the boat. I've got my own. I'll meet you at the Doge's Palace."

"Polly, don't be foolish," said Byron. "Whatever you're planning –"

Lips curling into a smile that didn't reach his eyes, he said, "I'll take care of myself, Milord."

The calm way he said it felt heavy and ominous, his voice taking on a sinister, deeper tone, as if conveying a hidden message only he and Byron understood. So many secrets. What else didn't I know about this man? Polidori's eyes fixed on me, and all our weeks' acquaintance melted away. I was looking at a stranger, one who gave me a bone-deep shiver. Polidori hadn't moved throughout the entire conversation, but he suddenly seemed to be taking up more space in the room. Before I could say any more, however, Byron picked up his cane and was pulling me out the door without another word.

"How are we going to get past those creatures?" I said as we started out into the hospital hallway. "They know we're in here. Aren't they going to be waiting for us?"

"Just keep moving," he said. "Polidori will distract them."

"What? We can't let him do that. They'll kill him."

He didn't answer me. Instead, my hand still held firmly in his, he hurried out the way we'd come. We clambered down the stairs, plaster crackling underfoot. Byron headed for the doors.

As he reached for the steel bar that blocked the exit, I heard a noise echoing from another part of the building, a deep guttural cry.

"Wait," I said. "We have to go back!"

But Byron didn't answer me. Lifting the bar free, he opened the door and tugged me out into the night.

"What if they've got him?" I said, half-stumbling in an effort to keep up.

We crossed the open weedy space before reaching the trees, and he whispered. "Don't worry about him. He's fine. Just worry about us. He said he'll meet us. He meant it. Now stop talking, and run."

Frowning, I looked back over my shoulder one last time, and as I did so I heard the echoing voice again, this time much louder, richer, deeper, more like a roar than anything human. From the rear of the building came answering voices, the sounds of the creatures. Polidori was calling them somehow.

I didn't have time to devote any more thought to it, however. Byron began running as fast as he could through the high weeds, ducking low hanging vines and tree limbs, and dodging obstacles in our path. Brambles caught on our clothes, and roots threatened to trip us both.

Suddenly, I stumbled over something in our path, falling hard to my knees. I threw my hands down, catching myself from landing face first on the ground, only to realize the whole place was covered in bones. They were sticking out everywhere, ancient and bleached. I had tripped over a skull that lay half buried in the ashy ground. The stink of rot clung to my hands and to my clothes, and I began to scream, scrambling to my feet and frantically trying to brush it off.

"There are bodies everywhere! Oh god! They're everywhere."

Rather than respond, Byron took hold of my arm and pulled me away toward the shore, not looking back. He didn't stop until we reached the place where we'd stashed the boat.

"Quick. Help me get it to the water," he said, already clearing away the brush he'd used to hide it.

I did as he asked, clearing away branches from the other side of the small craft. All around us, it was quiet, and then in the distance, back where we'd come, I heard rumbling. "Something's coming," I said, unable to hide the note of panic in my voice.

Byron nodded, grasping one side of the boat, "Let's move!"

Circling to the other side, I picked it up, and the two of us dashed toward the dock. We hurriedly put the boat into the water and leapt aboard. Byron let the little boat drift a little away from the shore, keeping his eyes on the treeline. I saw anxiety in his eyes, but I was too afraid to break the silence. Crashes from the foggy depths of the island echoed through the dark, followed by roaring cries.

I was just on the verge of asking Byron if we should go back when a figure emerged onto the pier. I knew it was Polidori because of the clothes he was wearing, but in all other aspects he had changed. Somehow, he seemed larger, menacing, a ferocious curl of his lips revealing fangs that glistened in the moonlight. His face was pale, his eyes haunted and dark. His hair was wild, and I saw streaks of blood and dirt on his shirt. I don't know what he did to get us free from that place, but I couldn't bring myself to ask. He gazed out at us, and I felt a chill down my spine.

Silently, Byron nodded at him and started the motor. We pulled away from the island, and I watched its outline fade in the distance before I let myself turn and look at the doctor once more. There were large shadowy figures beside him, and I realized what that meant. The creatures were his.

Night Comes on the Wing

Ernestine

The helicopter was the only way I could keep up with the monstrous hoard. They moved incredibly fast, leading me on a chase across northern Italy, skirting the mountains that border with Switzerland. The colony swept across the sky, shadowy figures so thick they blocked out the moon like scudding clouds, driven on the wind.

I didn't know what I would do once I caught up with them or how I would stop the thing which had been the Marquis, my father. I only knew I had to try. I held out very little hope in my ability to persuade him to stop. He was unable to speak as a result of his transformation, and I wasn't sure if he would understand my attempts to speak to him. Even if he could, I doubted there was any chance he would listen. If I had a week to prepare, I might have been able to muster weapons capable of bringing down the Master's transformed revenants. As it was, however, I would have to improvise and hope for the best. A gun would only work in close range, and I would have to make a direct hit straight to the heart. Otherwise, I knew the bullets would only enrage them. As for the Marquis himself, given a chance, I had little doubt he would turn on me and destroy me with the same ruthlessness he had shown to Raul. I prayed I was wrong.

Years had passed since the last time I had been to Venice, and then I had traveled by water, not by air. Still, it was impossible not to recognize the church spires and towers rising from the lagoon as a testament to determination and ingenuity. The swarm began circling the Piazza San Marco, and only then did I realize I had no place set to land. I had forgotten how close together all of the buildings were to one another. But the flying battalion was swooping down to land inside the courtyard of the Palazzo Ducale, their dark wings so thick, they blotted out the stones completely. I knew I had no choice but to take the only spot open to me, though the landing would be difficult. I took a deep breath, then began lowering the helicopter for a landing in the center of the Piazza San Marco. It was a tight fit between the buildings, and I could see chairs and tables from nearby restaurants overturning and rolling away in the fierce wind created by the helicopter blades. People scattered, but most had already seen the horror descending on them from above and taken shelter.

I shut down the engine, grabbed my pistol, extra magazines for quick reloads, and climbed out. Gripping the gun in both hands, I took off the safety and ran toward the Palazzo Ducale.

It wasn't difficult to find the way into the building. I simply ran the opposite direction from the people who were trying to escape. I leaped the turnstile that had been set up for tourists, heading through the main gate. Once the gate swung closed behind me, I flattened myself against the wall, trying my best to keep to the shadows. I didn't want to call attention to myself if I could help it.

In the center of the courtyard, revenants flew in concentric circles, like a hellish whirlwind of wings. Internally, I shuddered, though my feet froze momentarily at the preternatural swarm. There was nothing remotely human about them, and I felt a deep, primal terror wash over me. Everything in me was screaming to turn tail and run to escape that place. I knew I couldn't do that, however. If I ran now, I would only ensure these things would take over. I might not succeed in stopping them, but at least I would die putting up a fight.

Pausing for a moment, I closed my eyes to get control of my panicking mind. Then with a deep breath, I opened my eyes once more and crept along the wall for the stairs, following the sound of screams. I knew the Master would be leading the charge. If I could stop him, I thought, the rest of his army of revenants would be easier to stop since they would no longer have a leader to guide them.

As quickly as I could without attracting attention, I ran up the stairs, leading with the gun. Inwardly, I cursed that I was alone, but there was no help for it. The top of the staircase emptied out onto a long open-air space with columns facing out onto the courtyard. The cloud of revenants was at eye level. I lingered in the shadows for a moment, gathering my resolve. Their attention was on the people below, but I feared they would be drawn toward me once I moved. Still, I knew I couldn't stay there either. My only hope was in getting undercover inside the building, and that meant taking the risk of being spotted.

Suddenly, something below caught their attention, and they began to descend. That was my chance. Whoever or whatever was unlucky enough to be the target of those creatures would have to fend for themselves. Gritting my teeth, I made a run for it, crouching low so I wouldn't be seen over the balcony. Signs and arrows posted for tourists guided me forward, and from above I could hear the sounds of a struggle, voices crying out from an upper floor. This had to be where the Master had directed his attack.

The stairs were long. If I'd had time to pay more attention to my surroundings, I might have been able to appreciate the decorative terrazzo floors and opulent frescoes, but I was too filled with dread to spare more than a cursory glance to get my bearings. It seemed ironic to be so filled with fear and dread while surrounded by so much beauty.

On the next floor, I found the first bodies, broken and torn, limbs scattered, with blood pooling on the stone floor. He wasn't turning everyone, then. Somehow, I found this thought a comfort, but still, I didn't know how many more to expect as I went further on. A cry came from around the corner, and then I heard a repeated "pop, pop, pop" of gunshots. Ducking back into a doorway, back pressed against the stone archway, I hesitated for a moment, listening carefully. More shots. The sound of someone running. A gurgling cry. Then there was only silence. I bit my lip, waiting until I thought the struggle was over, and then I peeked out from around the doorframe.

A revenant was hunched over a body, tearing off great hunks of flesh with its razor-sharp teeth and swallowing them down. There was a hideous sort of purring sound coming from it as it ate. This thing was between me and the room beyond where I could hear the sounds of a skirmish.

I retreated back behind the doorway to consider my next move. It hadn't seen me yet, but I knew I had to get past it in order to stop what I knew the Master, my father, must be trying to do. I would only have one chance to kill the thing, and that meant shooting it in the heart. I couldn't afford to miss. If I was off even slightly, that thing would be on me, and I would end up just as the last two victims had, shredded and eaten. I would have to make it look up and pray I got lucky enough for an open shot.

"Hey!" I shouted, still hidden. My voice echoed against the stone floor, making it unclear exactly what my location might be. I heard the terrible chewing stop. It must have lifted its head to look around. Now or never. I counted to three in my head and then stepped out from my hiding place to face the revenant, gun upraised and held in both hands.

It was hideous. Gore dripped from its talons and spilled down its chin in rivulets, its eyes glowing red in the dim light. Those eyes fixed on me. It opened its maw, revealing extra rows of teeth. I glared back, unflinching, willing my feet to hold me steady. The wings unfurled, opening wide, and it lifted up in order to surge forward toward me. As it did so, the shoulders spread, back arching, leaving the chest open and exposed. I fired several rounds in a tight pattern directly into the heart, the gunshots echoing in those ancient halls. The creature shrieked and staggered. I fired once more. At last, it went down, landing on top of its kill in a heap.

I waited a moment. It didn't move. No others came out to see what had happened. Gun still leading, I walked cautiously over to it, and then kicked it over onto its back. It was dead. Still, I didn't trust this thing to stay that way. I needed to be certain it wouldn't get back up and come at me again.

Teeth clenched, I shifted the gun to my left hand, freeing the right. Then I drew back my fist and punched into its chest, directly over the bullet holes. Ribs cracked and crunched as I drove my hand through to the heart. Taking hold of it firmly, I pulled it free, tearing it loose from the body. I dropped the heart to the floor, then, breathing a small sigh of relief. I didn't know how many more of these I would encounter, but this creature definitely wouldn't be following me.

My relief was momentary, however. This was only one revenant in a place that was teeming with them. Though I wanted nothing more than to leave this place and never return, I had to push forward all the same.

Squaring my shoulders, I wiped my palm on my pant leg to clean off the blood as best I could, gripped the gun in both hands once more, and moved on toward the next room.

Hell is Empty and All the Devils are Here

Byron

We had left that cursed island behind us. Eyes fixed on the water ahead, I reached for Sybill's hand, gripping it tight within my own. Our fingers laced, I felt comforted and grounded by the connection, and I traced the edges of her thumb with mine, absently.

She didn't speak, though I knew she must have a million questions. I could hear them all, and they were the same ones I was pondering. How were we going to rescue Marie? What chance did we have, just the two of us alone against the Marquis and the coven's forces combined? I didn't have any answers. All I knew was if we were to die, I would rather die beside her, and I prayed the last sight I would ever see was her eyes meeting mine. Perhaps this was a selfish thought. Indeed, it probably was. I would fight to protect her with everything I had, but if today was to be my last day, I was glad to spend it with her.

The little boat skimmed the waves at top speed, bouncing slightly. When the city came into view, I slowed the motor.

"When we get there," I said, "I'm going in to try to find her. I suppose it's useless to ask you to stay here with the boat."

I knew the answer, of course, and wasn't disappointed when she squeezed my hand and said, "I'm not staying behind. Someone has to watch your back."

Laughing softly, I lifted her hand to my lips, kissing her fingers tenderly. "Stick close to me then. Promise me that at least."

"I promise," she said.

As soon as we got close enough to see the Palazzo Ducale, I gaped openmouthed at the sky where dark winged figures were swirling and then diving down within the walls, clearly heading toward the courtyard at the center of the complex.

"Good God," I whispered, my heart filled with a chill terror.

Sybill was silent, staring upward, clinging to my hand with all her might, her knuckles white from the strength of her grip. "Holy...what is that?"

"I don't know," I said. "I've never seen anything like it.

"Are they birds?" said Sybill. She let go of my hand to lean over the side of the boat for a better view.

"No bird is that huge," I said. "I don't know what —"

My words were cut off, however, by a man who rushed out of the main entrance to the Palace, screaming. As we watched, one of those things followed, swooped down, and tore into his flesh with enormous claws. The man struggled, falling onto the pavement, hands outstretched. He gasped for help, fingers scrabbling on the stones, but the thing dragged him away and began eating him right there on the embankment.

"That's definitely not a bird," she said, her eyes wide with shock.

People fled in all directions, many leaping onto boats in an attempt to escape the area. Praying the thing would be too preoccupied with its meal to notice us, I shot into one of the empty spaces left open by a fleeing water taxi driver. Sybill ran forward and jumped onto the pier to tie off the lines. She stayed low, her hands trembling. Grasping my cane, I pulled the sword free, leaving the hollowed cane sheath behind, and then I came ashore, clasping Sybill's hand once more.

I pulled her back into the shadows of an overhanging tree by the shore to assess the situation. The futility of a rescue attempt was obvious. The whole idea was ludicrous. There were scores of those things inside. But to her credit, Sybill didn't mention either of those facts. She didn't back down in fear. Instead, she looked at the creature, tearing great hunks of flesh from its victim with long dripping talons, squeezed my hand, and then nodded, jaw clenched with determination. She let go of my hand and pulled her small revolver from her waistband, taking off the safety and clasping it in both hands.

"Polidori said he would meet us, but we can't wait for him. He will have to find us if he can. Marie is in there," I said. "There's no time. Whatever those creatures are, they have to be stopped."

"Let's go," she said. "Before one of those things gets its hands on her."

She had never looked so beautiful to me than in that moment. I laughed in spite of the hopelessness of our situation, glancing over at her with a warm smile. "Sybill," I said, "just in case –"

"No. Don't say it," she said, her eyes still fixed on the creature as it kept eating.

"You don't know what I was going to say."

She looked over at me with a raised brow. "I swear to god, if you say it here I will never forgive you. You think I want to remember this moment that way? Then I'll have to say it back, and we'll both be all distracted going into that place. So just no."

I blinked.

Shaking her head, she rolled her eyes, a sly smile creeping at the corner of her mouth. "You have shitty timing," she said. "I'll say it back. Later."

"Nothing like incentive to send a man into a hopeless battle," I said, still staggered by her straightforwardness.

"Yeah? Well, you just better remember it and make it out in one piece. You'll ruin the whole thing otherwise."

"Come on," I said. "I'll swing for the necks. You aim straight for the heart. Don't miss."

"I've got this," she said.

Before I could respond, she stepped out into the open, under the gleaming streetlight, and waved her arms up and down. "Yo, ugly. Over here."

"Dammit," I muttered, gripping my sword tight.

The creature looked up and tilted its head appraisingly. Its eyes were red, glowing like coals, and they seemed to burn right into her. I had a moment to take in what I was seeing, and then I realized this thing once was human, but something had happened to render it into something completely unnatural and terrifying.

It raised its head and shrieked, wings opening wide. This thing looked like something straight from the bowels of hell. I felt my insides quiver in fear. But it was staring at Sybill with the same hungry expression it had worn before it took down the man who lay in tattered shreds on the pavement, and I had to do something in spite of that terror. Cursing under my breath, I ran forward just as it lunged for her, and with one great slicing blow, I severed its head from its body. Its momentum propelled it forward, though the wings were collapsing, and as the head dropped to the sidewalk and rolled into the water, the rest of the creature skidded across the stones, stopping right at Sybill's feet. A long crimson smear stained the pavement.

For a moment, we stared at the body, speechless. Finally, I looked up and began to wipe the blood from my blade with my jacket.

"Why the hell didn't you use that bloody gun of yours?" I said.

"I couldn't get a clear shot," she said. "I've only got six bullets in this revolver. And anyway, I didn't want to send the swarm after us."

Glancing toward the palace, I could see what she was talking about through the arched gate. How many of these creatures were there? Dozens, at least. My heart sank.

"Still time to leave," I said. "You could take the boat and just go."

"And miss all this fun?" said Sybill. "No way. Someday, this is going to be a really awesome story, and we'll laugh about it together."

"You are an extraordinary woman, Sybill Lysander," I said, unabashed awe in every word.

"Don't I know it," she said, winking. "Now let's go. You don't get to play hero today. Not without me."

This time, she took my hand rather than the other way around, and we ran forward together toward almost certain death. We passed the entrance barricade, then hung back against the wall of the main archway to get our bearings. Somewhere in an upper level of the building, we could hear gunfire. We weren't the only ones fighting these things. That meant someone was still alive. Maybe even Marie was among them. Though it was a small glimmer of hope, I latched onto it and let it give me courage.

Out in the courtyard, a myriad of dark shapes swirled and swooped above the courtyard, so thick they blotted out the moonlight. A man with a military grade semiautomatic rifle came out into the courtyard and began shooting at the creatures. They howled and screamed, but the bullets didn't seem to deter them at all.

Sybill shouted, "Aim for the heart," but her voice was too soft to be heard over the din.

The creatures began diving toward him, clawed hands reaching for him and for the gun. He shot holes in some of their wings and sent them careening to the ground, but that didn't stop them from running toward him in rage, and in very short order, the man was overwhelmed. Half a dozen of them swarmed around the body, the sickening sound of his scream suddenly cut short, and that was a rapid end to him. Unfortunately, he fell on top of his gun, and there was no way for us to recover it for our use. Nothing for it but the sword.

I gritted my teeth and then rushed forward, slashing at those creatures without mercy.

"Back you devils!" I said. "Go back to hell where you came from!"

I heard gunshots behind me, coming closer. Sybill was covering me from the rear. She brought down two of the things right away with direct shots to the chest. I cut off the heads to be sure they stayed down for good.

From that point on, Sybill and I worked together as a team, side-by-side, killing those creatures. We moved tirelessly, anticipating one another's actions. When she ran out of bullets, she drew their attention, and then I killed them at close range. I lost track of how long we went on that way, but we had a growing pile of bodies at our feet while the hoard circled overheard in ever-tightening circles. All the while, I prayed we were buying time for Marie and Casanova and that somewhere in the upper floors they had managed to escape. Chances were slim, I knew, but I could not bring myself to relinquish hope.

Suddenly, the flying creatures shrieked and began to focus on a new target behind us somewhere near the entrance. They started dive-bombing whatever or whoever it was, ignoring us entirely. The sound of their wings was deafening, whipping up the wind like a cyclone. Grit and dirt went flying through the air. All at once, I heard an answering monstrous cry that chilled me to the bone.

"Sybill," I said. "Run."

She was already way ahead of me, reaching for my hand to drag me away from the fray. We made our way behind a marble column, hiding in the shadows. I wrapped my arms around her protectively, holding her for a few moments while she tried to stop shaking.

We could hear the horrible sound of tearing flesh and bone, the flapping of wings, and roars and shrieks as a battle raged on.

"What...what is it?" Sybill whispered. "What's happening?"

"It's Polidori." I paused before I whispered back. "And his monsters. He's brought them to fight."

She buried her face against my chest and clung to me. "Oh god. We're going to die, aren't we?"

"Shh, lass," I said. "Shh."

That wasn't an answer, though, and she knew it. I had nothing else comforting to say. Instead, I simply stroked her hair and closed my eyes, tucking her head under my chin. We held one another and waited for the end to come.

Hell is Just a Frame of Mind

Marie

We walked through the armory back toward the main staircase. Our ramshackle quartet intended to go down by the smaller stairs to the lower levels of the museum's rooms, but the way was blocked by several members of the council of ten who had hidden there, afraid to go in either direction for fear of attack since they had no weapons. We could not see their faces, but when Casanova saw them huddled together on the landing, he pulled us back beyond their view.

"I won't go back to that cell again," he said, whispering low. "I can't. There must be another way out."

"Surely they would not continue with the tribunal. Not after this," I said, reaching to touch his arm.

"You give the council too much credit, my dear," he said. "There is no compassion left in any of them. They were quite happy to leave the guards to die in order to save themselves. Once they are free of this place and safe again, they'll need someone to blame for this incident. I make an easy scapegoat. If they believe it is to their advantage, they'll do whatever they wish. If we try to hide and wait this out, we will miss our chance to escape this place entirely. We must get out or die in the attempt."

I hated it, but he was right. Moreover, he had not said I would be treated the same way, but I knew if they had the chance, they would execute us both. "I agree," I said. "I have not survived for this long to be captured now."

"How are we gonna get out of here then?" Jenny said, glancing around with a furrowed brow.

"The only other stairs are back through the council chamber the way you came," he said, jaw set resolutely. "We must go that way instead. It's our only chance of survival. The longer we delay, the more likely it is we will all be captured and jailed for future execution."

Suddenly, from the corner of my eye, I caught sight of something moving outside the windows. Several somethings, in fact. Dark moving shapes blocking out the view, swooping and diving like enormous birds or bats. Impossible, I thought. I turned to look and stopped walking, staring.

"Something is outside," I said hesitantly, feeling as though if I didn't describe what I had seen, I could keep it from being real.

Casually, Jenny turned to look, and then she gasped and stood still beside me. Stunned, she whispered, "Holy shit."

At that, both men paused as well, silently looking out at the things we saw flying past.

Flying. They were flying. Huge creatures, like ominous shadows come to life, circled the courtyard. A cacophony of high pitched, infernal screeches shook the windows. These were the thing of nightmares.

When I was a little girl, I had a terror of the dark and insisted on sleeping with a lit candle beside my bed to keep the monsters from my dreams at bay. Even as I grew older, I felt my skin crawl in the deep shadows of night, sure that something was lurking, watching, waiting to attack me. I had told myself those fears were the product of childish imagination. I had believed it until I saw those things outside the palace walls. They were everything I had ever feared.

Though the guard had said the Marquis had brought an army of monsters to attack the Palazzo, I had not understood he meant what he said so literally, nor had I imagined anything so dreadful as what I saw through those windows.

I couldn't move. Filled with primal terror, I couldn't speak for fear they might hear us. All that separated us from those things were the panes of ancient glass facing out into the courtyard.

"We have to keep moving," said Casanova at last.

"And go where? You can't be thinking of trying to get past those things," said the thin man. "Did you see those claws? They'll rip us to shreds."

Casanova looked at him, his expression somber. "Sooner or later, they'll get inside here. Waiting here means certain death."

Her hand over her mouth, Jenny was still staring in disbelief. The thin man glanced over at her, his forehead furrowed with concern, then he looked back at Casanova and nodded. "You lead the way, then," he said. "You know this place better than the rest of us."

"Yes," Casanova said simply. Letting out a weary sigh, he then turned to me. "We must try, my dear."

Every instinct in me told me to curl up in the corner and hide. My rational mind overruled, however. Casanova was right. We couldn't linger. The choice was clear. We either fought our way through those things to freedom or we gave ourselves up to certain death. If those creatures didn't kill us, the guillotine would.

We all nodded, though we knew the chances of escape were low.

"Into the belly of the beast," said the thin man, turning and tilting his head back toward the council chamber.

"You really could have found a better way to say that," Jenny said.

"Come on," said Casanova.

With that, he led us forward, swords at the ready. I walked close behind him, followed by Jenny, and the thin man took up the rear. Every instinct in me was desperate to run, but those feelings were born of my rising panic, so I forced myself to ignore those impulses. All I could worry about and control was the immediate moment. Even five minutes into the future was too uncertain to spend time contemplating.

I began counting my steps as a coping mechanism to maintain my composure. *Five paces down to the next museum display case. Fifteen paces to the sign explaining the historical significance of the room itself. Turn slightly to the left. Three paces to the door. Just keep moving. Every step forward is that much closer to the exit.* We made it across the first room.

Stepping around the corner of the next doorway, however, we were confronted with our worst fears manifested. Three of those winged monsters were crouched over and feasting on a body that lay sprawled across the terrazzo floor. Casanova halted as soon as he saw them, but because it was so unexpected, he was unable to prevent us from piling up against his back. Each of us grunted in succession, though we tried desperately to remain silent. At the sound, the creatures looked up in unison. Those eyes were red and glowing, devoid of any vestiges of their original human state. At close range, they were even more hideous than I had imagined, skin bloated and covered in corpselike bruising. I could smell their fetid breath, as though they were rotting from the inside out. Upon seeing us, all three of them simultaneously curled their lips, revealing a mouth full of jagged teeth like razors. I shuddered and raised the sword defensively out of sheer terror.

No sooner had I done so, than they were flying toward us like devils sent from hell itself, their unnatural, piercing cries making my ears ache and my soul shrink in terror.

Jenny shot one in the heart with her crossbow, and miraculously, it fell, suddenly still and silent. She didn't have time to reload before the other two were nearly on her, however. Fumbling, she dropped an arrow and then fell backward onto the floor in panic. Both the thin man and Casanova stepped forward to protect her, stabbing the creatures and driving them back before their steel blades. I bent to help Jenny, picking up the arrow from the floor, and in that split second, one of the creatures managed to get around the two men and come toward me.

"Look out!" Jenny said, flinching instinctively.

My sword went up without my having thought about it. I sliced off the groping hand of the thing as it reached to clutch me. It screamed in pain, flapping backward as black blood spilled from the wound. My action gave Casanova the time he needed to maneuver once more, and he felled the beast, swinging his swords scissor-like to lop off the thing's head.

The thin man was still battling the third creature, but by then, Jenny had nocked another arrow.

"Get down," she said.

He ducked, and she shot again, hitting the heart with a clean shot.

The threat eliminated, we all paused for a moment to calm our frayed nerves. Then Casanova looked at Jenny with a raised brow.

"Where on earth did you learn to shoot an arrow like that?" he said.

She shrugged, though she was clearly pleased. "Iowa. Deer hunting is a thing in farm country."

As she spoke, she walked over to the creatures she had killed and pulled the arrows free. Though they were dripping with that inky blood, she was unfazed, wiping the arrows on her skirt and reloading the crossbow once more. This time, she kept the spare in her hand so she wouldn't be so slow to reload.

"Well," I said, breaking the tension, "that was thrilling. Shall we move on?"

They all turned to look at me, and then laughed in spite of our narrow escape.

"I knew from the first you and I would be good friends," Jenny said. "Thanks for having my back."

"Of course," I said, smiling back at her. "Thank you for having good aim."

She nodded. "Right back at ya."

All four of us took a collective breath, and then turned to face the closed doors we knew led to the council chamber.

"Onward, good sir," the thin man said to Casanova.

Gio set his shoulders, stood a little taller, and then led us on to stand beside the heavy wooden doors. We were silent, listening intently as sounds of a struggle grew closer and closer. A fight was going on in the chamber, and we lingered for a moment uncertainly, trying to assess what to do.

All of a sudden, a woman's voice could be heard, fierce and defiant, but somehow entreating in spite of the fear inherent in her tone. "Father, stop this. Please."

There was the sound of something heavy hitting the floor and the flapping of wings. Then a piercing and inhuman shriek echoed through those palace walls.

"Father, you know me. Please. You must stop this." She sounded tearful this time.

Lips pressed into a line, Casanova looked at each of us in turn before nodding. Then he took a deep breath and threw the door open wide. We rushed in behind him, weapons upraised, unsure what we would face, only knowing we could not leave this woman to die.

We entered the room to find the woman standing with a gun upraised, her feet planted firmly. At the opposite end of the room loomed another of those demonic, bestial figures, wings unfurled. She had clearly been addressing the creature in the center. He...it...seemed more sentient than the others. It looked up at her quizzically, as if trying unsuccessfully to comprehend her words. In its clutches was Signore Barbaro. The man lay limp in the creature's grasp, a smear of black blood across his lips. He groaned, skin growing livid and more like the thing that held him with each passing moment. There was no saving him, and if we didn't act quickly, he would be one more monster to fight.

As one, we moved to the woman's side, though we didn't know her. Jenny raised her crossbow, and the rest of us pointed our swords at the beast. It shrieked and dropped the man to the floor, stamping its foot.

We had thought our help would be a relief to her, but she became agitated, scowling.

"Get back," she said, keeping her eyes fixed on the creature before her. "I've got this. Don't hurt him."

Casanova looked at the man lying on the floor who was beginning to contort with the pain of his transformation. "We can't let him turn into one of those things, madam."

She frowned, though she still didn't break eye contact with the winged thing that stared at her menacingly. "I'm not talking about him. I'm talking about my father. All of you get back. He will listen to me."

I realized then she hadn't been talking about Signore Barbaro at all. This thing, hideous as it was, was who she had called father.

"He is gone," I said. "Whoever you think you are speaking to, that man is long gone. There is nothing left of him that knows you anymore."

Her eyes flitted over in my direction.

Several things happened in quick succession.

The man on the floor sat up and turned his head to look at us with crimson eyes devoid of recognition.

Jenny shot her crossbow at him, striking the man in the chest. He fell heavily to the stones and didn't move again.

The creature, infuriated, rushed forward, hands upraised and mouth open in with a piercing shriek. It was a terrifying blur of wings and claws and jagged teeth.

Shots rang out in quick succession, the woman's instincts overtaking her rational mind's reluctance. The bullets struck it in the chest, and I saw its eyes fix on hers with a look of recrimination and betrayal.

It stopped, staggering on its feet. Then it shrieked again.

All three of us with swords rushed toward the beast. I swung wildly, slashing at its claws, as did the thin man. Casanova went directly for the thing's throat, blades slicing cleanly through bone and sinew.

The head rolled to one side and hit the floor while the body of the monstrous thing fell at the woman's feet.

She dropped the gun, trembling uncontrollably.

"He's dead," she said. "He's dead."

For a moment, there was silence. Then from somewhere outside, we heard a mighty wail. The creatures in the courtyard somehow knew what had happened.

The woman went down to her knees beside the monstrous corpse, reaching out to touch the chest tentatively.

"I'm sorry, father," she said. "I couldn't save you. I'm sorry."

I knelt beside her reaching out to touch her shoulder. "What is your name, my dear," I said softly.

She looked at me then, really looked, and her eyes grew wide. For a long moment she was silent.

Then she whispered, "I'm your daughter, Marie Térèse."

A Distant Shore

Sybill

We clung to one another behind a marble pillar as the battle raged throughout the courtyard. I kept my eyes closed, face against Byron's shoulder, while monstrous cries and howls echoed against the palace stone. Both of us were simply waiting for death.

At one point, inexplicably, the flying creatures let out a terrifying wail, almost as one voice. From the ground, Polidori's creatures made an answering roar, and then we heard the fight grow more intense. Thudding crashes of bodies and sounds of torn flesh and broken bone filled the air.

I shuddered, huddling against Byron for strength to keep from collapsing. His arms were comforting. Dying in his arms, I thought wasn't the worst way to go.

Slowly, however, the din of the battle quietened, and then a strange silence fell.

Hesitantly, I opened my eyes only to find we hadn't died after all. Miraculously, we were still unscathed. I looked up at Byron who was just turning his head to peer around the column.

"Is it over?" I whispered.

He bit his lip and didn't answer. Turning to get a better look, his arms around me loosened, though he grasped my hands instead. I was afraid to look for myself, and instead kept my eyes fixed on him.

At first, his body was tense, ready to fight to the death if he had to, but then I saw his shoulders relax, and a smile of relief came over his expression.

"It's all right," he said.

With that, he stepped out from our hiding place, pulling me along with him.

The ground was littered with the bodies of those flying things. None remained overhead. I sobbed as the tension left me, covering my mouth with my hand.

That's when I saw him. Polidori.

He was standing in the center of the courtyard, splattered with that inky blood. Fanned out on either side of him stood nearly a dozen towering creatures, equally covered in gore. I knew the moment I saw them exactly what they were. They had been sewn together from the bodies of the dead. I could see the scars from the stitches. Some were more hideous than others, but all were fearsome. They bore deep scratches from the talons of those flying monsters, but they seemed unfazed by their wounds.

I remembered the first time I met Polidori. How he had been cutting open a skull in his laboratory in the monastery's basement. He had said then he was working on the body of a dead vampire.

Then I thought about what Byron had told me of the unnatural experiments on the island of Poveglia. Polidori was that doctor. He had to have been. These creatures were his creation.

Like Victor Frankenstein, Polidori had made these creatures what they were. He had fashioned them from the corpses of dead vampires. These things were not only terrifying, but they were immortal. I knew it with startling clarity. All the pieces fit into place.

And Byron had known.

They had both kept the truth from me and from Marie for reasons I didn't understand.

Speechless, I let go of Byron's hand, standing perfectly still while I let the realization sink in.

Byron crossed the courtyard and drew Polidori into a fierce embrace. I watched them, hanging back, trembling and uncertain. Then I cast my eyes to the creatures clustered together. They looked back at me, their faces defiant, as if daring me to react. They stood with fists clenched, and I got the feeling they expected another fight. I didn't move. I couldn't.

"Thank you," Byron said. "I thought we were done for. You did it."

Polidori patted his back and then pulled back from him with a hesitant smile. "You seemed to be doing all right without me," he said, but he was obviously pleased with the praise nonetheless.

His creatures glanced around uncertainly. Their eyes took in the statues, the decorative columns, and the sweeping archways of the palace with an almost childlike wonder mixed with an obvious anxiety. I was struck with a sudden realization, more profound than all the rest. This was likely the first time any of them had been away from that terrifying island. Had they ever seen anything else of the world until just now?

"We need to get them out of here," I said quietly.

He and Byron both turned and looked at me sharply.

My eyes still fixed on his creatures, I said, "There are other people coming. They won't understand. We need to go now before they are seen. They're in danger here."

Both men were silent for a moment.

"What about Marie?" Byron said, softly. "We came here to help her."

I looked at him directly then, and nodded. "And we did. We'll text her. Tell her we will find her later. But she won't understand this at all. We have to go now, or it will be too late."

The two men exchanged glances.

"Are you sure?" Polidori said.

Considering my answer carefully, I narrowed my gaze at him, full of conflicting thoughts. I was horrified by what he'd done. I pitied his creatures, and yet I found them absolutely terrifying. I was also full of questions, and I wasn't going to get answers by starting a fight. And without a doubt, if I did anything to indicate my displeasure with Polidori here and now, his creatures would come to his defense, and I would not stand a chance.

I opted to respond with caution, keeping my voice calm and my outward display of emotion in check.

"We're going to have a long talk," I said quietly. "No more secrets. You're going to tell me everything."

Jaw clenched, he hesitated, took a deep breath, and then nodded. "Very well."

"Deal," I said.

Byron moved to take my hand, and I allowed it, but I didn't squeeze it back. Instead, I glanced over in his direction, my face grave. "That goes for you too."

He blinked.

"I mean it," I said. "From this point on, you're going to tell me the truth, even if you think I won't like it."

A long moment passed, and then he nodded too. "All right."

I squeezed his hand then, letting out a deep breath. "Let's go."

Flesh and Blood

Ernestine

Staggered with disbelief, I studied the features of the woman standing before me.

It had been so long. Across the centuries, I had hunted her, hated her even, but still her face had all but faded from my memory. Yet here she was. Indisputably my mother. Those lips were like mine. Yes, it was her. I would know her anywhere.

Tentatively, she reached a hand to touch my cheek, eyes wide with wonder as she whispered, "I thought you were dead."

I flinched and moved away, stiffening, looking down at the Master's body at my feet. "I didn't think you'd notice one way or the other."

For a moment, she stared at me in surprise. Then without warning, she threw her arms around me and sobbed. "Oh, my darling. How I have missed you."

I didn't return her embrace. I couldn't. I froze in place, my mind and heart conflicted.

Time and again, the Master had told me she didn't want me and didn't care about me. He'd said she had discarded me along with the rest of the people she no longer needed. My mother was evil. She deserved to suffer and die for her crimes against the state, against the Marquis, and against me most of all.

In the deepest, most hidden part of my soul, a small part of me dreamed my mother looked for me. Of course I had. I had been only a child when the Marquis had brought me to his home to make me his daughter. Alone in my room at night, I used to cry myself to sleep because my mother had not come to bring me home. I longed for my lost childhood and the carefree days we had spent in the gardens of Versailles. She had built a miniature farm so we could pretend to be simple country folk. We knew it was only a game, but we had loved her for it. I had wept so often in secret, longing to return to those days before it all went wrong. Before I lost my innocence. Before I knew the truth about the sort of person she really was.

I had spent so many years suppressing the memory of her as a loving parent. The Marquis had taught me about her cruelty and selfishness, as well as her indifference to the pain and suffering of others. Because I could not reconcile his descriptions with my memories of her, I killed the sentimental attachment that lingered inside me. It was too painful to recall, and it was easier to forget rather than remember and know those days would never return.

Convincing the Marquis I could be trusted hadn't been easy. I had continuously been forced to prove my loyalty to him. I fought for the right to be the one who captured her. I had wanted to see the anguish in her eyes when I captured her. I wanted her to know how her abandonment of me had hurt. I wanted her to feel the pain and loss I had suffered because she never tried to find me. She had failed as a queen, and as a mother, even more so.

Her reaction was the opposite of what I had anticipated. Instead of indifference and coldness, she was holding me.

The Master would have told me those were crocodile tears. Hadn't he said she was a master manipulator?

This had to be a trick.

She and these other people with her had saved my life. In doing so, they had killed the man who had been my father. How could I be grateful for his death? And how could I stand beside his remains and allow myself to feel any sort of warmth toward her? Yet, to my shame, I felt both of these things.

At war with myself, conflicted in mind and spirit, my hands curled into fists, and I stood stone-faced.

Shouldn't I bring her in for punishment even now? Hunting her had become habit.

But as I stood there with her in my grasp, I realized I didn't have anyone to bring her to. I had wanted to capture her, yes, but I had wanted to do so as the ultimate proof of my loyalty to the man who now lay at my feet in pieces, his body changed beyond all recognition. There seemed little point in continuing on with the plan of punishing her since I was no longer beholden to anyone.

"You killed him," I said finally. "The Marquis. He's gone."

She pulled back, smiling, as though she had given me a gift. "Yes, my darling. He's gone."

"The world is full of wonders," said one of the men who until that moment had been standing silently, watching us both.

"Kit," said the other one. "This is not the time or place."

"Isn't it?" he said. "Queen and princess reunited? I'd say this is exactly the time and place to be amazed. They are only missing the prince, and the family would be complete."

The mother who had so long been my enemy released me then, turning to look at the men. "My sons are both dead."

"I beg your pardon, your majesty, but Louis Charles, heir to the throne, is not," said the thin man.

It was my turn to look outraged. "Who are you? My brother was taken away. He's long dead by now."

The man bowed, then looked up at us both with a smile. "I happen to know he is quite alive, your highness. As for who I am, I am no one special. Only a playwright. Christopher Marlowe, at your service."

He bowed again, this time a little deeper. Both my mother and I looked at him with astonishment.

"That's impossible," I said. "My brother's name never appeared in any of my databases. I would have known if he was still living."

"Christopher Marlowe? I have heard of you," said my mother. "I have seen performances of your plays. *Tamburlaine.* I remember that one. And *Doctor Faustus.* They were enjoyable."

"You honor me, madam," he said, clearly very pleased with himself at her praise.

"Tell what you know of my son," she said, her tone both warm and commanding. That was the way I had remembered her from my childhood.

He nodded and smiled. "Indeed, I know only a little, but I do know he traveled to the New World in the early twentieth century."

"And how is it you know this?" Her brow was raised, and she stood with a regal bearing. In that moment, she had become every inch the queen.

"Because I met him once by chance in New York City. At the theatre, of course. He was traveling the continent. Our acquaintance was very brief, but memorable nevertheless."

My little brother. Born to be king, though he would not ever wear the crown.

I pondered this for a moment, and then said slowly, "I knew there had been rumors he had been taken from the prison, just as I was, an imposter dying in his place. But I never dreamed they were true."

All this time, and I might have passed him on the street and never known. I glanced over at my mother and saw the same realization in her eyes as well.

"I must find him," she said simply. "I must go now, without delay."

Studying her face, I paused before taking a deep breath. "I have all the powers of my father's organization at my command. If he is out there, I can use those resources to find him."

"Your father?" Her forehead furrowed in confusion.

"That is what the Marquis asked me to call him," I said, though the words diminished what he was to me into something almost insignificant.

She looked toward me, taking in this information. I expected a wary suspicion, but instead she nodded, her expression resolute and without judgment. "We have much to discuss, it seems. I want to come with you. I need to know where he is and that he is all right. I need to hold my son again."

I stared at her, my mouth suddenly dry, my mind unable to formulate a response. It was overwhelming just having her near me. I had dreamed of this moment, though I had never believed it would come. Having her with me would make locating Louis Charles easier. Though I did not trust her, nor did I think I ever could, the possibility of finding my brother overcame my wariness.

"All right," I said at last. "Together, then."

"We have a great deal of catching up to do, you and I," she said. The breezy way she spoke those words made it sound as if we had only been parted for a few days. The words sounded hollow to my ears, and I didn't know how to respond. The breathtaking simplicity of her overstatement stirred up conflicted and complex emotions in me.

I glanced down once more at the Master's body. He had been my whole world for so long. I would have done anything to please him, and here at the end I had been unable to save him. I was keenly aware of the universe's perverse sense of timing.

"Indeed," I said, the words seeming to come from somewhere far away, though I knew they'd spilled from my own lips. "Catching up." Looking up at her, my eyes narrowed. "Raul, your progeny, was killed by the Marquis. By the thing he became, that is."

Her eyes fixed on mine with momentary shock. I had wanted to hurt her, and I could see my words had struck home. Rather than feeling triumph, however, I found myself wishing I could take them back. I expected her to respond in anger, but instead I saw only sadness, as though she had anticipated this news.

"I see," she said simply. "You will have to tell me about that too."

The Sweetest Pleasures are Those Which are Hardest to be Won

Casanova

All the while they had been talking, Jenny and I whispered together, stealing anxious glances over our shoulders toward the door. I didn't want to interrupt, but I had deep fears we would be discovered and all of us imprisoned once more.

Seeing a break in their conversation, I stepped in and said, "My dears, I understand the urge to continue this discussion after such a long separation, but we have some urgency of our own and must be gone from this place or all our efforts at escape will be for naught. Please, we must make haste. The council will return, and when they do, someone will become the scapegoat for what happened here today. We should all be long gone by then."

"I have a boat, boss," said Jenny. "It's down at the pier waiting for us. I've packed all your stuff and everything."

Moving toward Marie, I placed a hand on her arm to lead her away. Kit and Jenny did the same for Marie's daughter, and together we all made our way toward the golden staircase. We passed several slain creatures as we walked from room to room, and we anticipated meeting with others, but a strange silence had fallen over the palace, and we descended without encountering any more of them. Once we reached the lower level with the open colonnade facing out into the courtyard we saw why. Scores of them littered the ground below, all still and very definitely dead.

"Someone's slaughtered every one of them," said Marie in a hushed whisper.

"We'd better look out, then," said Jenny. "Whoever it is might just be waiting for us too."

But they weren't. We hurried down the final flight of stairs and then down to the stone courtyard, only to find we were the only ones in sight who weren't dead.

"Keep moving," said Kit. "I don't trust it. We still haven't seen those council members from the staircase, and they would just as soon clap us in irons again."

This advice was sound, and we took it, running out through the main gate and onto the quay beside the Piazza San Marco.

Jenny led us to where the boat was waiting, and she climbed aboard to start the motor. Kit followed, settling into the back of the little boat.

"We have to go," I said, taking Marie's hand in mine.

Rather than agree, however, she turned to met my gaze, still standing beside her daughter. and I knew in that moment, she and I were parting. She had already decided on a course of action that did not include me.

"You're going together to look for your son," I said.

She nodded. "I must. She's my family, and so is he. I need to find him."

Drawing a deep breath, I pressed my lips in a line and then smiled. "I understand. One day, perhaps you and I will meet again."

"I would like that," she said.

I bent to kiss her cheek, and then bowed low, lifting her hand to my lips. "You will always be my queen."

She chuckled, a pleased smile playing on her lips. "You are the best of men, Giocomo Casanova."

"That is the rumor," I said, laughing along with her.

With a wink, I pulled away and stepped carefully aboard the little boat.

Marie looked at me, her expression sad and tender. "I am afraid I have brought you nothing but trouble."

"Nonsense, dear lady." I shook my head and smiled. "It is an honor to be of service."

She looked down demurely, and then glanced back up through dark lashes. "Take care, Signore."

"And you, your majesty." With a bow, I took my seat, still gazing up at her directly. "Go safely, madame. We will see one another again one day."

Jenny started the engine and loosed us from the mooring, and then we pushed off, turning the boat away on the dark water. Marie quickly disappeared from view as we left the harbor, and I stared out at the waves ahead, brooding over where we would go from here.

Atonement

Marie

With a soft step, I entered the Basilica of Saint Louis, and my footfalls on the marble floor echoed in the silent space. Named for Louis the ninth, ancestor to my long dead husband, natives of Saint Louis simply call the building the Old Cathedral, though I felt strange saying such a thing since it was built nearly eighty years after I was born.

A week had passed since my daughter, Marie Térèse and I had flown together back to Saint Louis aboard a private jet. She had taken control of the Marquis' organization. Though she had wanted to go directly back to her headquarters in New York, I had convinced her that returning to Saint Louis first was necessary in order to begin our search for my little Louis. I had unfinished business, I told her, and it was necessary for me to tie up a few loose ends.

This visit to the basilica was one of those loose ends.

I walked down the center aisle. The air was still, as though something was waiting there for me. I hadn't been inside a church in years, and some part of me felt as though I was intruding. Yet, did I not have as much right as any to be there?

Though many believed that vampirism is the devil's work, it was clearly not so. I still retained a cross pendant and wore it on occasion, and it never burned me. I could pray just as I did in life. My soul was still mine. My thirst for blood and my unnaturally long life was a consequence of an illness, not a pact with a demon. Those prejudices rose out of fear and ignorance and not from God. I did not believe in organized religion, but I did believe in a higher power. In that place, I could feel that power all around me, as though it had been waiting for my arrival.

The candlelight glowed from the altar, and in a side chapel, I could see the host in it's monstrance on display. A priest was there holding vigil, sitting quietly on a pew and gazing up in contemplation. He did not turn to notice as I genuflected and sat in the row behind. I was grateful for his silent acceptance of my presence.

For a long time, I sat without moving or speaking, emptying my mind of fears and anxieties, just letting myself be in the moment.

At last, as though he had heard a voice instructing him to do so, the priest rose, genuflected, and went inside the confessional without a word.

At that moment, I realized why I came into the church. I was not seeking a mere quiet place of contemplation. I came because I needed to confess the things I had done. The realization shocked me.

Byron had told me once that "The beginning of atonement is the sense of its necessity." He was right about that. He was right about so many things.

Confession, to my mind, was not designed for God. God, if such a thing truly exists, is omniscient and must already know what we have done. Confession was intended to make us face our actions and acknowledge them, both to ourselves and to a witness. By stating aloud the things we were most ashamed of, we recognized our soul's desire to change for the better. And through acts of contrition and penance, we worked through our guilt and learned to forgive ourselves.

Knowing the purpose, however, did not make it easier for me to contemplate the act. I hesitated, unsure if I was ready to own up to my guilt and shame. I spent my life running from consequences. I let others do my fighting for me, facing the dangers that should have been mine alone. But after all my years of running from the Marquis, I needed to face my past in order to prevent it from controlling me as I moved past it into the future.

I had so many sins weighing on my heart, many of them still fresh. Crystal had died protecting my secrets. Raul had gone down a dark and destructive path. Mozart had died, and while I had been angry at his betrayal, when I learned of the way he met his end, I couldn't help feeling responsible. How many others had become collateral damage whose names I would never know?

Worst of all, I had lost the rest of my little family again. When I tossed away my phone, I lost any hope of reuniting with them. Byron, Sybill, and Polidori were gone, and all I could do was hope they were safe. Maybe one day I would find them again. I had brought them all loss and heartache. Perhaps they were better off without me.

With a deep sigh, I gathered my courage and rose from my seat. It was time. I walked to the confessional and stepped inside. I slid onto the seat, feeling the wood creak slightly beneath me. Closing my eyes, I began. "Forgive me, Father, for I have sinned. It's been 221 years since my last confession."

This Ends

Trial By Blood
Book Three Of The Blood Royal Saga

Keep Reading For An

Afterward
By The Author

Afterward by the Author

17 September, 2018

First things first. Thank you for reading. Thank you for going on this journey with me. Thank you for believing in me and the world that I created.

I hope you've enjoyed it as much as I have and that you will keep coming back for more. If you have enjoyed these books, please take time to leave a review on *Amazon* or *Goodreads* and recommend the series to your friends. It makes a big difference and helps ensure my ability to continue creating new books in the future.

When I began writing the first book in this series, I had no idea what was ahead of me. I had a vision for the story I wanted to tell. In fact, I wrote nearly all of the final chapter of this book before writing any of the rest. Though the story took me on some paths I hadn't foreseen, every twist and turn my characters took was always leading here.

I'm grateful beyond measure for the lessons I have learned along the way. Writing this series has changed me, expanded my beliefs in what's possible, and shown me the power of my own determination.

Writing used to be a dream, a game, something I did in private, and I fantasized about sharing it with others. Some people say writing is their hobby. It was never that for me. Telling stories was something I couldn't help doing. It was a vocation. I wrote in whatever spare time I had, and for me, sitting down at my keyboard or with pen and paper was the part of my day when I felt most free.

You know the feeling when you come home from work and take off your shoes, put on your most comfortable clothes, and let yourself relax after a long day? Writing was that for me.

I yearned for a time when I could write for a living, but somehow the time never arrived. There was always a long list of "have tos" in my life, so writing was relegated to stolen moments late at night and rare days off when I had time to myself to let my imagination take control. If I could just win the lottery, I thought, I could do this every day. It wasn't that I didn't like the work I was doing. I did. But it wasn't the work I felt I'd yearned for since I was small. It wasn't my calling.

Finally, I realized I couldn't keep waiting. All these stories were bursting out of me, and I had to start owning my days.

Leaving a job I enjoyed to pursue a career as a full-time writer felt strangely selfish at first. I was so used to denying the urge, I had to convince myself I had permission to create. Writing was what I did with my playtime, and in making this my job, I had to stop feeling decadent for doing something that didn't feel like work.

I had also never been my own boss before, and that shift required a new mindset. The only person I had to answer to was myself. I'd always been good at project management, but I had never applied it to storytelling before. I also didn't know how to plan my time because I didn't know what the workflow would be or how long each task would take.

I had to learn how to organize my time, run a business, design and produce the books from start to finish, market and promote myself, and be brave enough to share the end result of what I created. This work has a steep learning curve, and I will always be striving to improve and grow. Whenever I look back at what I've written, I can see different ways I might approach a scene I wrote earlier in the series if I were writing it now. I am my own hardest critic. I'm an imperfect person, but all I can do is my best. With each book, I will learn new lessons, and continue to evolve and improve. Still, I look back on my journey over the last couple of years, and I'm amazed at how far I've come. I'm proud of my hard work. I'm humbled by the way people have responded to my efforts.

These two and a half years felt like a marathon rather than a sprint. Sometimes, it was hard going, and all I could do was keep moving forward and trust that the finish line would greet me.

This job is the hardest and most challenging of my life, and my biggest obstacle was myself. I had to learn to think of myself differently. To trust in the universe to catch me when I made the leap. That trust has been rewarded in extraordinary ways.

Since I began this new chapter in my life, I've traveled all over the United States. I've met and learned from some extraordinary talented people who are mentors, friends, and colleagues. I've found a tribe of people who understand and support what I do. I've been to Romania to see the birthplace of Vlad Dracul himself, spoken at the ***International Vampire Film and Arts Festival*** alongside people whose work I admire, and won an award for my work. I've been asked to speak in libraries. I've spoken with readers from everywhere who are enthusiastic about my stories. And I've finished the third book in this story world. I am thankful for all that has come so far, and I'm hopeful as I look toward the future. I'm where I was always meant to be.

Now that this third book is finished and this first main story arch is complete, I'm going to be taking a short break from Marie and the rest of these characters to work on a few other projects I've had waiting in the wings. I'm also taking an extended holiday (my first since this journey began) while I move my writer's studio into a much larger space. I also have a couple of other book projects I want to work on as well.

But I will be back to this series. Never fear. There are other stories to tell in this little universe I've created, and I look forward to exploring them. Besides, my characters all insistent for me to get on with things. They have a lot left to say. I have outlines for three more books, and notes for three more beyond that. ***The Blood Royal Saga*** has only just begun.

Online at DeliaRemington.com

- /DeliaRemington
- @therealdelia
- /deliaremington/

Sign up for Delia's e-newsletter for quarterly updates and special discounts on new releases and much more.

See website for details!

About the Press

Eagle Heights Press, a division of *Eagle Heights LLC.*, publishes thriller, fantasy, science fiction, historical fiction, paranormal romance, speculative fiction, young adult, non-fiction, and more.

Find us on the web at eagleheightspress.com.